The Politics of *Star Trek*

The Politics of *Star Trek*
Justice, War, and the Future

George A. Gonzalez

THE POLITICS OF *STAR TREK*
Copyright © George A. Gonzalez, 2015

All rights reserved.

First published in 2015 by PALGRAVE MACMILLAN® in the United States—a division of St. Martin's Press LLC, 175 Fifth Avenue, New York, NY 10010.

Where this book is distributed in the UK, Europe and the rest of the world, this is by Palgrave Macmillan, a division of Macmillan Publishers Limited, registered in England, company number 785998, of Houndmills, Basingstoke, Hampshire RG21 6XS.

Palgrave Macmillan is the global academic imprint of the above companies and has companies and representatives throughout the world.

Palgrave® and Macmillan® are registered trademarks in the United States, the United Kingdom, Europe and other countries.

Chapter 3 appeared initially as: "*Star Trek*, American Military Policy and the Developing World," *Foundation: The International Review of Science Fiction* 43, no. 119 (2014): 16–28.

ISBN: 978-1-137-54940-2

Library of Congress Cataloging-in-Publication Data

Gonzalez, George A., 1969-
   The politics of Star trek : justice, war, and the future / by George A. Gonzalez.
     pages cm
   Includes bibliographical references and index.
   ISBN 978–1-137–54940–2 (alk. paper)
   1. Star trek (Television program) 2. Television programs—Political aspects—United States. I. Title.

PN1992.77.S73G66 2015
791.45'72—dc23   2015011423

A catalogue record of the book is available from the British Library.

Design by Scribe Inc.

First edition: September 2015

10 9 8 7 6 5 4 3 2 1

For Ileana and Alana

Contents

List of Figures	ix
Introduction	1
1 *Star Trek* (the Original Series): An Anti–Cold War Narrative	15
2 *Star Trek*, Utopia, and Pragmatism	31
3 *Star Trek*, American Military Policy, and the Developing World	55
4 *Star Trek* and the Clash of Civilizations: Traditionalism versus Modernity (Universalism)	73
5 *Star Trek* and World Government: Federation, Empire, or Neoliberalism	87
6 *Star Trek* and Technologies of Empire	103
7 *Star Trek*: Why Do Soldiers Fight in Modern Warfare? Preemptive Empire or Federation	117
8 *Star Trek*, the Dominant Social Paradigm, and the Lack of an Environmental Ethos	131
9 The Politics of State Building: *Star Trek: Enterprise*	145
10 Lost in the Developing World: *Star Trek: Voyager*	165
Conclusion: *Star Trek*: From Cold War to Post–Cold War	185
Notes	193
Index	217

Figures

Figure i.1	Captain Kirk and Lieutenant Uhura talking on the bridge of the *Enterprise*	3
Figure i.2	Captain Picard standing with Worf in Worf's hour of need (*Next Generation*, "Sins of the Father" 1990)	4
Figure i.3	Benjamin Sisko in command of *Deep Space Nine* ("Emissary," series pilot 1993)	7
Figure i.4	Kathryn Janeway, captain of the starship *Voyager* ("Caretaker," series pilot 1995)	7
Figure 1.1	Romulan from the original series	19
Figure 1.2	Klingons from the original series	20
Figure 2.1	Homeless family in the Sanctuary District (*Deep Space Nine*, "Past Tense" 1995)	40
Figure 2.2	Overhead view of the Sanctuary District (*Deep Space Nine*, "Past Tense" 1995)	40
Figure 3.1	Klingon warrior from *The Next Generation*	63
Figure 3.2	Cardassian officer	66
Figure 3.3	Romulan officers from *The Next Generation*	68
Figure 9.1	Jonathan Archer, captain of the starship *Enterprise*, twenty-second century	146
Figure 9.2	Vulcans from *Enterprise*	146
Figure 10.1	Kazon leaders	180
Figure 10.2	Trabe leader	182

Introduction

Aesthetics or art in the modern era has been critiqued as trivial (frivolous entertainment), solely epiphenomenal (purely reflecting social/political processes), or, worse yet, a kind of propaganda (the new opiate of the masses). This critique is seemingly sharpest for popular culture—especially television, and to a lesser extent, the movies.[1]

My argument in this volume is that *Star Trek*, perhaps the world's most renowned television franchise, actually makes an intellectual/analytical contribution to our understanding of the politics of the modern era. Thus while *Star Trek* is (1) certainly entertaining, (2) reflective of broader social/political phenomena, and (3) may very well be a kind of political/social somnolent, it nevertheless (4) significantly contributes to an analysis of the contemporary world. Indeed, what I show is that a thoughtful reading of the *Star Trek* text (its broadcast iterations) is indispensable to comprehending the twentieth and twenty-first centuries—that is, the American century. Most broadly, drawing from *Star Trek*, Chapter 2 outlines the argument that at the center of the American Mind is utopian Marxism and pragmatism/neopragmatism.

Star Trek as Entertainment

In asking why the *Star Trek* franchise is so entertaining for so many, we are engaging public opinion at the deepest levels. The Federation, across all *Star Trek*'s platforms, is a secular (at times antireligious) interstellar institution that is classless, and predicated on the total absence of gender/ethnic biases. In this way, the franchise is based on reason—that is, full and total equality. Thus *Star Trek*'s enduring popularity can/should be read as the broader public's adherence to reason and a rejection of premodernism (religion/aristocracy) as well as postmodernism (critiques of reason).

Nevertheless, *Star Trek* is a work of art and artistic choices must be made—for better or for worse. Critics have seized on some of these choices to make what amount to superficial readings of the *Star Trek* text, thereby obfuscating the truly progressive, liberating, and analytical elements of the franchise. Perhaps the most notable of *Star Trek*'s critics is Daniel Bernardi, who holds that the original series and *The Next Generation* are hopelessly marred by gender, ethnic, and sexual orientation biases.[2] Bernardi makes much of the fact that Lieutenant Uhura (the one African American bridge officer in the original series) is reduced to a bit role, the Klingons are dark skinned, *Next Generation* caregiver roles are assigned to women, and neither of the first two *Star Trek* series feature any gay/lesbian characters.

In criticizing the Uhura character, Bernardi is minimizing the fact that the original *Enterprise* had a black, female bridge officer (see Figure i.1). That Uhura had a minimal role in the show's plots is neither here nor there, as a true racist stance would never afford a bridge officer position to an African American. Also noteworthy is the fact that an African American actor (in the original series) plays one of the Federation's leading scientific minds.[3]

Bernardi is correct that the Klingons in *Next Generation* are a political trope, but not one that reflects American race politics per se, as he claims. As I argue in Chapter 3, the Klingons, Romulans, and Cardassians represent peoples of the less-developed world.

What is truly amazing about Bernardi's assertion of racism directed against the *Next Generation* is his treatment of the characters Geordi LaForge, Worf, and Guinan (all played by African American actors). These characters are admirable—of the highest intelligence, fortitude, and integrity. Nevertheless, Bernardi dismisses them because they are putatively disconnected from their history; he holds that at the core of the *Next Generation* "is a

Western and white standard."⁴ It is unclear how Bernardi expects African Americans on the *Enterprise* to behave. Should they be speaking Creole English (Ebonics)? An obvious message would be that African Americans, in spite of equal educational and social opportunities, cannot master standard English.

Bernardi inappropriately hones in on what are essentially artistic choices and makes a broader—and ultimately unsustainable—claim that *Next Generation* is profoundly racist. He makes hay of the fact that Captain Picard is played by Patrick Stewart and that Worf is a subordinate officer (a lieutenant commander). In misplaced (racist?) language, Bernardi makes the following distastefully worded observation: "[Worf] is trained and domesticated, becoming . . . a trusted officer who faithfully protects the *Enterprise* and its white captain."⁵ Bernardi cannot see beyond the skin tone of Picard and Worf to analyze their actual relationship—one built on professionalism and mutual respect, even admiration (see Figure i.2).

Figure i.1 Captain Kirk and Lieutenant Uhura talking on the bridge of the *Enterprise*

4 • The Politics of *Star Trek*

Figure i.2 Captain Picard standing with Worf in Worf's hour of need (*Next Generation*, "Sins of the Father" 1990)

Bernardi similarly makes a mountain out of a molehill by pointing out that a being that is conveyed as an evolutionary advancement is glowing white ("Transfigurations" 1990), while the beings from which all humanoids evolved have a tone that is tinged brown ("The Chase" 1993): "What is striking about 'Lucy' [the representation of the original humanoid species] is that the common ancestor to the bipeds of the universe is brown. Though dark or even colored is not where we're going ... it is apparently where we come from."[6] Bernardi goes on: "The course of evolution, of advancement and sophistication, is literally and metaphorically, physically and socially, white ... that's ... *The Next Generation's* version of the promised land."[7] If the special effects designers had made "Lucy" a little whiter or the advanced being darker, maybe we could have been spared Bernardi's pseudoracist rhetoric. I imagine, however, Bernardi would have something inappropriate or sardonic to say if Lucy were lily white.

Perhaps what is most baffling about Bernardi's approach to *Star Trek* is while he is focusing on the superficial (Picard's and Worf's skin tones), he elides the universality communicated in "Transfigurations" and "The Chase." In "Transfigurations," for instance, the alien that is going through a metamorphosis to a higher state of existence comments positively on the heterodox composition of the *Enterprise* crew: "Truly remarkable. They're all so different from one another yet they work together freely." The original humanoid species in "The Chase" were very highly advanced (even with their tanned skin tone): "Life evolved on my planet before all others in this part of the galaxy. We left our world, explored the stars." Lucy preaches solidarity and unity, emphasizing that all humanoids share a common genetic basis:

> Our scientists seeded the primordial oceans of many worlds, where life was in its infancy. The seed codes directed your evolution toward a physical form resembling ours. This body you see before you, which is, of course, shaped as yours is shaped, for you are the end result . . . It was our hope that you would have to come together in fellowship and companionship to hear this message [sent from the past in the form of Lucy]. And if you can see and hear me, our hope has been fulfilled. You are a monument, not to our greatness, but to our existence. That was our wish, that you too would know life, and would keep alive our memory. There is something of us in each of you, and so, something of you in each other. Remember us.

Lucy's message had a positive effect on a Romulan officer present during her speech. After everyone returns to their ship, he contacts Captain Picard: "It would seem that we are not completely dissimilar after all, in our hopes, or in our fears." Picard: "Yes." Romulan: "Well, then. Perhaps, one day [we can unify]." Picard: "One day." Bernardi is too caught up in a game of *gotcha* to meaningfully engage the *Star Trek* text and its political and social implications.

Bernardi again focuses on the superficial when he criticizes the fact that leading female characters in *Next Generation* hold caregiver roles on the *Enterprise*. Deanna Troi is the ship's counselor and Beverly Crusher is the ship's doctor. Bernardi says, "As in the original *Star Trek*, women in *The Next Generation* are consistently positioned as either helpers or fetishized objects. This is the case with both Dr. Crusher and Counselor Troi—their Federation jobs are supportive of their role as nurturers. The doctor and the counselor rarely give orders and almost always serve men."[8] (In drawing his criticisms, Bernardi fails to mention the female character of Tasha Yar, who was head of security during the first season of *Next Generation*.) First, in spite of Bernardi's judgmental tone, there's nothing wrong with women (or men) being nurturers, nor with women taking orders from men. Second, Bernardi puts forth no effort whatsoever to discuss the content of the Crusher or Troi characters (at this point, nothing in his hackneyed treatment of *Star Trek* surprises me). Crusher is not simply a nurturer but the ship's head doctor—hence, more than taking orders from men, she oversees medical care for the entire ship (a position of great responsibility, and one would imagine, prestige). Troi is not solely *Enterprise*'s counselor (chief psychologist), again a position of importance, but she is the captain's close advisor (her sage advice is regularly instrumental to the plot). Moreover, in the episode "Disaster" (1991), Troi takes command of the ship and saves the day. In pondering the treatment of women in *Next Generation*, it is important to note that female actors were frequently cast to play the roles of researchers, admirals, political leaders, and other positions of significant stature. Thus the decision to cast female characters as ship's doctor and counselor amount to nothing more than artistic choices, and most important, viewers watching the *Next Generation* would see women acting as decision makers, learned scientists, key advisors, and holding positions of great authority.

Significantly, Bernardi published his book on race and gender in the *Star Trek* franchise in 1998. By this time, *Deep Space Nine* and *Voyager* had already been running for years. (*Deep Space Nine* began airing in 1993 and *Voyager* in 1995.) In *Deep Space Nine*, the commanding officer is an African American male (see Figure i.3), with the first officer and science officer played by women. The starship *Voyager* is captained by a woman (see Figure i.4). Bernardi makes

Figure i.3 Benjamin Sisko in command of *Deep Space Nine* ("Emissary," series pilot 1993)

Figure i.4 Kathryn Janeway, captain of the starship *Voyager* ("Caretaker," series pilot 1995)

no comment on these shows or characters. Apparently, he and his publisher didn't let anything get in the way of their myopic, captious approach toward *Star Trek*.

Bernardi and critics of his ilk[9] are on stronger ground when they fault *Star Trek* for lacking openly LGBT characters. Efforts are made by *Star Trek*'s creators to favorably and thoughtfully treat LGBT issues—for example, *Next Generation* "The Outcast" (1992), where on a homosexual world, it is heterosexuals that suffer persecution. In the 1995 *Deep Space Nine* episode "Rejoined," one of the lead characters of the show does have a lesbian tryst. Nevertheless, it is painfully glaring in "The Host" (1991) when Dr. Crusher rejects the symbiont she has fallen in love with when it turns up in a female body—even though she earlier made love with the symbiont while it was in two different male bodies (one of them was Riker's, *Enterprise*'s first officer).

David Greven, in his outstanding book *Gender and Sexuality in* Star Trek, makes a very interesting observation on the sexual orientation politics of *Star Trek*. Greven holds that while the *Star Trek* franchise lacks LGBT characters, the franchise nonetheless presents a positive picture for the LGBT community. Greven's argument is that at the center of the *Star Trek* franchise is the claim that nonbiological family relations are just as valid and fulfilling as relations informed by biology or marriage. This is particularly important for the LGBT community, as historically its members were regularly estranged from their biological families and legally prohibited from forming new families—that is, denied the right to marry and adopt. Greven points to the fact that the relationship between Kirk, Spock, and McCoy is as vital and emotionally intimate as any relationship conveyed on American television (perhaps more so). A similar argument can be made of all *Star Trek* series, where few characters are married or have children, and same-sex friendships are the norm. Greven (who makes the point in his book that he is gay himself) comes very close (in my estimation) to holding that the addition of LGBT characters in the *Star Trek* franchise would have been overkill (artistically speaking), as the franchise is dominated by vibrant (nonbiological) relationships.[10]

Star Trek as Epiphenomenal

By necessity, all political art is to some degree derivative of the politics and societies of their times. Nonetheless, for aesthetics to qualify as political art, I contend it must stand outside of the politics of its time, even as it comments on those politics. Political art expands the field of politics to incorporate ideas/arguments outside of the "official," or those discourses deemed acceptable. Thus political art conveys the politics of the times but goes further in offering insights into the times and beyond.

The *Star Trek* franchise represents something of a natural experiment, where one iteration of the franchise is produced during the height of the Cold War (in the midst of the Civil Rights era and the student protest movements), and a later iteration is produced during the politically conservative Reagan Era and the denouement of the Cold War.

Therefore, the original series replicates the Cold War predominately through the Klingon-Federation geopolitical competition. As I outline in Chapter 1, *Star Trek* (the original series) is critical of the Cold War insofar as the series advises the United States/Soviet Union to make peace—that is, that they can/should bridge the divide between them. In this way, the original series leans decidedly away from official anticommunism and toward an argument in favor of detente.

Interestingly, the original series takes a strong stand against Nazism. Perhaps this is reflective of the fact that *Star Trek* creator Gene Roddenberry was a veteran of World War II. Regardless, that *Star Trek* seeks to identify Nazism as the true enemy of civilization and not communism, places the original series in the realm of political art, as it disrupts/challenges official discourse and propaganda and prods the viewer to look at all governments/politics through the lens of antifascism.

The *Star Trek* series that began in the late 1980s comes closer to uncritically replicating the official political ideology of its times. This is evident in its conveyance of interstellar geopolitical relations. These relations do not reflect the detente of the original series (and the ultimate hope for unity between the Federation/Klingons). Instead, interstellar relations are more reflective of neoconservative "clash of civilizations" reasoning (Chapter 4). Therefore, while the Klingons and the Federation are formal allies, the alliance is cast as uncertain, and war does occur between the Federation and the Klingons in *Deep Space Nine*. Also, a cold war persists with the Romulans, and an actual war almost occurs with the Cardassians. It is notable that the need for more military spending is expressed in more than one instance in *Next Generation*. In *Voyager*, peace is impossible with the Kazon (Chapter 10). Thus, seemingly consonant with realist foreign policy logic, later *Star Trek* holds that universal peace and unity is beyond reach—at least in the short to medium term.

Star Trek as Propaganda

With later *Star Trek* replicating/disseminating neocon biases, one might argue that these latter iterations of *Star Trek* are a form of propaganda. I resist this conclusion. For one, *Next Generation*, *Deep Space Nine*, and *Voyager* make sharp and explicit criticisms of the capitalist status quo. Indicative of *Star Trek*'s oppositional/subversive stance is the claim in *Voyager* that on Earth in the twenty-fourth century, "war and poverty simply don't exist" ("The 37s" 1995). Similarly, in *Enterprise*, the point is made that on twenty-second-century Earth, "war, disease, hunger . . . [were wiped] out in less than two generations" ("Broken Bow" 2001).

Perhaps more important, *Star Trek* outlines a revolutionary process whereby a classless Earth (without gender/ethnic biases) comes about. As I explain in Chapter 2 and revisit in Chapter 4, the *Star Trek* franchise conveys an American history that culminates with the antineoliberalism Bell Uprising of 2024. It is through this revolutionary process that the Earth of *Star Trek* attains classlessness and a world government, as well as overcomes gender/ethnic biases. An important caveat, the last *Star Trek* television series, *Enterprise*, provides a different Earth history—building on the movie *First Contact* (1996). In this iteration of Earth's history/politics, humans achieve global government and social justice because of its contact with Vulcans. With the manifestation of this "other," humans politically unify and remedy their social shortcomings (Chapter 9).

Interestingly, the *Star Trek* series that is most critiqued as a prop for American foreign policy is the original series. I take up these critiques in Chapter 1. Nevertheless, it is worth reiterating the fact that the original series (among all *Star Trek* series) is most critical and questioning of American foreign policy. This statement is arguably true in terms of all US television.[11]

Where *Star Trek* is least critical/questioning is in the realm of the environment. The original series does a better job on this matter (Chapter 2), whereas the later iterations (in my estimation) fail almost entirely on this score. Probably most significant is the fact that in the Federation, there are virtually no natural resource limits, and the matter of global warming is elided or badly distorted (Chapter 8).

Conclusion: *Star Trek* as Analytical Text

What distances later *Star Trek* series most from the realm of propaganda is that, even as it is replicating realist and neocon biases/reasoning, it is providing insight, meditations, and even critiques of these approaches to foreign affairs and non-Western societies. This is precisely why the *Star Trek* franchise can be deemed political art.[12] Even as it is conveying conservative ideation, *Star Trek* disrupts it and/or brings it to the fore, prompting the viewer to ponder and question international relations and the biases underlying American foreign policy. In Chapter 3 I show how, beginning with *Next Generation*, *Star Trek*'s creators expressly move away from directly commenting on American foreign policy. Chapter 4 outlines in detailed form how, starting with *Next Generation*, the Federation's foreign policy is predicated upon neoconservative ideology, thereby offering something of a sympathetic treatment of Samuel Huntington's controversial "clash of civilizations" thesis. This includes how the Borg is consistent with a critique of Western idealism (human liberalism) as it relates to traditionalist societies—that is, those shaped by patriarchy, political religion (theocracy), and obscurantism.

Star Trek is the quintessential text of the modern era. It provides the clearest analysis/understanding of social and political change, as well allows us to meaningfully explore/ponder the ideation at the heart of the American Century. Thus in Chapter 5 I argue that *Star Trek* demonstrates that the American Century manifests three routes, or strategies, to the attainment of global government—federation, empire, or neoliberalism. US world leadership manifests indications of all three. Moreover, *Star Trek* shows that empires (as distinct from federations) establish regimes of technologies. The United States has established a regime of technology consistent with empire (Chapter 6). In Chapter 7, I hold that *Star Trek* outlines that in the modern era, soldiers fight in wars for two prime reasons: (preemptive) empire or justice.

Thus while the likes of Bernardi are denouncing *Star Trek* in the strongest terms for its casting choices and its color schemes, he and others are stigmatizing arguably the most important political text of the modern era—falsely sullying *Star Trek* as sexist and racist, when in fact the franchise makes the clearest and most sustained appeal for gender/ethnic equality, as well as for social justice. Moreover, *Star Trek* allows us to see and understand the catastrophic perils and pitfalls (save for possibly global warming) that humanity faces in the modern era.

What I offer in this volume is a series of chapters wherein I approach the *Star Trek* franchise from multiple vectors. The *Star Trek* text is simply too rich in my opinion to put forth a single monograph that effectively analyzes its various themes, motifs, and meditations. The chapters of this book do overlap. I found this necessary to sufficiently work through the varied and important ideas inherent in the *Star Trek* text. Hopefully, readers agree.

CHAPTER 1

Star Trek (the Original Series)
An Anti–Cold War Narrative

The field of *Star Trek* studies (to coin a phrase) has been maligned by two hugely flawed assumptions: (1) that the original series is a metaphor for the Cold War (professor of US television history, Rick Worland: "The Klingons and the Federation were firmly established as two ideologically opposed superpower blocs")[1] and, even more egregious, (2) that the Federation represents a kind of pro-American political trope (professor of international relations, Mark P. Lagon: "The zealous desire of James T. Kirk, as the hero of the original *Star Trek*, to spread the Federation's way of life serves as a mirror to observe the American style of foreign policy").[2] (English professor, M. Keith Booker: "[Captain] Kirk is a walking icon of Americanism.")[3] These misplaced assumptions have worked to devalue *Star Trek* as pro-American Cold War propaganda.

I share historian Nicholas Evan Sarantakes's view that *Star Trek* cannot be reduced to pro-American Cold War propaganda. He makes this argument largely by appealing to the intentions of *Star Trek*'s creators.[4] I rely almost entirely on the *Star Trek* text to make my argument.

Star Trek is not a metaphor of the Cold War but a sharp critique of it. Moreover, the series is not pro-American but critical and questioning of US foreign policy. Judging from the content of the original series, *Star Trek*'s biases are not geared against Cold

War communism but against Nazism and fascism—not in favor of Americanism but modernism.[5] Reading the *Star Trek* original series text as holding a critical distance from the Cold War and American foreign policy allows us to view it as a work of "political art,"[6] lending important insight/meditations into the modern era.

Star Trek as Outside the Cold War

The first indication that *Star Trek* stands outside of the Cold War is the fact that, in the series, Earth is governed by a world government, and the United States/Soviet Union do not exist. More broadly, the series casts nationalism in a negative light. Thus earthlings are part of the Federation—a modernist nomenclature—an institution composed of heterodox peoples from throughout interstellar space. Notably, in *Star Trek*, it is peoples that politically identify themselves by their ethnicity (nationalism)—the Klingons, Romulans—that are seemingly warlike and aggressive.

Daniel Bernardi, in Star Trek *and History: Race-ing toward a White Future*, holds the *Star Trek* franchise (particularly the original series and *Next Generation*) exhibits racism, or more specifically, an "antiblack" attitude (a type of white nationalism).[7] Focusing specifically on *Star Trek*, the original series, Lieutenant Uhura (played by African American actor Nichelle Nichols) was reduced to a bit role, given almost exclusively throwaway lines. Nevertheless, this character was involved in a scene conveying arguably the clearest stance for ethnic equality and acceptance ever on American television. In "The Savage Curtain" (1969), an ersatz Abraham Lincoln[8] says to Uhura, "What a charming Negress." He quickly corrects himself, "Oh, forgive me, my dear. I know in my time some used that term as a description of property." Uhura responds, "But why should I object to that term, sir? . . . We've each learned to be delighted with what we are."

An even clearer rejection of nationalism (Americanism, whiteism) is made by Kirk and Spock (a Vulcan) in "Whom Gods Destroy" (1969). Kirk speaks of the founders of the Federation,

"They were humanitarians and statesmen, and they had a dream. A dream that became a reality and spread throughout the stars, a dream that made Mister Spock and me brothers." Indicative of how the Federation transcends all ethnic, religious, and species divisions, when asked, "Do you consider Captain Kirk and yourself brothers?" Spock replies, "Captain Kirk speaks somewhat figuratively and with undue emotion. However, what he says is logical and I do, in fact, agree with it."

Most important, *Star Trek* denies the validity of the normative core of the American position concerning the Cold War—that is, anti-Communism.[9] Thus *Star Trek*, far from replicating the American arguments against the Soviet Union, indicates that the Cold War is nothing more than a struggle between great powers over resources and territory. This point is made explicit when the Klingons (the main geopolitical rival of the Federation) are first introduced in "Errand of Mercy" (1967). When the Organians intervene to prevent a Klingon-Federation war, Captain Kirk and the Klingon at hand strongly object. In positing their objections, neither refers to the normative justifications/pretenses at the heart of the Cold War. Particularly significant is that Kirk does not refer to freedom, liberty, and so on—the typical Cold War rhetoric of the American side. Instead, Kirk's complaints are of the traditional great power sort: "We have legitimate grievances against the Klingons. They've invaded our territory, killed our citizens. They're openly aggressive. They've boasted that they'll take over half the galaxy." In 1987, during the pilot of *Next Generation*, *Star Trek*'s creators expressly cast the Cold War as "silly arguments about how to divide the resources" of the planet.[10] Taking the Cold War as simply an aggressive phase of great power politics, the following is a sharp rebuke of those that seemingly sought war with the Soviet Union. The Organian spokesman: "To wage war, Captain [Kirk]? To kill millions of innocent people? To destroy life on a planetary scale? Is that what you're defending [i.e., arguing for]?"

Significantly, when *Star Trek* does point to American normative values, the suggestion is made that in the context of the Cold

War, the United States has forgotten these values (McCarthyism?). In "The Omega Glory" (1968), the *Enterprise* crew encounters a planet identical to Earth, except that the Cold War resulted in a nuclear/biological weapons conflagration. The planet's population has been reduced to a veritable stone age. The group that represents the West (the Yangs) worships the American Constitution (the document), but they do not know what it means—that is, they are unable to read it. Ultimately, it is up to Kirk to remind them of the values that informed America.[11]

Again, far from accepting, conveying, and replicating the normative notions that were deemed insuperable during the Cold War, *Star Trek* suggests that peace between the great powers is achievable. The following is reported in "Day of the Dove" (1968): "For three years, the Federation and the Klingon Empire have been at peace." The action begins when the *Enterprise* rescues the crew from a Klingon vessel as it explodes. The *Enterprise* crew and the Klingons engage in hostilities, with hate, anger, and false accusations spewing from both sides. It turns out that they are being influenced and manipulated to hate and attack each other: "There's an alien entity aboard the ship. It's forcing us to fight . . . It subsists on the emotions of others." The alien entity "appears to be strengthened by mental irradiations of hostility, violent intentions. It exists on the hate of others. To put it simply." In the end, the Klingons and the *Enterprise* crew join forces to vanquish the alien creating the hostilities. To the alien: "Maybe you've caused a lot of suffering, a lot of history, but that's all over." The final scene of the episode shows the Klingons and the Federation crew standing shoulder to shoulder, laughing and jovial. The Organian in "Errand of Mercy" informs Captain Kirk and the Klingon commander that in the future, "you and the Klingons will become fast friends. You will work together."

The other great power in the *Star Trek* original series narrative is the Romulan Empire. The Romulans were introduced in "Balance of Terror" (1966; see Figure 1.1). A Romulan ship has invaded Federation space and destroyed outposts along the

Figure 1.1 Romulan from the original series

"Neutral Zone" (an ostensive reference to the "Demilitarized Zone" on the Korean peninsula). The Romulan "warbird" seeks to destroy the *Enterprise* using an invisibility ("cloaking") device. After sustaining heavy damage inflicted by *Enterprise*, the captain of the ship engages its self-destruct sequence. Indicating that the chasm between the Federation and the Romulans can be bridged, the captain of the doomed ship says to Captain Kirk, "I regret that we meet in this way. You and I are of a kind. In a different reality, I could have called you friend."

A particular strike against the idea that the original *Star Trek* can be reduced to a metaphor of the Cold War is that there is nothing Soviet/Russian about the Klingons.[12] It is noteworthy that the Klingons (of the 1960s variant and beyond) look like peoples of central Asia, not Russians[13]—with dark skin and dark hair (see Figure 1.2). Moreover, the Klingons employ no Soviet symbols or slogans. Unless we knew that *Star Trek* the original series was produced during the Cold War, we would have little reason to think that the Klingons are an allegory for the Soviet Union. Quite the

Figure 1.2 Klingons from the original series

contrary, highly suggestive of an attitude of detente in the original series, is the character Chekov, an *Enterprise* officer with a Russian/Soviet background and accent. Chekov's Russian/Soviet nationalist comments are benignly (and lightly) received by Captain Kirk and crew.

Star Trek as Critique of American Foreign Policy

Viewing *Star Trek* not as metaphor of the Cold War but as a commentary on great power politics of the era, the original series can be interpreted as offering a critical stance on the West's (the United States') conduct in its competition with the Soviet Union. At a minimum, the claim is made that the United States is no better in its tactics in the underdeveloped world than the Soviets. In "Private Little War" (1968), Kirk relates to a native on a primitive world, "There came a time when our weapons . . . grew faster than our wisdom, and we almost destroyed ourselves." So when the Klingons seemingly begin to supply particular tribes on this planet with advanced weapons, Kirk is reticent to do the same. In the context of US involvement in Vietnam, where the American military command measured success by the number of enemy dead, McCoy's comment that "killing is stupid and useless" can be viewed as a powerful condemnation. Kirk refers explicitly to the Vietnam War, "Do you remember the twentieth-century brush wars on the Asian continent? Two giant powers involved . . . Neither side could pull out." Drawing his inspiration from this historical precedent, Kirk concludes that the Federation will arm its allies on the planet with the same kind of weaponry given by the Klingons: "The only solution is what happened back then. Balance of power. The trickiest, most difficult, dirtiest game of them all, but the only one that preserves both sides."

In the episode "Arena" (1967), it is acknowledged that the West engages in aggressive, militaristic colonization. A Federation colony in a remote region of space is attacked, and Kirk is determined to destroy the offending ship to make an example of it:

> **SPOCK:** You mean to destroy the alien ship, Captain?
> **KIRK:** If the aliens go unpunished, they'll be back, attacking other Federation installations.
> **SPOCK:** I merely suggested that a regard for sentient life.
> **KIRK:** There's no time for that. It's a matter of policy. Out here, we're the only policemen around. And a crime has been committed.

Later, we learn that the matter is not as simple as Kirk believed. It turns out that the Federation colony was in Gorn space, and they viewed it as an invasion. Upon hearing the Gorn side of things, McCoy acknowledges, "We could be in the wrong" and "the Gorn simply might have been trying to protect themselves." In the end, Kirk decides to spare the life of the captain of the Gorn ship that destroyed the Federation colony.

"Patterns of Force" (1968) and "A Piece of the Action" (1968) can both be interpreted as critical of American intervention in underdeveloped societies. In "Patterns of Force," a renowned Federation historian is sent to a relatively primitive planet, Ekos, as a "cultural observer." Nevertheless, in an effort to stabilize the planet's society, the historian models its politics on Nazi Germany. When the historian, named Gill, is asked why he interfered in the primitive planet's politics/social organization, he responds (in a drugged stupor), "Planet . . . fragmented . . . divided. Took lesson from Earth history." Why Nazi Germany as a model? Gill responds, "You studied history. You knew what the Nazis were. Most efficient state . . . Earth ever knew." Thus just as the United States was doing during the Cold War in its relations with underdeveloped countries, Gill prioritized political stability and expediency over virtually all other values.

"A Piece of the Action" involves a remote planet (Sigma Iotia II) that a Federation ship visited one hundred years ago. This contact distorted the planet's society because the ship left behind a book dealing with "gangsters. Chicago. Mobs. Published in 1992 . . . They seized upon that one book as the blueprint for an entire society. As the Bible." As a result, the society of Sigma Iotia II organized itself into a set of competing mafia organizations, where the mobs themselves are the government. This is similar to the distortion that occurred in underdeveloped countries when they were incorporated into the American world system. In many underdeveloped societies, rentier/compradore classes came to dominate, as they offer raw materials and cheap labor to multinational corporations. Such countries are characterized by corruption and authoritarian practices.[14] The following exchange in "A Piece of the Action" occurs between a woman on the street and a mafia lieutenant:

> **WOMAN:** When's the boss going to do something about the crummy street lights around here, eh? A girl ain't safe. And how about the laundry pickup? We ain't had a truck by in three weeks.
> **MAFIA HENCHMAN:** Write him a letter.
> **WOMAN:** He sent it back with postage due. We pay our percentages. We're entitled to a little service for our money.

HENCHMAN: Get lost, will ya? Some people got nothing to do but complain.

Prioritizing stability and expediency, the *Enterprise* crew sets on the following course: "Oxmyx is the worst gangster of all [on this planet]. We quarrel with Oxmyx' methods, but his goal is essentially the correct one. This society must become united or it will degenerate into total anarchy." Just as the New York mafia did with Costa Nostra in the 1930s,[15] the *Enterprise* establishes a federated political structure employing the planet's mafia groups:

KIRK: You people, you've been running this planet like a piecework factory. From now on, it's going to be under one roof. You're going to run it like a business. That means you're going to make a profit.

"The Apple" (1967) also raises questions about intervention into underdeveloped parts of the world. Visiting the planet Gamma Trianguli VI, the *Enterprise* crew find that the inhabitants are content living a primitive life. They are sustained by an artificial intelligence also inhabiting the planet:

DR. McCoy: I just ran a check on the natives, and there's a complete lack of harmful bacteria in their systems, no decalcification, no degeneration of tissue, no arteriosclerosis. In simple terms, they're not growing old, and I can't tell you how old they are—twenty years or twenty thousand years.

The natives provide the machine (Vaal) with energy (food) to maintain it. McCoy objects to this arrangement but Spock objects to applying human values to the situation, regarding it as "a splendid example of reciprocity":

McCoy: It would take a computerized Vulcan mind, such as yours, to make that kind of a statement.
SPOCK: Doctor, you insist on applying human standards to non-human cultures. Humans are only a tiny minority in this galaxy.

McCoy: There are certain absolutes, and one of them is the right of humanoids to a free and unchained environment, the right to have conditions which permit growth.
Spock: Doctor, these people are healthy and they are happy. Whatever you choose to call it, this system works, despite your emotional reaction to it.
McCoy: It might work for you, Mr. Spock, but it doesn't work for me.

Kirk expresses a similar opinion in "This Side of Paradise" (1967) when his crew opts under an alien influence for a bucolic, sedentary life: "Man stagnates if he has no ambition, no desire to be more than he is."

Star Trek as a Caution against Nazism

As already noted, *Star Trek* does not treat the Cold War as an irrevocable normative struggle for the future of the planet. Instead, the series creators seemingly advise the great powers of the mid-twentieth century to ramp down the tensions of the Cold War, lest they risk an unnecessary, devastating conflict.

While *Star Trek* does not cast Cold War communism/Stalinism as an eminent ideological threat, the series creators do strongly caution against fascism/Nazism, indicating that it is predicated on genocidal hate and poses a profound threat to civilization. "Patterns of Force," as previously noted, portrays a Nazi regime on the planet of Ekos, which was instituted, sponsored, and overseen by a Federation official. With Nazism as the political basis of Ekos, the Ekosians organize around the vilification of Zeons, a population from the neighboring planet of Zeon. (Spock: "Why do the Nazis hate Zeons?" Zeonian: "Because without us to hate, there'd be nothing to hold them together. So the Party has built us into a threat, a disease to be wiped out.") In addition to massacring the Zeons on Ekos ("the eliminations have started. Within an hour, the Zeon blight will forever be removed from Ekos"), the Nazi regime organizes a planned genocide ("Their Final Solution") against Zeons on their home planet: "Our entire solar system will forever be rid of the disease that was Zeon."

In "City on the Edge of Forever" (1967), one of the *Enterprise*'s crew members, Doctor McCoy, inadvertently goes back in time and prevents the US entrance into World War II. The result being that the Nazis win the war, which subsequently prevents the formation of the Federation and even apparently stops humanity from ever being a space-faring race. ("Your vessel, your beginning, all that you knew is gone.")

Star Trek's Modernist Bias

Critics of *Star Trek* point to episodes like "The Apple" and "This Side of Paradise" to argue that the original series does little more than replicate American values and justifies their imposition on other societies. It does not matter to these critics that in altering the politics of these "primitive" societies, *Star Trek* (Spock) offers important (reflective) criticisms of these society-altering decisions. After Spock is freed from the alien (drug-induced) influence that led him to a sedentary, bucolic life in "This Side of Paradise," he says, "I have little to say about it, Captain, except that for the first time in my life I was happy." Professor Booker acknowledges, "Spock's point is potentially a highly subversive one, both in its rejection of capitalist competition and in its approval of drug-induced happiness." Nevertheless, Booker dismisses Spock's commentary for the odd reason that his character is "only half human," so his views "can hardly be taken as representative of *Star Trek*'s view of the human condition."[16]

Thus Booker rejects the idea that *Star Trek* is seeking to reflectively acknowledge and explore the biases in Western/modern reasoning. Instead, "the bulk of *Star Trek* tends to suggest . . . that the expansionist-colonialist impulse is natural."[17] In drawing this judgment, Booker makes no mention of "The Paradise Syndrome" (1968), where the *Enterprise* crew comes upon a group of Native American tribes transported to an alien planet. ("A mixture of Navajo, Mohican, and Delaware, I believe. All among the more advanced and peaceful tribes.") Significantly, no effort whatsoever is made to colonize or interfere with the transported natives. Instead, Kirk et al. succeed in ensuring that the tribes can continue their premodern existence.

An episode Booker does engage with is "Friday's Child" (1967). The ostensive moral of this episode is that if the United States wants to gain the allegiance of underdeveloped societies, it should respect their culture and politics. It is the promise of political and cultural autonomy that results in a "primitive" planet's joining of the Federation camp and not that of the Klingons. (Kirk: "The highest of all our laws states that your world is yours and will always remain yours.") Booker alleges that "Friday's Child" is pro-US Cold War propaganda, "much in the way the United States and the its allies vied with the Soviet Union and its allies in the 1960s to see which could make a more compelling case for itself as the legitimate foe of colonialism and friend of international liberation."[18] While a viewer watching in the late 1960s could share Booker's analysis of this episode, it is the obligation of the cultural critic to set aside his or her biases and assumptions in considering a work of art.

A similar charge of operating through bias/myopia can be made of Lagon's reading of "The Apple." After the *Enterprise* crew "free" the tribe of natives from Vaal, Kirk promises Federation assistance ("with our help") in transitioning to the point that they "learn" to "care for" themselves. Lagon conflates this promise of help with US rhetoric surrounding its foreign aid, which tends to serve American hegemonic designs: "The caveat 'with our help' points to a set of complicated questions for US policy: How long and at what cost will other societies require help to introduce democracy? Must they conform to our variety of democracy (limiting government intervention in economic affairs, based on a presidential rather than parliamentary system, and based on single member districts rather than proportional representation)? Should the United States use force to promote democracy?"[19]

Taking the *Star Trek* text seriously (something I think that the likes of Bernardi, Lagon, and Booker do not do), "The Apple" makes a case for modernism, not "American democracy" per se. Kirk uses what can be viewed as Enlightenment rhetoric when assuring the natives that their lives will be better post-Vaal, in spite of the fact that the machine provided for all their needs: "You'll learn to build for yourselves, think for yourselves . . . You'll like it a lot."

If we're going to read humanity's politics and history into this dialogue, it appears closer to an argument against religious paternalism (as the natives worshiped Vaal), than a justification/lauding of American intervention in the developing world. Consistent with this interpretation, in the denouement direct reference is made to religious allegory:

> **SPOCK:** Captain, you are aware of the biblical story of Genesis.
> **KIRK:** Yes, of course I'm aware of it. Adam and Eve tasted the apple and as a result were driven out of paradise.
> **SPOCK:** Precisely, Captain, and in a manner of speaking, we have given the people of Vaal the apple, the knowledge of good and evil if you will, as a result of which they too have been driven out of paradise.

Thus it is preferable to struggle for survival and develop your mind and society as a result than it is to live in comfort but in ignorance. Hence, despite Spock's claim that they drove the people of Vaal out of Eden, McCoy confidently holds, "We put those people back on a normal course of social evolution."

In considering whether or not "The Apple" is a stealth justification/invocation for American intervention in the developing world, or a meditation on the merits/demerits of promoting modernity, it is apposite to ponder the episode "Mirror, Mirror" (1967). "Mirror, Mirror" opens with a discussion between Kirk and the leader of the Halkans (named Tharn). The Halkans refuse to allow the Federation to mine the dilithium crystals on their planet because "dilithium crystals represent awesome power. Wrongful use of that power, even to the extent of the taking of one life, would violate our history of total peace." Kirk asks, "When may we resume discussion?" Tharn: "The council will meditate further, but do not be hopeful of any change." Tharn adds, "Captain, you do have the might to force the crystals from us, of course." Kirk: "But we won't."

Through a technical glitch, the *Enterprise* landing party is transported to an alternate universe. The *Enterprise* exists in this alternate universe, but instead of the Federation, the political authority is the Empire—where "behavior and discipline" is "brutal, savage." While in the Federation universe the *Enterprise* only pursues peaceful means with the Halkans, in the Empire universe, Kirk is "ordered to annihilate the Halkans unless they comply. *No alternative.*"

Booker and Lagon would presumably hold that "Mirror, Mirror" only obfuscates the fact that the United States engages in military interventions throughout the world, because the audience is supposed to associate the Federation with the United States and the Empire with the Soviet Union. Regardless, "Mirror, Mirror" is an explicit rejection/critique of military intervention into other societies, particularly for purposes of controlling natural resources—a censure that can be issued to the United States of the Cold War Era.

A critique of US foreign policy can also be read into the Federation's Prime Directive. It is a policy of noninterference, which expressly proscribes changing/influencing "the normal evolution" of non-Federation worlds ("A Piece of the Action"). While not always upheld by the *Enterprise* crew, the Prime Directive establishes that the Federation is prohibited from giving advanced technology to non-Federation planets, as well as influencing the politics and economics of said planets ("The Apple" 1967; "Private Little War" 1968; "Friday's Child" 1967; "Bread and Circuses" 1968; "A Piece of the Action" 1968). The Prime Directive would be directly at odds with modernization theory, embraced by foreign policy makers in the White House during the 1960s. Modernization theory amounted to a Cold War strategy to share advanced technology and foster particular economic policies within the pro-Western countries of the developing world in an effort to solidify their position within the American-led camp.[20]

Conclusion

The success of *Star Trek* (the original series) both as an entertainment vehicle and as political art is that it helps us reason through many of the key issues of the Cold War and the modern era more broadly. The reason that *Star Trek* does provide insights into the politics of the twentieth century, and even the twenty-first, is precisely because it is not a metaphor for the Cold War, nor pro-American. In this way, the original *Star Trek* is redolent of a Kennedy-esque liberal internationalism.[21] Hence the original series remains popular among international audiences as well as being instructive/elucidating.

Perhaps governed by the idea that an American television show made in the late 1960s (prior to the detente of the early 1970s) is incapable of maintaining a critical distance from US foreign policy, critics dismiss *Star Trek* as hopelessly biased/compromised. One is reminded of Mark Twain's (Samuel Clemens) visit to the twenty-fourth century in the *Next Generation* episode "Time's Arrow" (1992). Upon encountering the *Enterprise*, he cannot help but interpret it through his nineteenth-century understanding of history/politics. Thus he takes the existence of the ship as *prima facie* evidence of imperial politics: "Huge starships, and weapons that can no doubt destroy entire cities, and military conquest as a way of life?" However, Clemens comes to question his initial analysis and how it is colored by his knowledge of nineteenth-century-Earth:

> **CLEMENS:** So there're a privileged few who serve on these ships, living in luxury and wanting for nothing. But what about everyone else? What about the poor? You ignore them.
> **TROI:** Poverty was eliminated on Earth a long time ago, and a lot of other things disappeared with it. Hopelessness, despair, cruelty.

CLEMENS: Young lady, I come from a time when men achieve power and wealth by standing on the backs of the poor, where prejudice and intolerance are commonplace and power is an end unto itself. And you're telling me that isn't how it is anymore?
TROI: That's right.

Clemens comes to have a positive view of the twenty-fourth century: "Well, maybe it's worth giving up cigars for after all." Unlike Twain, critics of *Star Trek* are steeped in cynicism and an incapacity to step outside of twentieth-century history and politics.

My hope is that *Star Trek* is seen as the political art and political theory that it is. More than ever, we need to be inspired by the internationalism, optimism, anti-imperialism, antifascism, and social justice[22] of *Star Trek*.

CHAPTER 2

Star Trek, Utopia, and Pragmatism

The *Star Trek* franchise is the quintessential philosophical text of the American century. This is reflected in the popularity of the series, its tremendous financial success, and more impressive, its loyal and devoted following.[1] Interpreting *Star Trek* as philosophy[2] with a broad American audience[3] is consistent with Carlin Romano's claim in *America the Philosophical* that US society is highly philosophical.[4] Given that we are currently in the television age, it should not be surprising that political theory in the form of television-based fiction exists.[5] *Star Trek* does not simply reflect American political reasoning. It gives us insight into this reasoning.

Examining the political motifs and themes evident in the multiple broadcast iterations of *Star Trek*, my contention is that at the heart of the franchise (and American political thought) are two distinct normative paradigms: utopian Marxism and pragmatism. While embracing Marx's ontology of progressive social change and internationalism (world government), *Star Trek* issues a caution against pragmatism and neopragmatism—that is, intersubjective agreement.

Utopia

Authors in *The Cambridge Companion to Utopian Literature*, edited by Gregory Claeys, note how beginning in the nineteenth century—but especially in the twentieth century—science fiction and utopian literatures conflate.[6] It is seemingly the case that with the advent of modernity and its normative vaunting of technological progress, it is well-nigh impossible to distinguish between science fiction and utopian fiction.[7] Nonetheless, it is still analytically useful to point out that science fiction fantasy is substantively different from utopian fiction that is predicated upon presently unimaginable scientific revolutions. The most popular example of what I would classify as science fiction fantasy is the *Star Wars* franchise. In the first frame of the initial *Star Wars* movie, it is declared that its action takes place in a "galaxy far, far away," telling us that the narrative is a work of fantasy, and not one actively seeking to map current social, political, and economic trends into the future. Carl Freedman, in his essay "Science Fiction and Utopia," offers an observation that aids in distinguishing science fiction fantasy from utopian science fiction. Specifically, Freedman holds that a key aspect of utopian literature and art is "the future [as an] object of *hope* [for] a revolutionary reconfiguration of the world as a totality."[8]

Part of what makes *Star Trek* a powerful piece of political theory are the arguments it makes about how human society becomes a classless, prosperous, and thriving one—free of want and gender/ethnic biases. In this way, *Star Trek* is a political tract arguing/explaining how humans (more specifically Americans) will, can, and should achieve an ideal political, social, and economic system—that is, a utopia. Two points made by *Star Trek* as to how society can achieve an ideal state is the need for world government, and that social progress occurs through what can be deemed "revolutionary" events. This is consistent with Karl Marx's argument that one of the keys to political justice, freedom, and stability is internationalism. Marx also argues that political and economic progress occurs through a series of revolutions—culminating in a classless, just, and peaceful global society.[9]

Thus *Star Trek* is not solely a work of technological optimism—that is, the idea that technological advancement will alone drive social/political progress.[10] In fact, *Star Trek* renders cautions against unchecked/unregulated scientific/technological advancement.[11] One theme that appears in the *Star Trek* franchise is eugenics. In *Star Trek* historiography, in the Earth's past (or our near future) there is a Eugenics War: "An improved breed of human. That's what the Eugenics War was all about." The war resulted when "young supermen" seized "power simultaneously in over forty nations . . . They were aggressive, arrogant. They began to battle among themselves."[12] As a result of this experience, human genetic engineering is banned in the fictional world of *Star Trek*. The other prime caution that *Star Trek* yields against, "technologism"—that is, an uncritical faith in science and engineering—are the Borg. The Borg (first appearing in *The Next Generation*) embrace technology to such an extreme extent that they replace large parts of their bodies (and brains) with gadgets. Every Borg is mechanically altered—by force if necessary. The result is that the Borg do not create knowledge but can only appropriate (i.e., "assimilate") it from others.[13] Hence a prominent argument in *Star Trek* is that if technological development is to serve as a basis for justice, freedom, and societal well-being, humanity must get its politics right—otherwise technological and scientific advancement can result in eugenics, for instance, or other inherently oppressive and destructive outcomes like the Borg.

World Government

World government in *Star Trek* ostensibly comes about because the nation-state system is a major political liability.[14] *Star Trek*, the original series (1966–69), notes that humanity experienced a World War III in the 1990s—where tens of millions died. Spock, in "Bread and Circuses" (1968), lists Earth's three world wars in the twentieth century, along with specific numbers of dead: 6 million in World War I, 11 million in World War II, and 37 million in World War III. In "Space Seed" (1967), the following is rendered: "The mid-1990s was the era of your last so-called world war ... The Eugenics War." As was the case in World War I and II, nation-states (as noted previously) were the platforms for this fictional World War III. *Star Trek: The Next Generation* posits an episode with a world divided into two countries beset with hostility, loathing, and deep suspicion toward one another.[15]

Star Trek's fictional history, where Earth's wars become progressively devastating, is consistent with Lenin's theory of international relations. Accruing to Marxist theory, Lenin argued that as capitalist economies became more and more unstable due to declining investment returns (as theorized by Marx), the world's nation-state system would destabilize and result in wars of greater and greater proportion.[16] Lenin wrote during World War I.[17] The creators of the original series worked in the aftermath of World War II and during the height of the Cold War. Thus writing about a third world war occurring within a thirty-year frame was not much of a stretch. While this was a pessimistic view about humanity's inability to avoid another major war within a generation, *Star Trek* is optimistic about humanity's ability to overcome such devastating destruction and ultimately abolish one prime source of such devastation—the nation-state.

Present international politics point to the need for world government, as nation-states are continuing to serve as the basis for major military assaults. Thus the advent of America's global hegemony as the sole superpower with the collapse of the Soviet Union has not initiated a peaceful/stable global regime—that is, the "end of history." Indeed, just as the Soviet Union was being dismantled, a major war took place in the heart of Eurasia. I am referring to the first Persian Gulf War involving the Iraqi invasion of Kuwait (1990) and the coalition of countries that rolled back the invasion (1991). The September 2001 hijacking of civilian airliners and their use as weapons against iconic US structures (the New York Twin Towers and the Pentagon) brought about the US invasion of Afghanistan—seemingly among the remotest of regions of the planet. In 2003, in defiance of international law, the US organized and led "coalition of the willing" invaded and occupied Iraq. Libya, in 2011, had its government overthrown by another international coalition of nation-states. Writing in 2014, the United States is threatening Iran with military attack if Iran does not accede to America's (and its allies') demands to cease the development of nuclear energy. Globally devastating conflagrations are ostensibly possible, as the United States and Russia (the major nuclear weapon states) came into sharp opposition in 2008 over the country of Georgia. Similarly, in 2014, events in the Ukraine have again heightened political/military tensions between nuclear armed great powers (the United States, Russia, and the European Union).

With modern means of transportation and communication, the possibility of governing on a global scale appears absurdly obvious. This was even the case in the 1960s (à la *Star Trek*), before the current computer/Internet revolution. The opportunity for world governance is so patent in a context where people are constantly traveling and communicating across the globe[18] that darkly cast conspiracies of international government (the United Nations) are common fare among extremist nationalist groups—those most politically wed to their nation-states.[19] Extreme nationalism in opposition to global governance in the current epoch is consonant with the *Protocols of the Elders of Zion*—produced by the Russian Czar's secret police at the turn of the twentieth century—in which world government is cast as a dangerous cabal. The *Protocols of the Elders of Zion* can be perceived to be in direct response to *Angel of the Revolution*, written by H. G. Wells in 1892. Wells holds in this work of fiction that an Anglo-American–centered revolution defeats the forces of reaction and aristocracy worldwide, thereby establishing a global government founded on reason and justice.[20]

Regardless of whether world government is conceived as an objectionable impingement upon the sacred/venerable nation, or the institutional basis for peace and freedom, some type of worldwide regulatory regime is becoming more and more necessary. This is particularly evident with the climate change phenomenon.[21]

Collectively, the countries of the world are increasingly enhancing the heat trapping properties of the atmosphere.[22] With the dramatic decline of Arctic Ocean summer ice extent in 2012, the collapse of the Greenland ice sheet is a near- to medium-term likelihood. The result of all this would be a catastrophic rise in sea level and runaway global warming, as Arctic Ocean ice and Greenland ice anchor the planet's meteorology.[23] The nation-states of the planet have failed to negotiate a worldwide treaty to regulate/reduce greenhouse gas emissions.[24] Meanwhile, such gases are being emitted at faster and faster rates, as the so-called developed nation-states are holding their massive and disproportionate global warming emissions steady and, at the same time, the developing nation-states (e.g., India and China) are accelerating their emissions.[25] Pointing to the inherent difficulties of protecting the environment in the context of multiple nation-states that have absolute sovereignty, the 1986 movie *Star Trek: The Voyage Home* explains that in the late twentieth century, in spite of international agreements to prohibit whale hunting, particular countries continue to sanction their killing.[26]

Related to the global warming phenomenon is the expanding human population.[27] Over the course of the twentieth century and into the twenty-first, humanity has grown fourfold—from 1.6 billion to 7 billion—consuming increasing amounts of energy, food, and land.[28] Historian Matthew Connelly argues in his book *Fatal Misconception: The Struggle to Control World Population* that post–World War II population control efforts were marred by the perception and reality that such efforts were directed at specific countries and regions of the world.[29] The environmental movement of the late 1960s highlighted the threat of uncontrolled population growth.[30] "The Mark of Gideon" (1969), an original *Star Trek* series episode, conveys a planet where its population grows unchecked. This creates profound social and political problems. "The Conscience of the King" (1967) references a dilemma in which a colony was too large for its food supply.

Therefore, *Star Trek*, especially the original series, draws attention to problems and issues that could be resolved through global government. Unlike narratives and political arguments that view world government as unworkable or inherently oppressive, *Star Trek* holds that establishing political sovereignty on a planetary scale is a necessary step to achieve a peaceful and sustainable society.[31] World government is ostensibly more preferable to the current nation-state system that is serving as the basis for persistent, and potentially expanding, military conflicts. Moreover, environmental issues, particularly the global warming crisis, do lead to the conclusion that worldwide regulatory regimes are needed if humanity and civilization are to survive.

Transportation and communication technologies are not the only reason that *Star Trek* is optimistic about the possibilities and benefits of world government. American concepts of social and political assimilation—that is, "America the Great Melting Pot"—also inform *Star Trek*'s optimism.

The "Great American Melting Pot"

The internationalist pretenses of *Star Trek* are a product of the American belief that all humans are capable of being assimilated into modern Western political culture—the highest manifestation of this culture presumably being the United States. Hence the notion of the "American Melting Pot," where people from throughout the world can come to the United States and be accepted. Viewing this from an optimist stance, the claim put forward (and embedded in *Star Trek*) is that modernity is transparent and accessible to all, as well as places few political burdens on individuals. Especially important, there are no religious obligations, or any associated with ethnicity or lineage.[32] Captain Picard declares, "If there's one ideal the Federation holds most dear it's that all men, all [alien] races, can be united."[33]

Perhaps the core optimism conveyed in *Star Trek* is the ability of people from all ethnic backgrounds (and from other planets) to live peacefully together and fruitfully collaborate. During a *Next Generation* 1990 episode, a visiting alien is very impressed with the highly diverse background of the *Enterprise* crew: "Truly remarkable. They're all so different from one another yet they work together freely."[34] Operating through reason, science, and a common language (English), humans virtually throughout the *Star Trek* series and movies get along with little rancor or divisiveness. *Star Trek* is also distinctive for the intelligence and maturity of humans (and that of their fictional alien partners). A particular signature feature of *Star Trek* is the ability of its characters to maneuver complex (fictional) technologies. This is indicative of the putative transparency and accessibility of reason, science, and technology. It is also reflective of the belief that virtually every human has the mental capability to attain very high levels of knowledge, emotional maturity, and technical proficiency.

According to *Star Trek*, this plateau of human development is the result of revolutionary processes. Therefore, human advancement is not simply the result of natural progression but instead it is in part the result of conceptualizing America as a continuing project of "justice." Hence if America is exceptional, it is because it was founded on abstract principles of justice. Ideally, people from any place or ethnic background can join this project. Thus Lafayette, a Frenchmen, and Thomas Paine, a recently arrived Scotsman, could take prominent roles in the American Revolution—a fight against empire and aristocracy.[35] Later, in the nineteenth century, newly arrived immigrants from Ireland, Germany, and so on (and African Americans) would join together to militarily defeat the Southern slave-owning class in the American Civil War.[36]

Star Trek takes up the US entrance into World War II, where soldiers with greatly varying ethnic backgrounds served under the American banner. In "City on the Edge of Forever" (1967), one of the *Enterprise*'s crew members (Doctor McCoy) inadvertently goes back in time and prevents the US entrance into World War II. The result being that the Nazis win the war, which subsequently prevents the formation of the Federation and even apparently stops humanity from ever being a space-faring race. ("Your vessel, your beginning, all that you knew is gone.")

It is significant that McCoy profoundly alters the past when he prevents the death of a pacifist (played wonderfully by Joan Collins). Captain Kirk and Spock determine that this pacifist subsequently is able to form a movement that blocks the United States from fighting the Axis powers. Thus they make the difficult decision to let her die, which restores history. One interpretation of "City on the Edge of Forever" is that pacifism represents passivity in the face of injustice, corruption, malfeasance, warmongering, and so on. Put differently, justice, freedom, and even good governance require "eternal vigilance." The *Deep Space Nine* two-part episode "Past Tense" (1995) features the following exchange: Dr. Bashir asks, "Are humans really any different than Cardassians . . . or Romulans? If push came to shove, if something disastrous happened to the Federation, and we got frightened enough, or desperate enough, how would we react? Would we stay true to our ideals . . . or would we just [resort to authoritarian/oppressive means]?"

Captain Sisko responds, "I don't know. But as a Starfleet officer, it's my job to make sure we never have to find out."

To the American Revolutionary War (see later in this chapter), the US Civil War (see later in this chapter), and the American fight against fascism, *Star Trek* adds to America's revolutionary moments with the Bell Uprising. Aired in 1995, "Past Tense" is centered on this fictional uprising. The characters Sisko, Bashir, and Dax are accidentally sent back to 2024 San Francisco, where, like in "City on the Edge of Forever," they alter Earth's history for the worse. Upon being beamed to the past, Sisko and Bashir are separated from Dax. Without any identification (or money), Sisko and Bashir are forcibly interned in an urban detainment camp (a so-called Sanctuary District) for the poor and dispossessed (see Figures 2.1 and 2.2). It is described in script notes as follows: "Sisko and Bashir ENTER a street lined by dirty, dilapidated buildings, with boarded up windows and impromptu

Figure 2.1 Homeless family in the Sanctuary District (*Deep Space Nine*, "Past Tense" 1995)

Figure 2.2 Overhead view of the Sanctuary District (*Deep Space Nine*, "Past Tense" 1995)

campsites set up in the doorways and stairwells. It's a sharp contrast to the relatively clean city outside. The street is crowded with poorly dressed homeless men, women, and children, of all ages and races, many standing in a long food line."

Sisko, who is knowledgeable about twenty-first-century Earth, explains, "By the early twenty-twenties there was a place like this in every major city in the United States."

> **BASHIR:** Why are these people in here? Are they criminals?
> **SISKO:** No. People with criminal records weren't allowed in the Sanctuary Districts.
> **BASHIR:** Then what did they do to deserve this?
> **SISKO:** Nothing. They're just people. People without jobs or places to live.
> **BASHIR:** So they get put in here?
> **SISKO:** Welcome to the twenty-first century.

Writing in the mid-1990s about internment camps for the poor and homeless being in place in every major American city within thirty years is an explicit critique of the neoliberal project, which was well established by the 1990s.[37] Neoliberalism, whose proponents prioritize the free movement of capital, goods, and services, has been devastating to numerous urban centers, particularly in the former industrial American heartland.[38] Cities like Detroit[39] and Cleveland,[40] which were global centers of industrial production, have been hollowed out as the manufacturing base has been shifted to cheap wage venues in the South, Mexico, China, and so on. One of the displaced residents of the San Francisco Sanctuary District explains, "I used to be a plant manager at ChemTech Industries." The result has been pronounced urban decay in once wealthy and prosperous cities,[41] where a substantial homeless population is an enduring phenomenon.[42]

Moreover, the Great Recession of 2008 has caused persistently high unemployment.[43] A historically destabilizing factor of capitalism is the tendency of capital equipment (i.e., technology) to replace labor.[44] In a 2012 op-ed piece in the *New York Times*,

Princeton economist Paul Krugman holds, "There's no question that in some high-profile industries, technology is displacing workers of all, or almost all, kinds."[45] A Sanctuary District resident explains, "I came to San Francisco to work in a brewery . . . but they laid a bunch of us off when they got some new equipment . . . and so I ended up here." Another of the characters in "Past Tense" notes, "Right now jobs are hard to come by . . . what with the economy and all." The former plant manager plaintively explains, "Most of us agreed to live here [in the San Francisco Sanctuary District] because they promised us jobs. I don't know about you, but I haven't been on any job interviews lately. And neither has anyone else. They've forgotten about us."

Star Trek not only is critical of the economics and politics of neoliberalism but also takes aim at capitalism. In "The Neutral Zone" (1988), a wealthy businessman named Ralph Offenhouse from the late twentieth century is revived from a cryogenic chamber floating in space. Upon being awoken, Ralph explains, "I have a substantial portfolio. It's critical I check on it." Later, he adds, "I have to phone Geneva right away about my accounts. The interest alone could be enough to buy even this ship." Ralph dons an attitude of arrogance, entitlement, and authority. He tells Captain Picard, "I demand you see me." When Picard tries to put Ralph off by referring to the sensitive situation the ship is dealing with at the time, Ralph retorts, "I'm sure that whatever it is seems very important to you. My situation is far more critical." Ralph condescends the captain, "It is simply that I have more to protect than a man in your position could possibly imagine. No offense, but a military career has never been considered upwardly mobile." Picard, losing his patience, informs Ralph that his value system (and attitude) is misplaced and disdained in the current epoch:

> **PICARD:** A lot has changed in three hundred years. People are no longer obsessed with the accumulation of "things." We have eliminated hunger, want, the need for possessions. We have grown out of our infancy.

RALPH: You've got it wrong. It's never been about "possessions"—it's about power.⁴⁶
PICARD: Power to do what?
RALPH: To control your life, your destiny.
PICARD: That kind of control is an illusion.

Chastened, Ralph asks, "There's no trace of my money—my office is gone—what will I do? How will I live?" Picard explains, "Those material needs no longer exist." Ralph, invoking the values of the late twentieth century, responds by asking, "Then what's the challenge?" Picard, seemingly outlining the values of twenty-fourth-century Earth, retorts, "To improve yourself . . . enrich yourself. Enjoy it, Mister Offenhouse."

Similarly, in the *Deep Space Nine* episode "In the Cards" (1997), Jake Sisko exclaims "I'm Human, I don't have any money." Nog, a Ferengi—an alien race that operates on the profit-motive—is critical of twenty-fourth-century humanity: "It's not my fault that your species decided to abandon currency-based economics in favor of some philosophy of self-enhancement." Shifting humanity's (America's) values away from "currency-based economics" toward a "philosophy of self-enhancement" mirrors Karl Marx's point that in moving from capitalism to communism society would go "from each according to his ability, to each according to his needs!"—that is, communist politics would focus on "the all-around development of the individual."⁴⁷ Or as Jake told Nog, "There's nothing wrong with our philosophy. We work to better ourselves and the rest of humanity."

Indicative of how humans in the twenty-fourth century have undergone a profound paradigm shift in values and outlook, Quark, a Ferengi who traveled back to mid-twentieth-century Earth (more specifically, the United States), concludes from his dealings with humans (Americans) in this epoch, "These humans, they're not like the ones from the [twenty-fourth century] Federation. They're crude, gullible, and greedy."⁴⁸ Marx offers a consonant rebuke of the cultural/social ethos of capitalists: "Contempt for theory, art, history, and for man as an end in himself . . . is the real, conscious standpoint, the virtue of the man of money."[49]

Therefore, *Star Trek* takes the "Great American Melting Pot" idea to its logical conclusion—namely, that modernity, science, and reason can serve as the basis for a peaceful, highly productive, and thriving world. *Star Trek* is optimistic insofar as arguing that as global society accepts modernity, reason, and science—that is, the Enlightenment—humans will collectively achieve a higher plane of intelligence, knowledge, and emotional maturity. (This optimism is shared by Marx: "In communist society . . . the all-round development of the individual" will be achieved.)[50] *Star Trek*, however, in positing an earthly utopia, engages the issue of pragmatism—reflecting, I believe, the ambiguity that exists in the American mind on the issue of enduring justice versus intersubjective agreement.

Pragmatism and Intersubjective Agreement

While *Star Trek* draws on the argument that America is a project of the Enlightenment, its creators also comment on the dark themes and aspects of US history and politics. How can a nation that rebelled against the British Empire, incurred massive costs to defeat slavery, and fought a far-flung war to defeat fascism also have destroyed Native American societies/cultures, instituted Jim Crow segregation, supported/sustained corrupt/repressive regimes worldwide, engaged in an unnecessary land war in Indochina, and wantonly invaded Iraq in 2003?

American philosophers (most prominently William James and John Dewey) have sought to argue the position of pragmatism to account for—and perhaps explain—the "contradiction that is America."[51] Harvard historian Louis Menand points out that the core of pragmatism is "the belief that ideas [ethics, morality] should never become ideologies"—which early pragmatists saw as the cause of the American Civil War.[52] Therefore, pragmatists seemingly hold that concepts of justice or political principles should not precede the goal of maintaining social stability. To do so invites devastating conflict (the American Civil War) and chaos. It is political/societal stability, not justice (per se), that allows for social, economic, and technological progress.[53]

In the original series episode "Bread and Circuses" (1968), *Star Trek* is ostensibly critical of pragmatism and its overriding emphasis on societal stability—with the outcome being the persistence of slavery worldwide. The *Enterprise* crew comes upon a planet that is virtually identical to mid-twentieth century-Earth (America), except on this world, the Roman Empire never collapsed, and instead, spans the entire planet: "A world ruled by emperors who can trace their line back two thousand years to their own Julius and Augustus Caesars." The result is that slavery continues in part because the slave system was reformed to maintain its stability: "Long ago, there were [slave] rebellions . . . [but] with each century, the slaves acquired more rights under the law. They received rights to medicine, the right to government payments in their old age, and they slowly learned to be content." Spock: "Slavery evolving into an institution with guaranteed medical payments, old-age pensions." In defending this society, one of the characters explains, "This is an ordered world, a conservative world based on time-honored Roman strengths and virtues . . . There's been no war here for over four hundred years . . . Could your land of that same era make that same boast?" he asks of the *Enterprise* landing party (specifically Kirk and McCoy). Explaining why Federation citizens who had come upon this Rome-like world could not be allowed to leave (thereby having the opportunity to tell others of its existence), he says, "I think you can see why they don't want to have their *stability* contaminated by dangerous ideas of other ways and places"—that is, ideologies of freedom, democracy, equality, and so on that could be politically destabilizing. Spock, in response, opines, "Given a conservative empire, quite understandable."

In fashioning neopragmatism, Richard Rorty, an American philosopher writing in the early 1980s, argues that societies are based on intersubjective agreement.[54] Thus what is required for societal stability is enough consensus on a set of ideas—any set of ideas. Hence what matters is consensus, and not the ideas themselves. Presumably, when there is not enough intersubjective consensus/agreement, then social/political breakdown occurs.

More than ten years before Rorty published his pathbreaking notion of intersubjective agreement, the *Star Trek* episode "Mirror, Mirror" (1967) aired. Members of the *Enterprise* crew (including Kirk and McCoy), through a technical glitch, are beamed to an alternate universe. The *Enterprise* (including Spock) exists in this alternate universe, but instead of the Federation, the political authority is the Empire—where "behavior and discipline" is "brutal, savage." Captain Kirk (from the Federation) refuses to carry out the order to destroy a planet that refuses to comply with the Empire. Spock (sporting a mustache and goatee) notes to Kirk, "No one will question the assassination of a captain who has disobeyed prime orders of the Empire." Kirk: "I command an *Enterprise* where officers apparently employ private henchmen among the crew, where assassination of superiors is a common means of advancing in rank." McCoy asks, "What kind of people are we in this universe?"

> **KIRK:** Let's find out.
> **KIRK (TO THE SHIP'S COMPUTER):** Read out official record of current command.
> **COMPUTER:** Captain James T. Kirk succeeded to command I.S.S. *Enterprise* through assassination of Captain Christopher Pike. First action—suppression of Gorlan uprising through destruction of rebel home planet. Second action—execution of five thousand colonists on Vega Nine.
> **KIRK (INTERRUPTING THE COMPUTER):** Cancel.
> **McCOY:** Now we know.

The Captain Jonathan Archer (*Star Trek: Enterprise*) from the alternative universe declares, "Great men are not peacemakers. Great men are conquerors" ("In a Mirror, Darkly" 2005). The implication of "Mirror, Mirror" and "In a Mirror, Darkly" is, irrespective of their value system—whether Empire or Federation—humans can create and lead a vast interstellar political formation. Technological progress and political stability would essentially be the same.

The intersubjective agreement argument in "Mirror, Mirror" is brought into sharper relief in *Deep Space Nine*, where the alternate universe is revisited a century later.[55] We learn that Kirk's time in the alternate universe had a profound impact. "On my side, Kirk is one of the most famous names in our history." In "Mirror, Mirror," Kirk apprized Spock of a weapon (the Tantalus field). From one's quarters, a person could zero in on victims, and with the push of a button, make them disappear. This presages US drone technology, where operators in an air conditioned facility in Nevada guide small airplanes (drones) flying over remote regions of the world, and with the push of a button, fire missiles on unsuspecting individuals from fifty thousand feet.[56] Kirk counseled Spock to use such technology to profoundly change the Empire, and base it on the values of the Federation. When Spock, however, disrupts the intersubjective agreement that was the basis of the Empire, it collapses:

> Almost a century ago, a Terran starship captain named James Kirk accidentally exchanged places with his counterpart from your side due to a transporter accident. Our Terrans were barbarians then, but their Empire was strong. While your Kirk was on this side, he met a Vulcan named Spock and somehow had a profound influence on him. Afterwards, Spock rose to commander in chief of the Empire by preaching reforms, disarmament, peace. It was a remarkable turnabout for his people. Unfortunately for them, when Spock had completed all these reforms, his empire was no longer in any position to defend itself against us.

The end result is that the Earth is conquered and occupied.

While *Star Trek* dramatically depicts and explores the frightening aspects of pragmatism and intersubjective agreement, it posits a philosophical outlook wherein America is evolving through revolutions toward an ideal (utopian) society. The failure to pursue this path to justice will be disastrous for the United States and the world. We have already seen what happened in "City on the Edge of Forever" when the United States failed to engage fascism in the 1940s. The overriding need to pursue societal justice—that is, topple neoliberalism and capitalism—is made even clearer in "Past Tense." While in the Sanctuary District in 2024 San Francisco, Sisko intervenes into a fight, which accidentally results in the death of one Gabriel Bell—the would-be leader of the Bell Uprising. Like in "City on the Edge of Forever," this erases the entire history of the Federation. Meanwhile, back in the twenty-fourth century, all that remains of the original timeline is the ship (the *Defiant*) that beamed Sisko, Bashir, and Dax to the past. Uncertain when Sisko et al. are located, members of the *Defiant* crew randomly transport into Earth's past. They conclude Sisko et al. "arrived before the year 2048."

> **ODO:** How can you be sure?
> **O'BRIEN:** Because we were just there. And that wasn't the mid-twenty-first century that I read about in school. It's been changed. *Earth history had its rough patches, but never that rough.*

Therefore, the absence of the Bell Uprising to spark the revolution that would politically challenge the current neoliberalism regime would ostensibly result in Earth's society devolving into some type of nightmare scenario as early as 2048. One is reminded of Rosa Luxemburg's pronouncement that the "future is either socialism or barbarism."[57]

The original timeline is restored when Sisko takes the name Gabriel Bell and fulfills his role in history. One of the successes of the Bell Uprising was the ability of residents of the Sanctuary District to evade a government blockade of the "Interface"—that is, the Internet (which was a nascent technology when "Past Tense" aired in 1995)—and convey their personal stories to the world. One resident explains, "My name is Henry Garcia . . . and I've been living here two years now . . . I've never been in trouble with the law or anything . . . I don't want to hurt anybody . . . I just want a chance to work and live like regular people."

Confirming the interpretation of *Star Trek* as positing American history as a series of progressive events (revolutions) is "The Savage Curtain" (1969) and "The Omega Glory" (1968). The episode "The Omega Glory," like "Bread and Circuses," depicts a world with an identical history to that of Earth's, except in this instance, the Cold War resulted in globally devastating nuclear/biological war—where humans were reduced to a veritable stone age. Kirk ultimately realizes that the segment of the population that represented the West views the US Constitution as a sacred document. But they cannot read it, so Kirk explains to them, "That which you called Ee'd Plebnista was not written for chiefs or kings or warriors or the rich and powerful, but for all the people!" Kirk proceeds to read directly from this document (the Ee'd Plebnista), which is the Constitution: "We the people of the United States, in order to form a more perfect union, establish justice, ensure domestic tranquility, provide for the common defense, promote the general welfare, and secure the blessings of liberty to ourselves and our posterity do ordain and establish this constitution."

Asserting the revolutionary implications of the American Revolution and the Constitution that followed, Kirk declares, "These words and the words that follow . . . They must apply to everyone or they mean nothing!" Kirk adds, "Liberty and freedom have to be more than just words."

In "The Savage Curtain," the *Enterprise* crew meets the incarnation of Abraham Lincoln. While acknowledging that this is not the real Lincoln, Kirk insists that the crew treat him with the respect and deference due this great historical figure—the leader of what many consider to be the second American Revolution (i.e., the victorious Northern cause in the US Civil War).[58] Kirk notes, "I cannot conceive it possible that Abraham Lincoln . . . could have actually been reincarnated. And yet his kindness, his gentle wisdom, his humor, everything about him is so right." McCoy chides Kirk, "Practically the entire crew has seen you . . . treat this impostor like the real thing . . . when he can't possibly be the real article. Lincoln died three centuries ago hundreds of light-years away." Spock observes to Kirk, "President Lincoln has always been a very personal hero to you." Kirk retorts, "Not only to me." Spock: "Agreed."

Thus *Star Trek* is optimistic in that America is evolving toward an ideal, classless society (utopia). The American Revolution, the Civil War, the fight against fascism, the Bell Uprising—that is, the defeat of neoliberalism—are necessary stops on this road to (worldwide) utopia. This is reflective of American Marxists' view that US history is an unfolding revolutionary process, the end result of which is the establishment of an ideal socialist/communist society. Sidney Hook, for instance, writing in 1933 (when he was still a Trotskyist) reasoned, "America had gone through her second revolution to break up the semi-feudal slavocracy which barred the expansion of industrial capitalism."[59] Operating in the United States since the 1920s, Trotskyists hold that the American Revolution and the Civil War remain incomplete until the worker state is in place.[60] Put differently, these revolutions will be completed by the socialist revolution (the Bell Uprising?). (It is noteworthy and significant that in the episode where the Bell Uprising is conveyed, the phrase *neo-Trotskyists* is used; also, in another episode, a passage from the *Communist Manifesto* is read.)[61]

Hence, in spite of episodes like "Mirror, Mirror" and "Bread and Circuses," *Star Trek* rejects pragmatism and the concept (and implication) of intersubjective agreement, as the failure to achieve justice—that is, the utopia of Earth presented in *Star Trek*—would lead to unfathomable results.

The notion of humanity progressing toward an ideal utopia through a progressive and revolutionary teleology is further conveyed by commentary on (criticism of) societies that are prevented from engaging in this teleology. In *The Next Generation*, we are presented with peoples that are (genetically) incapable of participating in humanity's journey toward utopia. This portrayal leads to charges of racism. These issues are taken up next.

Unable/Incapable of Participation in *Star Trek*'s Teleology

Original series episodes like "Return of the Archons" (1967), "This Side of Paradise" (1967), and "The Apple" (1967) are critiqued as replicating (imposing) American biases (values).[62] (Spock's commentary in these episodes also represents instances when the show's creators issued sharply worded cautions against possible smugness/arrogance resulting from the putative superiority of American politics/values.)[63] Nevertheless, what is significant for this discussion is the concept of freedom that motivates *Star Trek* episodes like these. Namely, we are only truly "human" and free when participating in (forwarding) the progressive teleology outlined in *Star Trek*. In each of these episodes, some external force is keeping a society in some technologically, socially primitive, and backward state, thereby preventing people from progressing toward the utopian ideal represented by Earth (the Federation) and beyond.[64] These barriers to freedom/justice are destroyed/eliminated by Kirk et al.

Daniel Bernardi, in Star Trek *and History: Race-ing toward a White Future*, holds that *The Next Generation* conveys a bias against dark-skinned people.[65] Perhaps so.[66] Again, what is significant for this discussion is how the *Star Trek* franchise issues a potential insult. Seemingly among the greatest condemnations that exists in the world of *Star Trek* (and arguably in the American mind) is that someone (or some group of people) cannot participate in (contribute to) the teleology that is leading humanity toward utopia. This teleology (as outlined in *Star Trek*) is informed by (predicated upon) reason and conceptions of universal rights, peace, and freedom. Thus the Klingons are inherently outside of this process because, as famously stated in *The Next Generation* 1989 episode "The Icarus Factor," "there is, of course, a genetic predisposition toward hostility among all Klingons." Moreover, the clan politics and paternalism of Klingons (also caused presumably by their genes) renders them too parochial to participate in the Enlightenment project.⁶⁷ The people of Ligon II are also outside this project because they too are ostensibly hopelessly dominated by narrow tribal/clan concerns and rigid gender norms.⁶⁸

Conclusion

The *Star Trek* franchise indicates that significant segments of the US public have a favorable view of internationalism, and even of world government. The 1986 movie *Star Trek: The Voyage Home* makes the explicit point that meaningful environmental protection cannot be attained in a global political system fragmented into discrete sovereign nation-states. Environmental issues like climate change demonstrate the prescience of *Star Trek* in advocating for a global political regime. Such a regime/government could serve as the basis for a peaceful society and environmental sustainability.

Moreover, *Star Trek* argues for the replacement of the international neoliberal regime and of capitalist/materialist values with a value system and regime that prioritizes "human development"—that is, addressing social needs and fostering knowledge as well as emotional maturity. *Star Trek*'s argument that society should prioritize human development, not profit making, conveys Karl Marx's position that society should be revolutionized "from each according to his ability, to each according to his needs!" The Great Recession of 2008 (and the social decay that this recession has accelerated/exacerbated) again confirms the validity of *Star Trek*'s (and Marx's) insistence that society directly, robustly address human needs.

According to the ontology posited in *Star Trek*, political progress proceeds along revolutionary moments/events, which is consistent with Marxist ontology—and more specifically, the American Trotskyist view of US history. Importantly, the series *The Next Generation* makes the ostensive suggestion that not all groups can participate in this progressive ontology, which leads to allegations of racism. More generally, this suggests that within the American mind exists doubts/skepticism that all groups can contribute equally to the teleology that is at the core of the *Star Trek* narrative.

Significantly, *Star Trek* makes an active argument against using pragmatism and intersubjective agreement as touchstones for social/political development. Normatively, an emphasis on stability—that is, pragmatism—would keep such morally reprehensible practices as slavery intact. Additionally, prioritizing intersubjective agreement can lead to nefarious (imperial) politics. Most damning of all (apart from the alternative reality motif), *Star Trek* makes the claim that a politics dominated by pragmatism and maintaining intersubjective agreement (for its own sake) leads to social/political breakdown (the end of civilization).

In the final instance, the outstanding contribution of *Star Trek* to political theory is that it demonstrates that while terms such as *socialism* and *communism* may be irreparably stigmatized in the American mind, a very significant segment of Americans enthusiastically embrace the normative values of Marx (a "philosophy of self-enhancement"), as well as Marxists' understanding of world politics (V. I. Lenin) and of US history (American Trotskyist). Therefore, *Star Trek* promotes a utopian Marxist metaphysics and politics, and explicitly rejects the normative commitment to stability found in pragmatism/neopragmatism. Judging from the immense and enduring popularity of *Star Trek*, so do many, many Americans.

CHAPTER 3

Star Trek, American Military Policy, and the Developing World

In the preceding chapter, I outlined how a progressive ontology/teleology informs the *Star Trek* franchise. Nevertheless, there is a notable shift in *Star Trek* that occurs between the original series and *The Next Generations*. This chapter focuses on this shift. Importantly, the original series sought to directly comment on US foreign policy and the Cold War, whereas *The Next Generation* explicitly forewent these issues. Moreover, while the original series hinted at the clash of civilizations between the Federation, the Klingons, and the Romulans,[1] *The Next Generation* centers its narrative on this clash, and the idea that the world system is inherently unstable—as are the politics of the developing world. Very significantly, *The Next Generation* expands on the original series' notions of social justice and universalism.

Social Justice and Universalism in *Star Trek*

The key commonality of the original series and *The Next Generation* is their shared commitment to social justice and universalism. Both shows point to the possibility of societies free of class distinctions, as well as of ethnic and gender biases. *Star Trek*, the original series, indicates that Earth in the near future is based on a selfless politics and economics when in "City on the Edge of Forever" (1967) Captain Kirk explains to Edith Keeler that by the early twenty-first century the socially minded notion of "let me help" will assume greater importance than the more individualistic concept of "I love you."[2] as noted in Chapters 1 and 2, *The Next Generation* takes this suggested critique of selfish profit making and posits an overt rejection of capitalism when Picard chastises Ralph Offenhouse for his twentieth-century obsession with personal wealth and power.

Both *Star Trek* and *The Next Generation* hold that peoples from all backgrounds can live together and meaningfully participate in a single polity—the Federation. Again, as noted in Chapter 2, in "Whom Gods Destroy" (1969), "The Savage Curtain" (1969), "Transfigurations" (1992), and *Nemesis* (2002), *Star Trek*'s creators affirm the franchise's commitment to universal solidarity and total ethnic equality. Significantly, in the 2009 rebooting of the *Star Trek* movie franchise, Spock rejects admittance to the Vulcan Science Academy because of its racism, and instead enrolls into Starfleet Academy—ostensibly because all ethnic groups (species) are treated/considered equal there.

While both of the initial *Star Trek* series share an optimism about social justice and the ability of humanity to overcome all social, economic, and ethnic divisions, they take differing tacks on the specific issue of US foreign policy. The original series does provide sharply worded critical comments and scenarios that can be readily interpreted as directed against US (Western) relations with the developing world. *Next Generation*, in sharp contrast, expressly begs off any commentary on US foreign policy. Moreover, whereas the original series indicated that the global system is fundamentally stable, *The Next Generation* suggests instability is the rule in international relations, and makes an explicit appeal for more military expenditures. The instability in the international system follows from the unstable and bellicose politics of the developing world.

Foreign Relations in Original *Star Trek*

As outlined in Chapter 1, in the original series, episodes like "Private Little War" (1968), "Patterns of Force" (1968), "A Piece of the Action" (1968), "Arena" (1967) and "The Apple" (1967) offer critical meditations and judgments on American (Western) foreign policy. While *Star Trek* of the 1960s posited commentary and appraisals of American foreign policy and US involvement in the underdeveloped world, *The Next Generation* series in the 1980s rebuffed critiques of America's role in the world. "Encounter at Farpoint" (1987), the series pilot, expressly absolves the Federation (the United States) of any present misdeeds. Before a court convened by the all-powerful entity Q, Captain Picard proclaims, "We agree there is evidence to support the court's contention that humans have been murderous and dangerous. I say 'have been'... and therefore we will respectfully submit to a test of whether this is presently true of humans." The *Enterprise* crew, with its state-of-the-art ship, passes this test by freeing a creature that was being enslaved/exploited at Farpoint Station. Picard to Q: "You accuse us of 'grievous savagery'? No, the one proven guilty of that crime is you!"

As for the Cold War itself, it is swept aside as "nonsense." In the 1987 episode "Lonely among Us" (1987), Picard asks, "Do you understand the basis of all that *nonsense* between them?" Riker: "No sir. I didn't understand that kind of hostility even when I studied Earth history." Picard: "Oh? Well, yes, but these lifeforms feel such passionate hatred over differences in ... strangely enough, economic systems." Similarly, in the "The High Ground" (1990), when Doctor Beverly Crusher begins to question Federation policy/politics toward a planet in turmoil, Picard dismisses her concerns by suggesting that she is mentally impaired as a result of her hostage experience:

> PICARD (ABOUT THE REBELS): They're mad.
> CRUSHER: I don't know any more. The difference between a madman and a committed man willing to die for a cause ... it's begun to blur over the last couple days.
> PICARD: Beverly, I don't have to warn you about the psychological impact of being a hostage.

A similar minimization of colonial intervention is made in "Journey's End" (1994). A peace treaty has been negotiated with the Cardassians, and certain Federation planets are being ceded. One of them (Dorvan V) contains a tribe of Native Americans who relocated there: "The North American Indians were forcibly displaced from their ancestral lands. This group on Dorvan V originally left Earth two hundred years ago because they wanted to preserve their cultural identities."

Picard objects to the forced removal from Dorvan V: "There are certain . . . disturbing historical parallels here. Once again, these people are being asked to leave their homes because of political decisions made by a distant government." As explained by a Starfleet Admiral, however, "the Indians colonized Dorvan 20 years ago . . . and at that time they were warned the planet was hotly disputed by the Cardassians . . . It took three years to negotiate this treaty . . . some concessions had to be made . . . and this is one of them." Picard is ordered to carry out the removal of the Native Americans, and the Admiral giving the order remarks, "I don't envy you this task . . . but I do believe it is for the greater good." Of course, in reality, natives in the United States and elsewhere were never removed for peacemaking purposes, but for entirely venal reasons. In the end, the Indians on Dorvan V opt to live "under Cardassian jurisdiction." In US history, Native Americans were not offered an "equitable solution" or allowed to "take that risk" of staying.

Returning to the original series, the episode "Errand of Mercy" (1967) suggests that a global conflagration is unlikely in the near term. The Federation and the Klingons are amassing their considerable military forces and are on the verge of an all-out war. The action centers on the planet Organia, which is deemed of high strategic importance in the seemingly upcoming Klingon-Federation war. The inhabitants of the planet, the Organians, live technologically simple lives, and are ostensibly oblivious to the machinations the Klingons and the Federations are engaged in around them. Just as the Klingons and the Federation are to begin an interstellar war, the Organians intervene to prevent it. It turns out that far from being a primitive culture, the Organians are a highly advanced people—capable of rendering both the Federation and Klingon military machines "inoperative." On Organia, Captain Kirk and a Klingon commander speak for the dogs of war (objecting to the Organians' intervention): "What gives you the right? . . . You can't interfere."

> **KIRK:** We have legitimate grievances against the Klingons. They've invaded our territory, killed our citizens. They're openly aggressive. They've boasted that they'll take over half the galaxy.
> **KLINGON COMMANDER:** You've tried to hem us in, cut off vital supplies, strangle our trade! You've been asking for war!
> Kirk and the Klingon officer bark at each other.
> **KIRK:** You're the ones who issued the ultimatum to withdraw from the disputed areas!
> **KLINGON COMMANDER:** They are not disputed! They're clearly ours.
> **KIRK (TO THE ORGANIAN LEADER):** you have no right to dictate to our Federation.
> **KLINGON COMMANDER:** Or our Empire!
> **THE ORGANIAN:** To wage war, Captain? To kill millions of innocent people? To destroy life on a planetary scale? Is that what you're defending?

The Organians impel the Klingons and the Federation to conclude a peace treaty. Reading these fictional events into the geopolitics of the 1960s, the suggestion being made is that fear of the consequences of a global war will prevent such a war from occurring. Thus, at least in the short term, humanity's better angels (and cooler heads) will prevail—as happened with the 1963 Cuban Missile Crisis. Striking a hopeful note, the Organian informs Captain Kirk and the Klingon commander that in the future, "You and the Klingons will become fast friends. You will work together."

While the original series cast the world system inhabited by the Federation (the United States) as stable (at least in the short term), *The Next Generation* depicts a geopolitical system fraught with dangers and the explicit point is made that more resources need to be dedicated to the defense of the Federation. When the Borg appear poised to attack the Federation, Starfleet is not prepared, as the weapons being developed to confront the Borg will not be ready any time soon: "I can't believe any of [Starfleet's] new weapons systems can be ready in less than eighteen months." It was worse than that because Starfleet command was projecting 24 months before their new weapons would be ready for deployment ("The Best of Both Worlds" 1990). When civil war breaks out in the Klingon Empire and the Federation intervenes to prevent the Romulans from surreptitiously determining the outcome of the war, Starfleet's resources are deemed insufficient for the task: "Starfleet is stretched pretty thin across the quadrant . . . The only other ships available are either in spacedock for repairs or still under construction. Most of them don't even have full crews yet." When asked if his plan to expose Romulan duplicity can succeed with the number of ships available, LaForge responds, "It's possible" ("Redemption" 1991). When a rogue Starfleet ship commander threatens to destabilize relations with the Cardassians, a Starfleet Admiral tells Picard, "I don't have to tell you the Federation is not prepared for a new sustained conflict" ("The Wounded"). In the movie *Star Trek: Insurrection* (1998), the following observation is rendered: "In the last 24 months," the Federation has "been challenged by every major power in the quadrant."

The Next Generation and the Developing World

In chapter four of Star Trek *and History: Race-ing toward a White Future*, Daniel Bernardi holds that *The Next Generation* conveys a racist or, more specifically, "antiblack" attitude.[3] My position is that the series, contrary to Bernardi's argument, is not racist per se, but that it tends to cast the developing world as populated by corrupt, violent regimes. Although it can be argued that the series offers partial and incomplete metaphors for various developing world peoples, it nevertheless makes what amounts to very negative commentary on Africa, the Arab Middle East, Latin America, and East Asia.

Africa

Bernardi's argument is based largely on two factors: one, the episode "Code of Honor" (1987), and two, the treatment of the Klingons. "Code of Honor" focuses on what appears to be a metaphor for sub-Saharan Africa. Bernardi aptly acknowledges that the planet depicted in this episode, Ligon II, bespeaks black Africa:

> The Ligonians [who are all played by black actors] . . . carry spears and staffs. The men have deep scars on their faces and chests, suggesting hand-to-hand combat and primitive tribal rituals. They wear turbans, poufy pants, and sashes cut in the figure of an "X" so that their dark, muscular bodies are plainly visible. The planet is ruled by a bombastic chief, Luttan, whose followers are prone to beating sticks in rhythmic response to his emphatic proclamations. The Ligonian world is reminiscent of the African safari, as we see silhouettes of trees and shrubs against a saturated reddish-orange sky. Even the music-bed, with its heavy bass and slow beat, is reminiscent of classic Hollywood jungle movies and National Geographic documentaries of the "dark continent." The representation of these "closely humanoids" in this way suggests that Ligon II is not only a black world, but one that "parallels" real African tribes.[4]

The Ligonians are dominated by tribal and clan politics, and this insularity threatens the *Enterprise*'s mission—which is to save a Federation colony afflicted with a deadly infection by retrieving a precious medicine (a natural resource) only available on Ligon. The Ligon leadership appears little concerned with the fate of the colonists, and instead draws the *Enterprise*'s crew into its tribal/clan politics.

While "Code of Honor" is a negative portrayal of Africans (not African Americans), Bernardi focuses solely on American race relations in his treatment of this episode: "The episode reveals a dramatic shift in the articulation of race in the *Trek* mega-text, perhaps due to a sociopolitical context less concerned with the practices of the civil rights movement than with a neoconservative ideal." Bernardi further centers his analysis on US domestic politics when he writes, "The mid-1980s through the early 1990s, the period of the production and initial reception of *The Next Generation*, is marked by a sociopolitical climate quite different from that of the 1960s, the period of the original *Trek*'s production. In what is now commonly referred to as the Reagan-Bush years, the civil rights movement was no longer the dominant arbiter of the meaning of race."[5]

Bernardi again overlooks the seeming reality that "Code of Honor" is an unflattering portrayal of Africa when he adds that this episode, and *The Next Generation*, are consistent with a backlash against the US civil rights movement: "With its roots in the 1970s and earlier, the neoconservative movement came to power during this period with the stated goal of curtailing and even rolling back many of the sociopolitical inroads that had been made in the 1960s."[6]

The Middle East

Like with "Code of Honor," Bernardi reads the treatment of Klingons in *The Next Generation* as a broad indictment of dark-skinned people. He writes, "Biological notion of blackness is displaced onto the Klingons while a civilized notion of whiteness is ascribed to the Federation."[7] Bernardi correctly notes that Klingons—who are brown skinned (see Figure 3.1)—are described as inherently violent. In "The Icarus Factor" (1989), the point is explicitly made by the steadfastly objective Lieutenant Commander Data that "there is, of course, a genetic predisposition toward hostility among all Klingons." In "Heart of Glory" (1988), Klingons are portrayed as wolf-like when they howl as part of a funeral ritual.

As in the case of "Code of Honor," my argument is that Klingons can be most productively read as members of the developing world, and not dark-skinned people writ large. Although

Figure 3.1 Klingon warrior from *The Next Generation*

Christian Domenig notes that the Klingons from the original series physically resembled peoples from Central Asia,[8] he links their culture, however, to the traditions and practices of medieval Europe.[9] While the Klingons, particularly beginning with *The Next Generation*, exhibit medieval customs, such as the observance of ritual and a belief in ethnic identity, their physical appearance—brown skin, dark and wavy hair—associates them with an Arab identity. In "Heart of Glory," a Klingon speaks like a Muslim/Arab fundamentalist when he says, "We are, after all, brothers lost among infidels." Arab societies tend to be patriarchies, as is Klingon society, with women prohibited from sitting on the Klingon's supreme political body, the "High Council." Political decisions for the family/clan are made by the eldest male, and the crimes of fathers implicate their sons.[10] A comparison can also be drawn with the rise of political Islamism in the episode "Rightful Heir" (1993), which focuses on the figure of Kahless (who is described in Mohammed-like terms). Kahless is the founder of the Klingon state who is revered as a demigod: "To believe in Kahless and his teachings . . . and to become truly Klingon." According to Klingon theology, Kahless "united" the Klingons, gave them "honor and strength," and "promised to return one day." In the story, Kahless is cloned from ancient DNA and his clone is made head of the state for the Klingon Empire.

The political instability/corruption of Klingon politics and the uncertainty of the Federation-Klingon alliance are evident in "Sins of the Father" (1990), "Reunion" (1990), "The Mind's Eye" (1991), and "Redemption" (1991). In "The Mind's Eye," a Klingon colonial governor (Vagh) suspects that the Federation is arming an independence movement in the colony (Krios) he governors. The brutality of the Klingons is conveyed when a Klingon ambassador (Kell) is asked, "You are prepared to grant [the inhabitants of Krios] independence?" and Kell responds, "Perhaps. But we will conquer them again later if we wish to." At one point, war between the Federation and the Klingon Empire almost occurs when the *Enterprise* is seemingly caught red-handed delivering weapons to the rebels. (The weapons were transported from the *Enterprise* by Chief Engineer Geordi LaForge, who, under the control of the Romulans, was actively seeking to destabilize Klingon-Federation relations.) The *Enterprise* is surrounded by a number of Klingon battleships and ordered to stay in planetary orbit. It is reported that Governor Vagh "is fully prepared to fire upon the *Enterprise*."

In "Sins of the Father," Worf's father is posthumously found to have betrayed the Klingons to the Romulans (a rival nation-state), resulting in the destruction of a Klingon space station. Worf (who is Klingon) challenges this verdict. It turns out that the allegation against Worf's father was fabricated to maintain the stability of Klingon politics (as it was the patriarch of a currently powerful family/clan that was the actual traitor). "If the truth were known, it would . . . almost certainly plunge [the Klingon Empire] into civil war." When Captain Picard refuses to accept the outcome of a corrupt judicial/political process, the Klingon chancellor (K'mpec) warns him, "If you defy the orders of the High Council in an affair of the empire, the alliance with the Federation could fall to dust." (Initially, in order not to jeopardize Federation-Klingon relations, Worf accepts the punishment of execution, but is spared because he publicly accepts his father's guilt to save his brother's life—who would have been executed as well were it not for Worf's admission.)

In "Reunion," we learn that "the Klingon Empire is at a critical juncture." It "may be facing civil war." It is further observed that "Klingon wars seldom remain confined to the Empire... the Federation won't be able to stay out of it for long." The action is precipitated by the fact that the Klingon chancellor is dying. (He was slowly poisoned.) The internal Klingon political situation is so uncertain that Captain Picard (a non-Klingon) is asked to serve as "arbiter of succession"—thereby overseeing the process whereby a successor chancellor will emerge. In "Redemption," civil war among the Klingons does subsequently erupt. One of the two factions vying for political power is led by the Duras family: "The Duras family is corrupt and hungry for power... They represent a grave threat to the security of the Federation." (The Federation, under the leadership of Captain Picard, exposes the military relationship between the Duras clan and the Romulans, thereby allowing the pro-Federation Gowron-led faction to win the Klingon civil war.) In "Reunion," during the succession deliberations, a Duras foot solider carries out a suicide attack (with a bomb placed inside his arm) in an effort to disrupt the proceedings.

While *The Next Generation* casts Klingons as politically unstable, genetically combative and hostile, and seemingly incapable of engaging in a settled/permanent peace, the original series indicates that the Klingons and the Federation could form a durable/lasting peace. The following is reported in "Day of the Dove" (1968): "For three years, the Federation and the Klingon Empire have been at peace. A treaty we have honored to the letter." The action begins when the *Enterprise* rescues the crew from a Klingon vessel as it explodes. The *Enterprise* crew and the Klingons engage in hostilities—with hate, anger, and false accusations spewing from both sides. It turns out that they are being influenced and manipulated to hate and attack each other: "There's an alien entity aboard the ship. It's forcing us to fight . . . It subsists on the emotions of others." The alien entity "appears to be strengthened by mental irradiations of hostility, violent intentions. It exists on the hate of others. To put it simply." In the end, the Klingons and the *Enterprise* crew join forces to vanquish the alien creating the hostilities. To the alien: "Maybe you've caused a lot of suffering, a lot of history, but that's all over." The final scene of the episode shows the Klingons and the Federation crew shoulder to shoulder, laughing and jovial.

Latin America

The Cardassian Alliance also poses a security threat to the Federation. Introduced in *The Next Generation*, the Cardassians could be viewed as representing Latin Americans with their straight black hair and light, greenish-gray skin tone (see Figure 3.2). Perhaps

Figure 3.2 Cardassian officer

what the Cardassians have most in common with Latin America is a history of military dictatorship. In "Chain of Command" (1992), Cardassia's military regime is both defended and vaunted by a Cardassian as he tortures Picard, "We acquired territory during the wars . . . we developed new resources . . . we initiated a rebuilding program . . . we have mandated agricultural programs. That is what the military has done for Cardassia."

In "The Wounded" (1990), we learn that the Federation and Cardassia were recently in a war. "It has been nearly a year since a peace treaty ended the long conflict between the Federation and Cardassia." The action in the episode centers on a rogue Starfleet captain who ordered his ship (the Phoenix) into Cardassian space. The rogue captain (Benjamin Maxwell) destroyed what the Cardassians describe as a science station. In justifying his actions to Captain Picard, Maxwell contends the "Cardassians are arming again. That so-called science station? A military supply port . . . There's no good reason for a science station in the Cuellar System . . . but it's a hell of a strategic site for a military transport station . . . a jumping off point into three Federation sectors. They're running supply ships back and forth . . . and nobody's gonna tell me it's for scientific research."

Maxwell is finally apprehended by the *Enterprise*. Nevertheless, Picard is convinced that Maxwell was correct and the Cardassians are preparing for war—or at least engaging in military moves menacing to the Federation. Picard confronts the Cardassian military liaison officer on board the *Enterprise* during its pursuit of the Phoenix: "Maxwell was right. Those ships weren't carrying scientific equipment, were they? A 'research' station within arm's reach of three Federation sectors? . . . Cargo ships running with high energy subspace fields that jam sensors? . . . If I had attempted to board that ship . . . I am quite certain that you and I would not be sitting here now. And that ships on both sides would be arming for war." Picard issues the following warning: "Take a message to your leaders . . . We know. We'll be watching. We'll be ready."

In "Chain of Command," the Cardassians are discovered to be marshaling their forces along the Federation border and readying for an invasion. The invasion is only stopped because the *Enterprise* is able to attach explosives to the Cardassian attack fleet—the Cardassians agree to forego their planned assault in exchange for the disarming of the explosives attached to their ships.

East Asia

In the world of *Star Trek*, the Romulans represent the region of East Asia. Romulans have straight black hair coming down to just above their eyes and ears (see Figure 3.3), very similar to the peoples of East Asia (China, Korea, Japan). "Unification" (1991), in part takes place in the capital city of the Romulan home world. Picard and Data visit to find Spock, who is undertaking a private mission. The script notes describe the Romulan city scene as follows: "Colorless, bleak . . . pedestrians only . . . this is a poor neighborhood, life here is a struggle."[11] This could be the description of a Chinese or Korean town in 1991 when "Unification" aired.

Figure 3.3 Romulan officers from *The Next Generation*

Enterprise officer Geordi LaForge in "The Enemy" (1989) does make common cause with a Romulan soldier when they are trapped on a barren, inhospitable planet. Nevertheless, the Romulans in *The Next Generation* are cast as implacable and dangerous foes. They are described as "violent beyond description." Also, "their belief in their own superiority is beyond arrogance" ("The Neutral Zone" 1988). Picard asserts, "The Romulans have always been willing to take enormous risks in order to gain any advantage over the Federation" ("Redemption"). In "The Mind's Eye," the Romulans kidnap LaForge and psychologically torture him. They brainwash LaForge and turn him into a pawn in their machinations against the Federation-Klingon alliance. The episode "Unification" exposes a Romulan plot to invade the Federation planet Vulcan under the guise of reuniting the Romulan and Vulcan peoples, who are apparently the same species.

The darkest plot turn in the *Star Trek* franchise involves Romulan perfidiousness ("The Next Phase" 1992). The *Enterprise* comes to the rescue of a critically damaged Romulan ship. Picard: "Romulan ship, this is the *Enterprise*. We are en route to your position." The Romulan ship reports that it's in dire straits: "*Enterprise* . . . critical that you . . . core breach imminent." The *Enterprise* saves the Romulan ship. The *Enterprise* crew aids the Romulan ship in repairs, including giving it critical equipment and transferring power from the *Enterprise* (via transfer beam). In spite of the fact that the *Enterprise* crew risked life and limb to save the Romulans (and their expression of gratitude), the Romulans hatch a plan to destroy *Enterprise* and her crew: "We will set up a muon feedback wave inside the transfer beam. The particles will accumulate in their dilithium chamber. When they go to warp speed, their engines will explode."

The action of the movie *Star Trek: Nemesis* (2002) begins with the killing of seemingly the bulk of the Romulan Senate—including the governing ministers (Praetors). Behind this mass murder is the military high command, which is plotting an attack against the Federation. The leader of the military explains to the new head of government (Shinzon), "We supported you because you promised action." Shinzon: "In two days the Federation will be crippled beyond repair." The Romulan plot against the Federation is centered on the destruction of Earth. Shinzon developed a weapon (Thalaron radiation) that was barred "because of its biogenic properties . . . I can't overestimate the danger of Thalaron radiation . . . A microscopic amount could kill every living thing on this ship in a matter of seconds." Picard (speaking of Shinzon): "He would have built a weapon of that scope for one reason. He is going after Earth . . . Destroy humanity and the Federation is crippled."

Conclusion

The original *Star Trek* was produced in the midst of the political and social turmoil of the mid to late 1960s—the US civil rights movement, Lyndon B. Johnson's policy dream of the "Great Society," the escalation of the Vietnam War, and the emerging counterculture. In this context, the writers posited thoughtful criticisms and commentary of the Cold War, including US foreign policy and the impact of incorporating developing nations into the capitalist world system, while presenting that system as fundamentally stable. *The Next Generation* was produced in the late 1980s and early 1990s, during the fall of the Berlin Wall in 1989 and the subsequent collapse of the Soviet Union. In a world-system that was now unstable and dangerous, represented by the uncertain alliance with the Klingons and multiple enemies (Q, the Cardassians, Romulans, and the Borg), the protagonists were less avatars of progressive modernism—signified by Kirk's hero-worship of Lincoln (noted in Chapter 2)—and more often participants operating as best they could within political structures beyond their control.

Nevertheless, both *Star Trek* and *The Next Generation* share an enduring belief in social justice, and the idea that such justice can ultimately allow humanity to overcome and erase all political divisions. The contribution of both series is that they pose arguably the prime question that confronts humanity at the beginning of the twenty-first century: can humanity transcend the stereotypes, suspicions, and fears that are sharply outlined in *The Next Generation* in time to fulfill the promise and optimism introduced in the original *Star Trek*?

CHAPTER 4

Star Trek and the Clash of Civilizations
Traditionalism versus Modernity (Universalism)

Samuel P. Huntington, in his "clash of civilizations" concept, argues that much of the world is rooted in "traditionalism." Traditionalist societies (mostly underdeveloped countries) are resistant to modernity—that is, secularism, democracy, gender equality, and so on. In juxtaposition to modernity, traditionalists advocate state-imposed religion (theocracy), paternalism (male dominance), and obscurantism. Significantly, much of the broadcast *Star Trek* franchise illustrates Huntington's conceptualization of world politics—particularly beginning with *The Next Generation* series (as outlined in Chapter 3).

Most important is Huntington's argument that world politics is centered on civilizations, each with their own distinct culture and politics. *Star Trek* depicts this "clash of civilizations" politics, gives insight into it, and allows us to see what is at stake. The world of *Star Trek* is populated by a number of civilizations, most prominently the Federation, the Klingons, the Borg, the Romulans, and the Cardassians. The Federation civilization reflects the modernism of the Western world; the Borg represent hyper- (or dystopian) modernity; and the Klingons, Romulans, and Cardassians are traditionalist societies.

Universal Civilization versus Traditionalism

Huntington points to the concept of "universal civilization": "The idea implies in general the cultural coming together of humanity and the increasing acceptance of common values, beliefs, orientations, practices, and institutions by peoples throughout the world."[1] Huntington holds that the notion of a universal civilization is misplaced and instead claims that people are irrevocably wedded to their idiosyncratic group characteristics: "People define themselves in terms of ancestry, religion, language, history, values, customs, and institutions. They identify with cultural groups: tribes, ethnic groups, religious communities, nations." Huntington describes "politics," in large part, as an effort of "people . . . to define their identity." Moreover, "nation states remain the principal actors in world affairs . . . [and] their behavior is shaped . . . by cultural preferences, commonalities, and differences." Therefore, concepts of universal civilization are unworkable because "humanity is divided into subgroups—tribes, nations, and, at the broadest level, civilizations."[2] Ultimately, Huntington asserts that most civilizations cling to traditionalism, and in the West's conceptualization of a universal civilization, the values of modernity are in actuality only the values of the West. Moreover, the West needs to protect itself and its values from the threat of traditionalist civilizations.

Prior to the *Enterprise* series, *Star Trek* rejects Huntington's critique of universal civilization and openly argues that humanity must embrace such a notion if it is to establish a thriving society. The concept of universal civilization advocated by *Star Trek* is rooted in Marxist ideas of political change and Marxist social/economic ideas. This suggests that when Huntington holds that the idea of universal civilization is, in an essence, a fiction, he is in fact rejecting Marxism.

Federation, Modernity, and Marxism

As outlined in Chapter 2, the federation concept of polity in *Star Trek* is ostensibly predicated on the Marxist ontology of social change and revolution. Karl Marx argued that a classless society based on modernity would occur through a series of progressive revolutions. Leon Trotsky, as leader of the Russian Revolution, held that this revolution would inspire other societies to have their own socialist revolution, and thus the revolutionary polity would be expanded globally through such examples as set by Russia (and presumably) et al.³

While viewing *Star Trek* through the prism of American Trotskyism, the franchise can be read as offering a telos that results in a socialist revolution. Consistent with the interpretation of *Star Trek* as positing American history as a series of progressive events (revolutions) is "The Savage Curtain" (1969) and "The Omega Glory" (1968). Also outlined in Chapter 2, reflecting Trotskyist reasoning/hope in terms of US history, to the Revolutionary War and to the Civil War, *Star Trek* adds to America's revolutionary moments with the Bell Uprising—a critique/rejection of neoliberal economics and politics. As also noted in Chapter 2, *Star Trek* not only is critical of the economics and politics of neoliberalism but also takes aim at capitalism, as reflected in the episode "The Neutral Zone." In Chapter 2, I additionally explain that according to *Star Trek*, humans by the twenty-fourth century have undergone a profound paradigm shift in values and outlook (*Deep Space Nine*, "Little Green Men" 1995). The point is made that humanity's (America's) values have shifted away from "currency-based economics" and toward a "philosophy of self-enhancement" (*Deep Space Nine*, "In the Cards" 1997).

With humanity basing itself on a "philosophy of self-enhancement," humans come to lead the Federation, and most important, its expansion is predicated on voluntary mergers/unions. ("The Federation is made up of over a hundred planets *who have allied themselves* for mutual scientific, cultural and defensive benefits" [*Deep Space Nine*, "Battle Lines" 1993]; "The Federation consists of over one hundred and fifty different worlds *who have agreed to share their knowledge and resources in peaceful cooperation*" [*Voyager*, "Innocence" 1996].) Kirk, speaking of the founders of the Federation, says, "They were humanitarians and statesmen, and they had a dream. A dream that became a reality and spread throughout the stars, a dream that made Mister Spock and me brothers" ("Whom Gods Destroy" 1969).

Seemingly indicative of how the social justice politics (broadly conceived—i.e., universalism) of the Federation transcends all ethnic, religious, and species divisions, when asked, "Do you consider Captain Kirk and yourself brothers?" Spock replied, "Captain Kirk speaks somewhat figuratively and with undue emotion. However, what he says is logical and I do, in fact, agree with it" ("Whom Gods Destroy," original series 1969). Captain Picard declares, "If there's one ideal the Federation holds most dear it's that all men, all [alien] races, can be united" (*Star Trek: Nemesis* 2002). During a *Next Generation* episode, a visiting alien is very impressed with the highly diverse background of the *Enterprise* crew: "Truly remarkable. They're all so different from one another yet they work together freely." ("Transfigurations" 1992).

The *Voyager* episode "The Void" (2001) provides insight into the normative values and political processes that are at the center of the Federation. *Voyager* is trapped in a void in space, where there is no "matter of any kind." Other ships trapped in the void have taken up the practice of attacking and raiding other trapped ships for supplies as a means of surviving: "There are more than 150 ships within scanning range but I'm only detecting life signs on 29 of them."

Through collaboration and solidarity, Janeway argues that the ships in the void can work together to escape. In shaping this reasoning, Janeway draws inspiration from the example of the Federation: "The Federation is based on mutual cooperation—the idea that the whole is greater than the sum of its parts. *Voyager* can't survive here alone, but if we form a temporary alliance with other ships maybe we can pool our resources and escape." *Voyager* shares its limited food and medical supplies, as well as joins in common defense, to build trust and establish (what Janeway calls) the "Alliance." Through the Alliance, *Voyager*'s food supplies are enhanced: "One of the crews that joined us had technology that tripled our replicator efficiency . . . We can feed five hundred people a day now using half the power it took us a few days ago." Led by *Voyager*, the Alliance ships escape the void. Those that refused to become members stay behind.

Therefore, *Star Trek* posits the argument that a stable, ethical society can only be based on a classless society based on modernism—one that is free of gender and ethnic biases. *Star Trek*, however, does offer a critique of modernity. This critique is rendered through the Borg. Additionally, the creators of the franchise offer a somewhat sympathetic treatment of a traditionalist society via the Klingons.

The Borg: A Traditionalist Critique of Modernity

The Borg are introduced in *The Next Generation*. The seemingly obvious interpretation of the Borg is that they are a pessimistic/dark view of modernity—that is, modernity run amok. Through the literary device of the Borg, modernity is cast as totalizing, oppressive, dehumanizing, expunging creativity, and blanching away individuality. The Borg are described as "a mixture of organic and artificial life" ("Q Who" 1989). They inform their victims, "Resistance is futile. Your life as it has been is over . . . We will add your biological and technological distinctiveness to our own. Your culture will adapt to service ours." Among the Borg, individuality is erased: "You are not dealing with an individual mind . . . It is the collective minds of all of them," Troi said ("Q Who").

The Borg travel in giant grayish cubes, and inside these lit cubes there are no signs of recreation, creativity, or family life. The straight lines, precise right angles, and dark hues inside the Borg ships bespeak extreme utilitarianism—a perfectly efficient, rationalist use of space and color bereft of anything that could be distracting or that makes life worth living ("Best of Both Worlds" 1990). Borg are referred to as "drones," and their social organization is labeled a "hive" (*Voyager*, "Drone" 1998). Hence the Borg are an ironic critique of modernity.

Samuel P. Huntington, apparently ascribing traditionalist values to everyone outside of the West, asserts, "What is universalism [modernity] to the West is imperialism to the rest."[4] Guinan reports that her species was ravaged by the Borg: "My people encountered them a century ago. Our cities were destroyed—our people scattered across the galaxy. They are called the Borg—protect yourself or they will destroy you" ("Q Who"). The Borg say, "Freedom is irrelevant. Self-determination is irrelevant . . . Your people will be [forcibly] assimilated" ("Best of Both Worlds").

Traditionalism in *Star Trek*: The Klingons

Unlike the Federation, which is based on the universal ideas of equality, fairness, and equal treatment, Klingons are traditionalists. Traditionalist societies tend to be patriarchies, as is Klingon society, with women prohibited from sitting on the Klingon's supreme political body, the High Council. Political decisions for the family/clan are made by the eldest male, and the crimes of fathers implicate their sons ("Sins of the Father" 1990; "Redemption" 1991).

The fictional Klingons base their polity on ethnic identity—hence the name of their polity, the Klingon Empire. (Klingons in fact are not a different species from humans, as Klingon-human couplings can result in offspring.)[5] Klingons look to their past and religion to shape and legitimatize their politics. The episode "Rightful Heir" (1993) focuses on the figure of Kahless, who is credited with founding the Klingon state. According to Klingon theology, Kahless "united" the Klingons, gave them "honor and strength," and "promised to return one day and lead [them] again." Kahless is described as a prophet-like figure in the following: "To believe in Kahless and his teachings . . . [is] to become truly Klingon." Kahless is cloned from ancient DNA material, and the Kahless clone is made the head of state of the Klingon Empire.

Pointing to the traditionalism of the Klingons, ancient (traditional) rituals serve as an important part of their society.[6] Significantly, instead of using modern (democratic and transparent) means of selecting a head of government, the Klingons employ the "rite of succession"—an oblique ritual/tradition—to select their political leader. In this rite, the "Arbiter of Succession" (with no clear criteria) decides who are the "strongest challengers" to vie for the chancellorship ("Reunion" 1990).

Daniel Bernardi, in Star Trek *and History: Race-ing toward a White Future*, holds that *The Next Generation* conveys a bias against dark-skinned people.[7] He writes that the "biological notion of blackness is displaced onto the Klingons while a civilized notion of whiteness is ascribed to the Federation."[8] Bernardi correctly notes that Klingons (who are brown skinned) are described as inherently violent. In "The Icarus Factor," the point is explicitly made by the steadfastly objective Data that "there is, of course, a genetic predisposition toward hostility among all Klingons."

Bernardi, in my estimation, is wrong to argue that the Klingons represent dark-skinned people writ large. Instead, as I have already indicated in Chapter 3, the Klingons represent traditional societies (à la Huntington). The Romulans in *The Next Generation* are cast as implacable and dangerous foes. (Significantly, Romulans are not generally dark skinned.) They are described as "violent beyond description," and "their belief in their own superiority is beyond arrogance" ("The Neutral Zone" 1988).

Another polity rooted in ethnic identity (traditionalism) is the Cardassian Alliance. In "Chain of Command" (1992), the Cardassians are discovered to be marshaling their forces along the Federation border and readying for an invasion. The invasion is only stopped because the *Enterprise* is able to attach explosives to the Cardassian attack fleet. The Cardassians then agree to forego their planned assault in exchange for the disarming of the explosives attached to their ships.

While traditionalist societies in *Star Trek*—especially in *The Next Generation*—are cast as violent and dangerous, they are also cast as the technological equal of the Federation, the quintessential modernist society. This leads to two important conclusions. First, according to *Star Trek*, in terms of technology, modernist societies are not superior to traditionalist ones. This is an explicit rejection of the Enlightenment claim that technological advancement occurs most freely where social progress (political equality and equal treatment) is predominate.[9] Second, traditional societies (the underdeveloped world) are not dependent and subordinate to modernist (Western) societies. Both these conclusions support Huntington's claim that traditionalist societies can outmaneuver modernist societies and that the modernist/traditionalist bifurcation is the prime tension in the contemporary world system. Put differently, colonialism, resource and labor exploitation, and Western military interventions are peripheral to the fact that developing world politics and economics are essentially autonomous and can overrun the West.

Modernity as a Form of Traditionalism

Huntington's most controversial assertion is that the West should abandon the notion that modernism (e.g., Marxism) is truly universal and accept the conclusion that modernity is a type of traditionalism. More precisely, Western concepts of political equality, secularism, and equal treatment are exactly that—Western. More ominously, unless we in the West give up the misguided idea that democracy (in all its dimensions) is a universal principle, the West may succumb to competing civilizations—those rooted in conventional notions of traditionalism. Huntington holds that "the survival of the West depends on Americans reaffirming their Western identity and Westerns accepting their civilization *as unique not universal* and uniting to renew and preserve it against challengers from non-Western societies." Worse still, the West has to accept the patriarchy, authoritarianism, and political religiosity of traditional societies—that is, not seek to change them. Huntington, somewhat pessimistically, asserts, "Avoidance of a global war of civilizations depends on world leaders accepting and cooperating to maintain the multicivilizational character of global politics."[10]

What *Star Trek* shows is that a world dominated by this outlook, where there is no universalism but only parochialism and sectarianism, is a world dominated by instability, war, authoritarianism, and racism. As outlined in Chapter 3, the political instability/corruption of Klingon politics and the uncertainty of the Federation-Klingon alliance are evident in "Sins of the Father" (1990), "Reunion" (1990), "The Mind's Eye" (1991), and "Redemption" (1991). The Cardassians have a military dictatorship, also noted in Chapter 3. They invaded the neighboring planet of Bajor and occupied it for decades—enslaving its population and exploiting its natural resources. Similarly, the Romulan government maintains a regime of terror as "thousands of dissidents . . . live in fear of their lives" (*The Next Generation*, "Face of the Enemy" 1993)

Perhaps the worst aspect of a world permanently cleaved into civilizations is the xenophobia and racism that would seemingly be forever part of global politics—in both the developed (or advanced) world and the rest. The xenophobia of traditionalism (the Klingons) is evident when Worf is chided for bringing "*outsiders* [humans] to our Great Hall" ("Sins of the Father" 1990). In another instance, one Klingon is opposed to another Klingon marrying a non-Klingon: "She believes that by bringing aliens into our families we risk losing our identity as Klingons." This is acknowledged as "a prejudiced, xenophobic view" (*Deep Space Nine*, "You Are Cordially Invited" 1997).

The racism inherent in the concept of civilization posited by Huntington is particularly evident in *The Next Generation* episode "Birthright" (1993). The action centers on a prison camp established by the Romulans more than twenty years earlier to house a group of Klingons who could not return home. They were stigmatized by the fact that they were taken prisoner—Klingons are expected to fight to the death or commit suicide if captured. As an act of kindness, and at great sacrifice, a Romulan officer agrees to oversee the camp—otherwise the captured Klingons would be executed. Worf, whose father was falsely rumored to be at the camp, discovers it. He objects to an arrangement whereby Klingons live as prisoners of the Romulans even though they are treated well, have complete freedom on the planet they reside on, have given birth to children, and share a strong sense of community. Worf, nevertheless, tells the Romulan camp commander (Tokath), "You robbed the Klingons of who they were. *You dishonored them.*" Tokath, pointing to the irrationality of Worf's position, retorts, "By not slitting their throats when we found them unconscious?" Worf explicitly resorts to racialist thinking to justify his position: "I do not expect you to understand. *You are a Romulan.*" Hence there is something particular about Klingons that is inscrutable to non-Klingons. Tokath explains, "We've put aside the old hatreds. Here, Romulans and Klingons live in peace." Worf is unmoved: "Do not deceive yourself. These people are not happy here. I see the sadness in their eyes."

Worf adopts an openly hateful attitude when he comes to discover that a woman (Ba'el) he is romantically interested in is an offspring of one of the Klingon prisoners and a Romulan. Worf is kissing Ba'el, draws back her hair, and sees her pointed ears (characteristic of Romulans). Outraged, Worf exclaims, "*You are Romulan!*" Unabashed in his racism, he asks with a tone of disgust, "*How could your mother mate with a Romulan?*" He declares, "*It is an obscenity!*" Fully venting his racism, Worf tells Ba'el, "Romulans are *treacherous, deceitful.* They are without honor." Ba'el says, "My father is a good man. He is kind, and generous. There is nothing dishonorable about him."

Earth-Vulcan Relations in *Enterprise*

The most demoralizing aspect of Huntington's "clash of civilizations" claim is the view that the West is unique in its commitment to (or suitability for) modernism (democracy, equality, and fairness), which would invariably lead to a type of hostility in the West toward societies that are at least perceived to be doomed to traditionalism (as argued by Huntington).[11] Most notably, Huntington holds (as outlined previously) that the West is in competition with the rest of the world. This reasoning is at the core of the last *Star Trek* television series, *Enterprise* (2001–5). Perhaps the most salient aspect of the *Enterprise* narrative is that, unlike the original series where the Vulcans and earthlings are part of the same Federation polity/civilization, in this series Earth and Vulcan have an uneasy relationship and seemingly form two discrete (competing) civilizations.

It is significant that in *Star Trek: First Contact*, by 2063 San Francisco is destroyed.[12] In "Past Tense" (*Deep Space Nine*), San Francisco is where the antineoliberalism Bell Uprising (the basis of a new global politics) occurs in 2024. Thus, according to the 1996 movie, Earth's global polity is not formed as a result of the replacement of the neoliberal order. Instead, according to the movie *First Contact*, Earth's politics is predicated on a we/they distinction. This is consonant with Huntington's point that "for peoples seeking identity and reinventing ethnicity, *enemies are essential.*"[13]

Therefore, the political foundation of humanity in the mid-twenty-first century is the we/they dichotomy, with the Vulcans serving as "they." This is the basis of *Enterprise* (set in the twenty-second century, whereas the original series is set in the twenty-third century, with *Next Generation*, *Deep Space Nine*, and *Voyager* in the twenty-fourth). In *Enterprise*, conflict and competition with the Vulcans do occur. The episodes "The Forge" (2004), "Awakening" (2004), and the "Kir'Shara" (2004) make up a story arc whereby Earth's embassy on Vulcan is bombed, killing Admiral Forrest (Captain Archer's mentor), and the *Enterprise* crew gets swept up in internal Vulcan religious and political strife—with an attempt made against Captain Archer's life, and the *Enterprise* and Vulcan military ships coming to a face-off. In the denouement, we learn that elements within the Vulcan government were behind the bombing of the Earth embassy, and that a faction still in the government wants to pull the planet toward a political/military alliance with the Romulans. This is ominously threatening to Earth, as it suggests the formation of a Vulcan-Romulan civilization (they are the same ethnicity).

Enterprise conveys Earth's polity as afflicted with xenophobia and racism. The series concludes in 2005, and the penultimate episode centers on the group "Terra Prime" (also the episode title). Initially, this organization is described as xenophobic: "They want to stop all contact with alien species . . . They believe it's corrupting our way of life." Later, we learn that Terra Prime is racist: "This is an alien-human hybrid. Living proof of what will happen if we allow ourselves to be submerged in an interstellar coalition. Our genetic heritage . . . That child is a cross-breed freak. How many generations before our genome is so diluted that the word human is nothing more than a footnote in some medical text?" The leader of Terra Prime declares, "I'm returning Earth to its rightful owners." Referring to signs of broad sympathy for Terra Prime and its agenda, the Vulcan Ambassador Soval notes, "The fact that [Terra Prime] has the support of so many of your people is . . . troubling."

Of great significance for a discussion based on Huntington's vision of world politics informed by the idea of conflictive civilizations are the Xindi, introduced in *Enterprise*. The Xindi are the former inhabitants of the planet Xindi. The Xindi are cleaved into five distinct civilizations, with each civilization corresponding to a distinct species—one insectoid, one humanoid, one aquatic, one apelike, and one reptilian. As a result of their competition, the Xindi destroyed their planet: "The war went on for nearly a hundred years . . . The insectoids and reptilians detonated massive explosions beneath the eight largest seismic fissures. I'd like to think they didn't realize how devastating the result would be" ("The Shipment" 2003).

Conclusion

Star Trek, beginning with the original series, conveys the positive/inclusive politics predicated on the universalism of modernity. As explained in Chapter 2, this type of politics, and the process that brings it about, is ostensibly shaped by the social justice politics inherent in Marxist and, more specifically, Trotskyist thinking. Beginning with *The Next Generation* series, *Star Trek* begins drawing on ideas and arguments consonant with the "clash of civilizations" ideation posited by Samuel P. Huntington. Particularly significant is the development of the Klingons, who represent a traditionalist society. Also noteworthy are the Borg, which can be viewed as a traditionalist critique of modernity—that is, the utilitarianism, rationalism, and universalism of the West. Other traditionalist societies conveyed in *Star Trek* (those centered on ethnic identity) are the Romulans and the Cardassians. These traditionalist polities are perennially hostile and militarily aggressive toward each other and the modernist Federation (the "clash of civilizations" as envisioned by Huntington).

In illustrating the "clash of civilizations" concept, *Star Trek* shows that to accept this clash as the permanent basis of global politics is to consign humanity to perpetual authoritarianism, instability, and war. Perhaps most disconcerting is that cleaving the globe into distinct civilizations results in irreparable racialist reasoning and ethnic-based hate (e.g., "Birthright"). *Enterprise* shows how operating on the assumption of competing civilizations leads to xenophobia, racism, and hate even in the West. Ultimately, the clash of civilizations risks planetary destruction, as with the Xindi.

The analytical brilliance of *Star Trek* is found in its creators' ability to effectively and credibly convey both Marxist politics and values and the "clash of civilizations" ideation, as well as to entertainingly and convincingly juxtapose these competing worldviews. As a result, *Star Trek* makes an outstanding and invaluable contribution to political theory and international relations theory. Most significantly, it demonstrates the hope and optimism evident in Marxism and the demoralization and pessimism that inheres in Huntington's "clash of civilizations" view of humanity and global politics.

CHAPTER 5

Star Trek and World Government
Federation, Empire, or Neoliberalism

As outlined in Chapter 2, humanity is desperately in need of world government. Global political/military tension and upheaval among nation-states suggests the very real possibility of the outbreak of a planetary conflagration—even involving nuclear weapons. Additionally, the global warming phenomenon/crisis indicates the outstanding need for a worldwide regime governing humanity's interaction with the environment. The *Star Trek* franchise posits a future with Earth having a world government, pointing to both the geopolitical and environmental reasons for such a government.

Star Trek indicates three distinct means to establish a world government: (1) federation, (2) empire, and (3) neoliberalism. The federation path to world government is predicated on the concept of justice known in the academic literature on *Star Trek* as "liberal humanism"—a classless society, free of gender/ethnic bias.[1] The justice—that is, liberal humanism—evident in federation inspires others to become part of the global polity. The empire strategy of establishing global governance relies on national (for *Star Trek*, species) identity. Within empire, a particular identity group seeks to politically impose themselves on other (species) societies. They do so through military (violent) means and deception, claiming racial/political superiority in the process. The proponents of the neoliberal state argue for a global regime based on practical considerations—expanding trade relations and bolstering international security. *Star Trek* indicates that a political basis of neoliberalism is the we/they distinction, à la Carl Schmitt. Utilizing these templates as set out in *Star Trek*, it can be concluded that the American-led global hegemonic system contains characteristics from all three templates. *Star Trek* suggests, however, that only the federation route to global government is viable.

Federation

As outlined in Chapter 2, the federation concept of polity in *Star Trek* is ostensibly predicated on the Marxist ontology of social change and revolution. Karl Marx argued that a classless society based on modernity would occur through a series of progressive revolutions. Leon Trotsky, as leader of the Russian Revolution, held that this revolution would inspire other societies to have their own socialist revolution, and thus the revolutionary polity would be expanded globally through such examples as set by Russia (and presumably) et al.

With humanity basing itself on a philosophy of self-enhancement and liberal humanism (see Chapter 2), humans come to lead the Federation, and most important, its expansion is predicated on voluntary mergers/unions. ("The Federation is made up of over a hundred planets *who have allied themselves* for mutual scientific, cultural and defensive benefits" [*Deep Space Nine*, "Battle Lines" 1993]. "The Federation consists of over one hundred and fifty different worlds *who have agreed to share their knowledge and resources in peaceful cooperation*" [*Voyager*, "Innocence" 1996].)

Voyager episode "The Void"—as explained in Chapter 4—provides insight into the normative values and political processes that are at the center of federation. *Voyager* shares its limited food and medical supplies, as well as joins in common defense, to build trust and establish (what Janeway calls) the "Alliance." Led by *Voyager*, the Alliance ships escape the void.

The United States as Federation

The US-led world system was constructed in significant part because the American government inspired admiration and loyalty à la federation. The United States could be said to have been a good friend to Europe—helping defeat the Kaiser and the Nazis, as well as giving Western and Central Europe huge sums in the post–World War II period in the form of the Marshall Plan. Also, the United States committed itself to defending Europe from the Soviets during the Cold War through the North Atlantic Treaty Organization. Of course, in carrying out these "friendly" acts, the United States committed vast resources and incurred massive costs, including the potentially catastrophic risk of nuclear war. These acts and sacrifices are arguably the key reasons the United States is the leader of the current world system.

Moreover (at least in the American mind), US global leadership is ostensibly justified because it is a locus of global justice and freedom—for example, the American Revolutionary War, the US Civil War, the fight against fascism, the New Deal, the Civil Rights Movement. *Star Trek*'s creators explicitly hold that victory over the Axis Powers (World War II) could not have been attained without American involvement (original series, "City on the Edge of Forever" 1967). Through the *Deep Space Nine* platform, *Star Trek* renders a very effective lauding of the struggle for racial equality in the United States during the 1950s and 1960s ("Far Beyond the Stars" 1998).

Has the United States, however, shifted from federation to empire in its worldwide dealings? This question is treated in the next section.

Empire

Star Trek offers an excellent opportunity for the comparison of empire and federation. It does so in significant part through the episodes "Mirror, Mirror" (1967) and "In a Mirror, Darkly" (2005). *Star Trek* also illustrates the means of empire through the fictional Klingon Empire, Romulan Empire, and the Dominion. Whereas in a federation, persuasion and inspiration are the means through which a polity seeks to expand its influence and sovereignty, in an empire, conquest and deception are how political control is expanded and maintained.

While in the Federation universe, the *Enterprise* only pursues peaceful means with the Halkans, in the Empire universe, Kirk is "ordered to annihilate the Halkans unless they comply. *No alternative*" ("Mirror, Mirror"). The *Star Trek: Enterprise* Captain Jonathan Archer from the alternative universe declares, "Great men are not peacemakers. Great men are conquerors" ("In a Mirror, Darkly" 2005). Captain Picard points to the Romulan Star Empire's "massacres in the Norkan outposts," which the Romulans labeled "the Norkan Campaign" ("The Defector" 1990). The following describes how the Dominion accrues territory: "They destroyed our communications center, they executed our leaders, and before we realized it, [the Dominion] had seized control of the entire planet" (*Deep Space Nine*, "The Jem'Hadar" 1994).

When the Klingon Empire invades Cardassia based on unsubstantiated rumors that the Dominion was surreptitiously leading the new civilian government, the Federation-Klingon alliance ended as the Federation intervened to protect Cardassian territory/sovereignty. In explaining why the Klingon Empire decided to attack Cardassia, it is noted that "fear of the Dominion" is only "an excuse." Klingons "were born . . . to conquer." It's later added that if the Klingons defeat the Cardassians, "They will occupy the Cardassian home world, execute all government officials, and install an imperial overseer" (*Deep Space Nine*, "The Way of the Warrior" 1995). The brutality of the Klingon Empire is conveyed when a Klingon ambassador (Kell) is asked, "You are prepared to grant [the inhabitants of Krios] independence?" and Kell responds, "Perhaps. But we will conquer them again later if we wish to."

Empire and Claims of Superiority

A hallmark of empire is the claim made by the governing group that it is somehow superior to the subject peoples of such political formations. Captain Archer of the Empire denounces his counterpart in the Federation because "he sold out Earth's future to a group of subhuman species." Put differently, the subject peoples of humanity's Empire are "subhuman species." When a Klingon commander is confronted with the charge that Klingons have "boasted that they'll take over half the galaxy," he retorts, "Why not? We're the stronger!" (original series, "Errand of Mercy" 1967). The leadership caste of the Dominion is composed of a species that mostly live in a liquid state, called the Founders. They justify their empire through the idea that "many years ago we set ourselves the task of imposing order on a chaotic universe." As a species, the Founders are known as Changelings, and one Changeling tells another (named Odo, who was separated from the Founders), "It's not justice you desire, Odo, but order. The same as we do. And we can help you satisfy that desire in ways the Solids [i.e., humanoids] never could" (*Deep Space Nine*, "The Search" 1994).

Deception and Empire

In pursuing the invasion of Cardassia and thereby ending the decades old Klingon-Federation alliance, the Klingon head of government, Chancellor Gowron, declares, "*History is written by the victors*" (*Deep Space Nine*, "The Way of the Warrior" 1995). Contrary to this sentiment that the perception of reality (facts) is malleable and can/should be shaped to serve any (corrupt) agenda, Captain Picard declares, "The first duty of every Starfleet officer is to the *truth*. Whether it's scientific truth, or historical truth, or personal truth. It is the guiding principle upon which Starfleet is based" ("The First Duty" 1992). In another instance, Picard, speaking to one of the leading political figures of the Federation, declares, "Sarek of Vulcan never confused what he wanted with the *truth*" ("Sarek" 1992).

The deception arguably at the core of empire is aptly depicted in the *Next Generation* episode "The Next Phase" (1992), which involves the Romulan Empire. In spite of the fact that the *Enterprise* crew risked life and limb to save a Romulan ship (and the commander's expression of gratitude), the Romulans, nevertheless, hatch a plan to destroy *Enterprise* and her crew.

The United States as Empire

In the 2003 invasion of Iraq, the United States reflected the characteristics of empire as outlined in *Star Trek*. First, of course, the United States conquered Iraq. Thus just like all the imperial formations depicted in *Star Trek*—the Empire universe, Klingon, Romulan, and Dominion—the United States seeks to expand its political influence through conquest. Second, the Bush Administration justified the invasion in part by claiming that the Iraqi political system was inferior, and America would bestow its democracy onto the Iraqis.[2] Third, the Bush Administration used deception in its conquest of Iraq—most glaringly, the false claim that Iraq possessed weapons of mass destruction.[3] With regard to US claims about bringing democracy to Iraq, shortly after the invasion it was explained by a reporter that the United States in Iraq "is seen as a military occupier that supports democracy and free speech when they serve its interest, but suppresses both when they don't."[4]

According to *Star Trek*, building a stable global polity on Earth through empire is not possible outside the Empire universe. This claim is seemingly made in the original series episode "City on the Edge of Forever" (1967). Thus the establishment of a presumably worldwide Nazi Empire evidently leads to the collapse of human civilization.

With the last *Star Trek* television series (*Enterprise*), *Star Trek* creators move away from liberal humanism as the basis of Earth's government and the creation of the Federation. Instead, they rely on the we/they distinction to explain a worldwide polity on Earth, and neoliberalism to account for the intergalactic formation that humanity would lead—that is, the Federation.

Neoliberalism

Enterprise is set in the twenty-second century, whereas the original series took place in the twenty-third century and *Next Generation*, *Deep Space Nine*, and *Voyager* in the twenty-fourth. *Enterprise* directly takes up the question of the creation of the Federation.

The argument is made that the Federation is established not as a harbinger of justice and freedom but for pragmatic reasons altogether. This more closely mirrors the formation of the European Union than the history of the creation and strengthening of the American federal government. The effort to create a European-federated structure in the post–World War II period grew predominantly out of two entirely practical considerations: defense (from the Soviet Union) and economic stability—trade, energy security, and so on.[5]

The pressing need for a regional security regime is established in the second *Enterprise* episode, "Fight or Flight" (2001). The *Enterprise* comes across an alien ship that has been attacked and whose crew is dead. With no protocol or any officials to notify, the *Enterprise* initially leaves the damaged ship and her dead crew adrift in space.

The need for a regional security protocol is again treated in "Babel One" (2005), "United" (2005), and "The Aenar" (2005). These make up a three-episode arc involving Romulan subterfuge, whereby they launch a remotely controlled ship in an attempt to destabilize Earth's region of space. The Romulan ship can take various forms, and attacks ships under the guise that the offending ship is from one of the other powers in Earth's sector of space.

The economic difficulties created by the lack of a security framework are outlined in the following episodes: "Fortunate Son" (2001) and "Marauders" (2002). "Fortunate Son" revolves around the fact that without a protective military presence, cargo ships are regularly subject to raiding (from a species known as Nausicans). Archer to the Nausican raiders: "You're not sneaking up on an old freighter this time. This is an NX Class Starship. Take a good look, because you'll be seeing more of them." In "Marauders," a small alien colony is eking out a living producing and trading a source of energy (deuterium), but a group of Klingon marauders force the colonists to pay them tribute.

Therefore, according to the creators of *Enterprise*, the prime motive underlying the creation of the Federation is security and trade. This represents the obligations of the neoliberal state—that is, guaranteeing the secure and free movement of goods, services, and capital.

In making the case for a federated interstellar political system, Captain Archer tells an audience of delegates of the would-be United Federation of Planets the following:

> Up until about a hundred years ago, there was one question that burned in every human, that made us study the stars and dream of traveling to them, Are we alone? Our generation is privileged to know the answer to that question. We are all explorers, driven to know what's over the horizon, what's beyond our own shores. And yet, the more I've experienced, the more I've learned that no matter how far we travel, or how fast we get there, the most profound discoveries are not necessarily beyond that next star. They're within us, woven into the threads that bind us, all of us, to each other. The final frontier begins in this hall. Let's explore it together. ("Terra Prime" 2005)

Thus in advocating for a federation among planets, *Enterprise* does not make any specific justice claims (the elimination of poverty, the promotion of democracy, etc.). Instead, Captain Archer's position is rooted in practical considerations—namely, the logic of coordinating planet members' space travels ("Let's explore [space] together").

We can see the implications of (the minimal) neoliberal political obligations in a federated world system in the original series episode "Cloud Minders" (1969). Captain's Log: "A botanical plague is devastating a planet in the quadrant of the galaxy where the *Enterprise* is operating at present. It threatens to destroy the vegetation on the entire planet, leaving it uninhabitable." The *Enterprise* goes "to the planet Ardana, where the only source of zenite exists. It is the one substance that can halt the plague." In effective imagery, the political, economic, and social realities of the planet are portrayed—with the privileged/governing caste living a life of aesthetic splendor in a "cloud city" (Stratos) floating in the heavens, while the laboring classes (referred to as Troglytes) live on the (barren) planet working the mines (extracting zenite). The *Enterprise* mission is in jeopardy because of civil/political strife on Ardana. Led by "Disrupters," the Troglytes are blockading the shipment of zenite. Consistent with a neoliberal conception of international politics, Kirk informs the Ardana leadership that as a member of the Federation, it has an obligation to make the zenite available to other Federation planets. Kirk says, "I must concern myself with [the conflict on Ardana] if it should interfere with the delivery of zenite to Merak Two . . . Ardana is a member of the Federation, and it is your council's responsibility that nothing interferes with its obligation to another member of the Federation."

When Kirk directly engages the Troglytes to discuss reforming Ardana's society, Kirk is informed, "Your Federation orders do not entitle you to defy local governments." When Kirk decides to proceed with his plan for reform in the face of the opposition of Ardana's government, Spock warns him, "If you are apprehended deliberately violating the [Ardana] High Advisor's orders, he will be within his rights to have you executed." Evidently, Federation rules do not extend to the treatment of member planets' citizens.

A later iteration of *Star Trek* stresses the fact that Federation member states are expected to maintain *just* domestic polities. When the planet Bajor reconstitutes a caste structure (the D'jarra system), it is informed, "Caste-based discrimination goes against the Federation charter. If Bajor returns to the D'jarra system, I have no doubt that its petition to join the Federation will be rejected" (*Deep Space Nine*, "Accession" 1996).

Enterprise (2001–5) indicates that the normative core of a neoliberal polity is the "friend/foe" dichotomy posited by political theorist Carl Schmitt. *Enterprise* further indicates that neoliberalism and empire polities share the normative claim among their dominate groups of political/ethnic superiority.

The "Friend/Foe" Dichotomy and Star Trek

Carl Schmitt (1888–1985) held that at the center of politics is the distinction "between friend and enemy."[6] Social and political cohesion is based on this friend/foe bifurcation. Reflective of Schmitt's friend/enemy reasoning, in *The Next Generation* episode "Face of the Enemy" (1993), the point is made that Romulans have an "absolute certainty about . . . who is a friend and who is an enemy." Political scientist Shadia B. Drury renders the following observation: "Schmitt . . . believes that politics is first and foremost about the distinction between WE and THEY. [He] thinks that a political order can be stable only if it is united by an external threat."[7]

The *Star Trek* movie *First Contact* (1996) is predicated on a we/they distinction. The action of the movie takes place in the year 2063. The Borg go back in Earth's history to prevent humanity's first contact with the Vulcans. This initial exposure to an alien culture occurs because Zephran Cochrane conducts humanity's first successful warp drive experiment. (Warp speed represents a speed faster than light.) When the Vulcans detect Cochrane's ship achieving warp speed, they decide to introduce themselves to earthlings—first contact. In *First Contact*'s iteration of *Star Trek*'s historiography of Earth, in 2063 humanity is in what is referred to a "Second Dark Age."[8] What rallies humanity from its disarray is its contact with the Vulcans:

> **RIKER:** It is one of the pivotal moments in human history, Doctor [Cochrane]. You get to make first contact with an alien race, and after you do, everything begins to change.
>
> **TROI:** It unites humanity in a way no one ever thought possible when they realize they're not alone in the universe. Poverty, disease, war. They'll all be gone within the next fifty years.

Therefore, the political foundation of Earth's polity in the mid-twenty-first century is the we/they dichotomy—with the Vulcans serving as "they": "The political enemy is not necessarily morally evil." Instead, Schmitt held that the potential enemy "is merely the other, the stranger, and it is sufficient that according to his nature he is in a special intense way existentially something different and alien, so that in the extreme case conflicts with him are possible."[9]

In *Enterprise*, conflict with the Vulcans does occur. "The Andorian Incident" (2001) concludes with the exposure of a Vulcan spy station by Captain Archer, which earns the ire of the Vulcans. The Vulcan ambassador to Earth complains, "The Andorians wouldn't have found the [spy] station if your people hadn't interfered." The *Enterprise* has "been in space for six months and they've already destabilized an entire sector" ("Shadows of P'Jem" 2002). "Fusion" (2002) involves a set of Vulcans who, contrary to Vulcan norms, embrace their emotions. A dissident Vulcan explains that "I always knew there had to be more to life than just logic and reason." This Vulcan telepathically "rapes" T'Pol (a Vulcan and *Enterprise*'s first officer), and Captain Archer engages in an intense fist fight with the transgressor. The episodes "The Forge" (2004), "Awakening" (2004), and the "Kir'Shara" (2004) make up a story arc whereby Earth's embassy on Vulcan is bombed, killing Admiral Forrest (Archer's mentor), and the *Enterprise* crew gets swept up in internal Vulcan religious and political strife—with an attempt made against Captain Archer's life, and the *Enterprise* and Vulcan military ships coming to a face-off. In the denouement, we learn that elements within the Vulcan government were behind the bombing of the Earth embassy, and that a faction still in the government wants to pull the planet toward a political/military alliance with the Romulans—an intention ominously threatening to Earth.

The we/they or friend/foe dichotomy at the heart of Earth's politics in *Enterprise* and *First Contact* is in sharp contrast to earlier iterations of *Star Trek*, where (as noted previously) state-building was accomplished through the progressive expansion of political rights and social justice. It is significant that in *First Contact*, by 2063 San Francisco is destroyed.[10] In "Past Tense" (*Deep Space Nine*) San Francisco is where the antineoliberalism Bell Uprising (the basis of a new global politics) occurs in 2024.

The result is, far from being impressed by human social practices and political formations, the Vulcans are leery of humanity. T'Pol: "You have yet to embrace either patience or logic. You remain impulsive . . . It remains to be seen whether humanity will revert to its baser instincts" ("Broken Arrow" 2001). Such pronouncements strike against the very foundation of the *Star Trek* franchise—namely, that humans are socially, politically, and technologically progressing toward a utopian ideal (e.g., *The Next Generation*, "Transfigurations" 1990).

With the we/they dichotomy serving as the basis of Earth's politics, unsurprisingly a wave of racism grips the planet in *Enterprise*. The *Enterprise* series concludes in 2005 and the penultimate episode centers on the group "Terra Prime" (also the episode title). Initially, this organization is described as xenophobic:

> **GOVERNMENT OFFICIAL ON EARTH:** "They want to stop all contact with alien species." "They believe it's corrupting our way of life." Later, we learn that Terra Prime is racist:
> **LEADER OF TERRA PRIME:** "This is an alien-human hybrid. Living proof of what will happen if we allow ourselves to be submerged in an interstellar coalition. Our genetic heritage." "That child is a cross-breed freak. How many generations before our genome is so diluted that the word human is nothing more than a footnote in some medical text?"

The leader of Terra Prime goes on to declare, "I'm returning Earth to its rightful owners." The group seeks to scuttle the formation of the Federation by promising to destroy Starfleet command (in San Francisco) unless all aliens leave Earth. Referring to signs of popular support for Terra Prime and its agenda, the Vulcan Ambassador Soval notes, "The fact that Paxton has the support of so many of your people is . . . troubling." An Andorian ambassador makes the point, "Earthmen talk about uniting worlds, but your own planet is deeply divided. Perhaps you're not quite ready to host this conference [promoting interstellar cooperation]."

Neoliberalism and the United States

The United States has led in the formation of the neoliberal world system,[11] which has brought substantial changes to the global economy.[12] As noted previously, *Star Trek: Enterprise* indicates that the normative core of neoliberalism is the we/they distinction. In the case of the current world system, neoliberalism became hegemonic in the 1980s, in a context where the Reagan Administration was ramping up the Cold War.[13] More specifically, President Ronald Reagan (shifting away from the rhetoric of detente) held that the United States was "a bright beacon of hope and freedom,"[14] and the Soviet Union was an "evil empire."[15] After the collapse of the Soviet Union, a different foe was identified in Islamofascism—a global movement aimed at secular, modern governments and societies.[16] A similar position was reflected in the "clash of civilizations" thesis—namely, that traditional/religious societies are pitted against modern/secular ones.[17] In 2014, there are efforts to recast Russia as a threat to civilization. Senior Senator and former Republican nominee for President John McCain, for instance, recently castigated Russian President Vladimir V. Putin for being an "unreconstructed Russian imperialist and K.G.B. apparatchik." He contrasted this with the idea that "America's greatest strength has always been its hopeful vision of human progress."[18] *Enterprise* indicates that these efforts to establish a foe reflect a need to shore up the normative core of the American neoliberal global project.

In pointing out that the normative foundation of neoliberalism is the friend/foe distinction, *Enterprise* indicates that the normative core of empire and neoliberalism are roughly similar. Notably, Islamofascism is used to anchor the neoliberal world system, and it was used by the Bush Administration to justify the conquest of Iraq.[19] The main component of Hitler and the Nazis' political/propaganda argumentation was directed at an imaginary coalition of Western bankers and Eastern communists conspiring against Germany. According to Nazi mythology (myopia), Jews were at the center of this worldwide anti-Germany coalition.[20] The Vulcans, in First Contact and Enterprise, are cast as the "they" to humanity's "we" in the neoliberal Federation. In this context, it is noteworthy that Leonard Nimoy (who was Jewish himself) held that Vulcans are a metaphor for Jews.[21]

Just like *Star Trek* indicated in "City on the Edge of Forever" that global empire is doomed to failure, global neoliberalism will also condemn humanity to catastrophe. The overriding need to pursue societal justice—that is, topple neoliberalism/capitalism—is made clear in "Past Tense." While in the Sanctuary District (in 2024 San Francisco), Sisko intervenes into a fight, which accidentally results in the death of one Gabriel Bell—the would-be leader of the Bell Uprising. Like in "City on the Edge of Forever," this erases the entire history of the Federation.

Conclusion

Going back to the 1960s, *Star Trek* made an effective case for world government, pointing somewhat presciently to both the geopolitical and environmental liabilities of the current nation-state system. *Star Trek*, however, goes further than making a normative case for global government. Its creators also offer three different templates on how to achieve such a world government: (1) federation, (2) empire, and (3) neoliberalism.

In this way, *Star Trek* helps us to reason through the momentous perils that confront humanity in the modern era—that is, globally devastating war and impending environmental catastrophe (i.e., climate change). Will humanity choose to achieve a global polity through liberal humanism—a concept of universal justice and equality? Alternatively, will we turn to a project of conquest and imperial control to establish stability and environmental sustainability? Finally, will humans rely on an argument of practicality (neoliberalism) to manage global affairs?

In outlining the federation, empire, and neoliberalism paths to world governance, *Star Trek* describes the normative principles of each. For federation, the normative value propelling the creation of a global polity is liberal humanism—that is, the idea of a classless society, free of ethnic/gender biases. Empire relies on concepts of national (species) superiority and deception. Neoliberalism, while its proponents hold that practical concerns are sufficient to create an international governance structure, *Star Trek* (*Enterprise*) posits the compelling argument that concepts of national (species) superiority also serve as the normative foundation of neoliberalism.

Analytically, each of these templates of federation, empire, and neoliberalism can be identified in America's present leadership of the global economic/political system. Nevertheless, *Star Trek* (drawing ostensibly on American Trotskyism) demonstrates a bias for the federation form of government—indicating that the solidarity and justice at the heart of federation is the only way to establish an effective, viable, and long-lasting global governance regime. Otherwise, humanity will face ultimate disaster as it seeks to establish world government through empire or neoliberalism.

CHAPTER 6

Star Trek and Technologies of Empire

The *Star Trek* franchise outlines the key political tension/disagreement in modernity: pragmatism versus the attaining of justice (as explained in Chapter 2). At the heart of *Star Trek* is an explicit critique/rejection of pragmatism—that is, an excessive fixation on stability—and the active argument that free, thriving, and stable societies are those that are based on justice, and not on intersubjective agreement (neopragmatism).

The consensus in the academic literature that centers on the *Star Trek* franchise is that the concept of justice that inheres in the multiple broadcast iterations of the franchise is liberal humanism. The seeming claim (via *Star Trek*) is that the liberal humanism conception of justice is manifest (exists) as a classless society—without want and gender/ethnic biases.[1] In *Star Trek*, the antithesis of liberal humanism justice (the Federation) is Empire. Whereas the basis of the Federation is the concept of justice as elaborated in liberal humanism, the philosophical foundation of Empire is pragmatism and the maintenance of intersubjective agreement (neopragmatism).

One of the means that *Star Trek* uses to convey Empire (as opposed to Federation) is technology. As such, *Star Trek* makes the explicit claim that particular technological regimes will exist within Empire that would not ostensibly exist in Federation. The technologies of Empire are evident in *Star Trek* through weapons of mass destruction and torture. In laying a claim that the politics of technology is decidedly different in Empire from that of Federation, *Star Trek* allows us to identify a "politics of intersubjective agreement" in contradistinction to the "politics of justice." One conclusion of this analytical comparison/juxtaposition is the United States in the contemporary era could be viewed as operating within a politics of empire.

Pacifism: Pragmatic or Principled?

As noted earlier, *Star Trek* cautions against pragmatism. One of the issues that *Star Trek* grapples with is whether pacifism is pragmatic or principled. This is especially germane for a discussion centered on differentiating the politics of empire from those of federation (liberal humanism). *Star Trek* indicates that pacifism is a pragmatic (maintaining stability) tactic and should be avoided. There are key instances when pacifism is cast negatively in *Star Trek*. An obvious rebuke of pacifism to maintain stability (avoiding war) is offered in the 1990 *Next Generation* episode "Allegiance." Captain Picard, along with someone from the planet Mizar Two, is being held captive. The character from Mizar Two (a Mizarian)—with some pride—alludes to his planet's pacifist tradition: "My race has no enemies." Picard, incredulously, retorts, "*None?* In the last three hundred years of Mizarian history, your planet has been conquered six times!" Arguing that pacifism is a practical/appropriate response to oppression (military occupation, etc.), the Mizarian (named Tholl) explains, "We've survived by not resisting." Finally, Tholl holds that pacifism (pragmatism) is morally superior to fighting for democracy, freedom, equality, and so on. "Mizarians value peace above confrontation." One of the other captives denounces Mizarians as "A race of cowards"—the viewer cannot help but to agree.

One (perhaps generous) view of humanity is that people prefer death rather than endure pronounced/obvious injustice. This view is vaunted in the *Star Trek* original unaired pilot "The Cage."[2] A powerful alien race is planning on breeding and exploiting humans. They, however, come to conclude that humans are not appropriate for such a project because they cannot be adapted to unjust circumstances (specifically, imposed captivity): "We had not believed this possible. The customs and history of your race show a unique hatred of captivity. Even when it's pleasant and benevolent, you prefer death. This makes you too violent and dangerous a species for our needs."

The ostensive importance of being willing to sacrifice oneself for justice is succinctly and artfully conveyed in the 1982 movie *Star Trek: Wrath of Kahn* when David tells his grieving father, Captain Kirk, "How we face death is at least as important as how we face life." In other words, to live a meaningful (even enjoyable) life, people have to be ready to die for just/appropriate causes—for example, striking out against a perpetual regime of forced captivity, or willingly giving one's life to save your ship and crew mates (as Spock did in *Wrath of Kahn*).

Arguably the most salient and broad-ranging critique of pacifism in American television/literary history is rendered in the original series episode "City on the Edge of Forever" (1967). Upon learning that "Edith Keeler must die" in order to restore history, Kirk and Spock express agreement that peace is a laudable goal, but the desire for peace has to be tempered against broader considerations (the fight against fascism). Kirk: "She was right. Peace was the way." Spock: "She was right, but at the wrong time."

The parable convened in "City on the Edge of Forever" is that pacifism represents passivity in the face of injustice, corruption, malfeasance, warmongering, and so on. Put differently, justice, freedom, and even good governance require "eternal vigilance." The *Deep Space Nine* episode "Past Tense" (1995) features the following exchange: "Are humans really any different than Cardassians . . . or Romulans? If push came to shove, if something disastrous happened to the Federation, and we got frightened enough, or desperate enough, how would we react? Would we stay true to our ideals . . . or would we just [resort to authoritarian/oppressive means]?"

Captain Sisko responds, "I don't know. But as a Starfleet officer, it's my job to make sure we never have to find out."

Star Trek's prime contribution to an analysis of pragmatism—that is, stability as the prime normative value—is that there is a straight line from this mode of thought to dictatorship and torture. *Star Trek*'s claim (discussed in the next section) is that dictatorship and torture are overt, explicit efforts (means) to maintain societal and political stability.

Dictatorship and Torture in Service of Stability

Through the *Deep Space Nine* platform, *Star Trek*'s creators issue a clear warning that political elites can/do use stability (safety/security) concerns to establish regimes of dictatorship. In the denouement of "Homefront" (1996), Earth experiences a planetary-wide blackout. Starfleet Admiral Leyton said, "Earth's entire power relay system has been knocked off-line. Even Starfleet's emergency backups have been affected." This leaves Earth completely vulnerable to attack.

> **ODO:** Take down the power relays, and you neutralize sensors, transporters, surface-based defense installations.
> **SISKO:** In other words, Earth's defenseless.
> **LEYTON:** If the Dominion attacks now, we don't stand a chance.

A state of emergency has been declared. The subsequent *Deep Space Nine* episode "Paradise Lost" (1996) begins by showing troops patrolling the street and everyone submitting to security screening (blood tests) to establish that they are not enemies (Changelings). One of these blood tests is falsified to implicate Captain Sisko when he comes into opposition to the militarization of Earth. We learn that the power outage was perpetrated by elements within Starfleet (the Federation's military apparatus).

> **SISKO (TO THE PRESIDENT OF EARTH):** We believe that Admiral Leyton and his supporters weren't satisfied with the limited

security procedures you authorized. They were convinced that extraordinary measures were necessary to counter the Changeling threat . . . They were determined to prove to you and to everyone else just how vulnerable Earth was to a Dominion takeover. So they sabotaged the global power grid.

Thus *Deep Space Nine* issues a caution against the use of national security threats to suspend civil and political rights, as well as democratic decision-making processes:

> **SISKO:** What you're trying to do is seize control of Earth and place it under military rule.
>
> **ADMIRAL LEYTON:** If that's what it takes to stop the Dominion.

To fully comprehend how the normative prioritization of stability justifies (causes) authoritarian governance and regimes of torture we must consider the logical conclusion of pragmatism—intersubjective agreement (neopragmatism). In fashioning neopragmatism, American philosopher Richard Rorty, writing in the early 1980s, argues that societies are based on intersubjective agreement.[3] Thus what is required for societal stability is enough consensus on a set of ideas—any set of ideas. Hence what matters is consensus, and not the ideas themselves. Presumably, when there is not enough intersubjective consensus/agreement, then social/political breakdown occurs.

Intersubjective Agreement and the Politics of Empire

With the neopragmatism conceptualization of society as little more than intersubjective agreement, the prime goal of institutions is achieving societal cohesion by fashioning, fostering, and/or imposing such agreement. Therefore, authoritarian (dictatorial) regimes, as well as torture practices/technologies, can be effective (even appropriate) means to maintain (impose) intersubjective agreement—thereby establishing political/social stability.

As outlined in Chapter 2, *Star Trek* introduced the concept (not the term) of intersubjective agreement and the implications of such political theorizing in the 1967 episode "Mirror, Mirror." One important conclusion from *Star Trek*'s treatment of the intersubjective agreement argument is those societies that prioritize achieving such agreement, as opposed to those that base their cohesion on the attainment of liberal humanism, develop/deploy technologies intended to impose political consensus—or, at least, to suppress/punish those that would challenge this consensus. In the Empire of "Mirror, Mirror" (the original series 1967) and later "In a Mirror, Darkly" (*Star Trek: Enterprise* 2005) torture technologies called an "agonizer" and an "agony chamber" exist. When used, they cause extreme pain without causing tissue damage. "In a Mirror, Darkly" the following is explained of the "agony booth": "Traditional forms of punishment can overwhelm the nervous system. After a time, the brain ceases to feel anything . . . These sensors continually shift the stimulation from one nerve cluster to another, keeping the subject in a constant state of agony." Thus pain can endlessly be inflicted. Such fictional technologies presage the Bush Administration's notorious 2003 memo authorizing torture. In this memo, perpetual, intense pain was deemed legally allowable. Only "death, organ failure, or permanent damage resulting in a loss of significant body functions will likely result" was prohibited.[4] While the Bush Administration didn't develop infinite pain machines like agonizers or agony chambers (as far as we know), technologies/practices like waterboarding (where drowning is simulated) were used hundreds of times on individual victims.[5]

It is through such means that the Empire maintains stability—most important, threatens/menaces those that seek to operate outside of (or challenge) its intersubjective agreement regime. Communicating the political theory at the heart of the Empire, Spock explains, "Terror must be maintained or the Empire is doomed. It is the logic of history."

The original series episode "Cloud Minders" (1969) depicts a society on the planet of Ardana where torture technology (the rays)—and unsurprisingly, racism—are used to maintain/stabilize a caste system. (Ardana is a seeming stand-in for South Africa.) In effective imagery, the political, economic, and social realities of the planet are portrayed—with the privileged/governing caste living a life of aesthetic splendor in a "cloud city" (Stratos) floating in the heavens, while the laboring classes (referred to as Troglytes) live on the (barren) planet surface working the mines (extracting zenite). The residents of Stratos are fair skinned and fair haired and partake in the high arts. The Troglytes are dark haired, dark skinned, and unwashed.

The rays are deployed in an effort to break a political movement in opposition to the governing regime—that is, defying society's intersubjective agreement. A prisoner is pressed to provide the names of the putative leaders of the mining caste's rebellion:

> PLASUS (ARDANA GOVERNMENT LEADER): You still refuse to disclose the names of the other Disrupters.
> TROGLYTE: There are no Disrupters!
> PLASUS: Very well, if you prefer the rays.

She screams in agony, discomforting onlookers. Spock, in his famous calm, equanimous voice, observes, "Violence in reality is quite different from theory."

> RESIDENT OF STRATOS: But what else can [Troglytes] understand, Mister Spock?
> SPOCK: All the little things you and I understand and expect from life, such as equality, kindness, justice.
> PLASUS: Troglytes are not like Stratos dwellers, Mister Spock. They're a conglomerate of inferior species.

The use of the threat of torture (and worse) to politically cow a populace is dramatically depicted in *The Next Generation* episode "Face of the Enemy" (1993). *Enterprise*'s ship counselor, Deanna Troi, is impressed into impersonating an officer from the Romulan secret police, known as the Tal Shiar. Troi is forced into a mission whereby, as this officer (named Major Rakal), she is to oversee the transport of special cargo to the Federation. As a Tal Shiar officer, Troi is able to order a Romulan ship captain into transporting this secret shipment—high ranking members of the Romulan government who wish to defect. They are in boxes, suspended in "stasis."

Troi, at first, is disoriented and frightened—as she was drugged, kidnapped, surgically altered (without her knowledge), and literally thrust into the role of a Tal Shiar officer abroad an enemy military ship. (If Troi were to be found out, she "will be killed.") Troi, however, has empathic abilities—that is, she is able to sense the emotions of others—and she quickly realizes that the Romulans on the ship are petrified of her, a Tal Shiar officer. ("They're all terrified of me.") Her Romulan collaborator explains to Troi, "The purpose of the Tal Shiar is to ensure loyalty [i.e., subservience to the Romulan intersubjective agreement]. To defy them is to invite imprisonment . . . or death." We learn that the Romulan government maintains a regime of terror to maintain political stability as "thousands of dissidents [i.e., those who challenge their society's intersubjective agreement] . . . live in fear of their lives." When Major Rakal (Troi) decides to take command of the ship, she threatens the bridge crew and their families, "If any one of you defies the Tal Shiar, you will not bear the punishment alone. Your families . . . all of them, will be there beside you." They dutifully accede to her orders.

Troi, as Major Rakal, and the Romulan ship captain (Toreth) engage in an exchange that sums up the difference between a regime based on intersubjective agreement and one based on justice (liberal humanism). The captain openly resents the Tar Shiar and their crushing of dissent, recounting how it "disappeared" her father for ostensibly questioning the hegemonic intersubjective agreement. ("Was the Empire threatened by the words of an old man, a devoted citizen who merely tried to speak his mind? . . . He was just an idealistic old man . . . and I never saw him again.") Having lost all patience, Major Rakal barks, "*I don't need your devotion, Commander. Just your obedience.*" Toreth retorts, "*That is all you have.*" Thus regimes predicated on maintaining intersubjective agreement compel (force) loyalty, compliance, subservience, and so on. Whereas regimes based on justice (presumably liberal humanism) impel (inspire) sacrifice, service, commitment, and so on. The different political tacks of federation and empire yield decidedly different technological regimes. More specifically, the politics of empire yield technologies of empire.[6]

The Politics of Assassination[7]

Star Trek makes the empirical claim that certain technologies exist in empire that do not exist in federation. As noted previously, in the Empire exists an agony booth. Notably, when the Captain Archer of the Federation feels compelled to torture someone (to save planet Earth), he is forced to use conventional technology (an airlock) to do so. In the process, Archer comes close to killing a person (the torture victim) who has vital information (*Enterprise* "Anomaly" 2003).

The intersubjective agreement argument in "Mirror, Mirror" is brought into sharper relief in *Deep Space Nine*, where the alternate universe is revisited a century later ("Crossover" 1994). We learn that Kirk's time in the alternate universe had a profound impact. "On my side, Kirk is one of the most famous names in our history." In "Mirror, Mirror," Kirk apprized Spock of a weapon (the Tantalus field). From one's quarters, a person could zero in on victims, and with the push of a button, make them disappear. Kirk counseled Spock to use such technology to profoundly change the Empire, and base it on the values of the Federation. As noted in Chapter 2, the end result is that the Earth is conquered and occupied.

Focusing on the Tantalus field, this is explicitly a technology of the Empire, as it does not exist in the Federation universe. The Tantalus field communicates key aspects of the structure and practice of political power in the context of empire—that is, a polity whose priority is the maintenance of intersubjective agreement. Importantly, the concept of intersubjective agreement does not directly speak to the question of how many people, or precisely who, has to participate in an agreement in order for society to be stable. Authoritarian polities (empires) seek to concentrate political and institutional authority in a small number of people who exercise institutional control and work together to impose their intersubjective agreement on the whole of society.

In turn, this is precisely why the phenomenon of palatial politics occurs—people maneuver among the coterie of power wielders to hold and/or attain power. In the *Deep Space Nine* episode "When It Rains . . ." (1999), the argument is made that the Klingon Empire's current head of government (Chancellor Gowron) has no significant accomplishments other than successfully mastering Klingon "palace intrigue"[8]: "What has he done except plot and scheme his way to power?"

In a context where political power is highly concentrated, assassination becomes an effective means of advancing a military/political career (agenda), as rivals/obstacles are vanquished. In the Empire universe of "Mirror, Mirror," "Captain Kirk's enemies have a habit of disappearing" (via the Tantalus field). Spock (to Captain Kirk): "I do not intend to simply disappear as so many of your opponents have in the past." As alluded to previously, Spock of the Empire uses the Tantalus field to gain the leadership of the Empire and to fashion a new intersubjective agreement. The Klingon Empire's Chancellor, K'mpec, is poisoned to open the path to power for an ambitious clan (*The Next Generation*, "Reunion" 1990). In the *Deep Space Nine* episode "Inter Arma Enim Silent Leges" (1999), a clandestine operation is successfully executed to manipulate the politics of the Romulan Star Empire by politically destroying (i.e., character assassination) a senator to ensure the appointment of a reliable Federation ally to the Romulan Continuing Committee—the highest policymaking body in the Empire. Assassination resulting in the protection/entrenchment of a policy regime brings to mind the President John F. Kennedy assassination, as his killing seemingly cleared the way for a more reliable "Cold War Warrior" in Lyndon B. Johnson to ascend to the American presidency.[9]

Weapons of Mass Destruction

In the *Next Generation* episode "Time's Arrow" (1992), Mark Twain (Samuel Clemens) is transported to the twenty-fourth century and assumes that the Federation represents/institutes a regime of conquest and control. His reasoning is based on the existence of the starship *Enterprise*—that is, the political/economic regime he thinks it represents: "Huge starships, and weapons that can no doubt destroy entire cities, and military conquest as a way of life?" One factor that proves Clemens wrong about the *Enterprise* and the Federation is the technology it does not employ—the cloaking device. The cloaking device is introduced in the original series as a weapon deployed/developed by the Romulan Empire. Later, the Klingon Empire adopts this technology as well. It allows starships to travel under a shield (cloak) of invisibility. The cloaking device is a tremendous tactical weapon—as ships can approach enemies totally undetected, thereby allowing devastating surprise attacks. A Romulan commander tells of a battle where Klingon "warships decloaked, they took us completely by surprise. The Klingons managed to destroyed half my squadron before we even opened fire" ("Face of the Enemy" 1993). Glaringly and significantly, when a Starfleet officer surreptitiously develops cloaking technology for the Federation, his actions (once discovered) are denounced as criminal and expressly in violation of the law: "As Captain of the *Enterprise*, I'm placing you under arrest" (*Next Generation*, "The *Pegasus*" 1994).

The fact that the Federation foregoes cloaking/stealth technology communicates that its starships—to the extent that they have military capabilities—are deployed solely for purposes of defense. Cloaking/stealth military technology is expressly offensive in nature—solely intended for the vanquishing of enemies, including rebellions. The fact that Federation ships do not have this offensive capability serves to substantiate the claim that the *Enterprise* "is a ship of peace. Not of war" (*Next Generation*, "Yesterday's *Enterprise*" 1990). Notably, the United States pioneered the development/use of Stealth Bombers—designed to evade enemy radar and execute surprise bombing attacks.[10] Another stealth technology pioneered by the United States are predator drones,[11] where operators in an air conditioned facility in Nevada guide small airplanes (drones) flying over remote regions of the world, and with the push of a button, fire missiles on unsuspecting individuals from fifty thousand feet.[12]

Along the lines of stealth military technology are weapons of mass destruction. Such weapons are also weapons of empire— capable of intimidating/destroying those that challenge/resist particular intersubjective agreements. It is noteworthy that the United States pioneered in the development and use of nuclear weapons. Importantly, it has historically led in the advancement of the delivery of nuclear weapons—making them ever more effective/menacing.[13]

Star Trek takes up the question of losing control of weapons of mass destruction. First, pursuit of such weapons is self-defeating, as other powers develop these weapons—prompting an arms race. Speaking of a massive machine that can consume entire planets, Kirk draws a comparison to the Cold War[14] arms race at the time: "It's a weapon built primarily as a bluff. It's never meant to be used. So strong, it could destroy both sides in a war. Something like the old H-Bomb was supposed to be" ("The Doomsday Machine" 1967). Such a strategy, however, does not ensure stability. The episode "The Omega Glory" (1968) depicts a world with an identical history to that of Earth's, except in this instance, the Cold War resulted in globally devastating nuclear/biological war—where humans were reduced to a veritable stone age. *The Next Generation Enterprise* crew comes upon a planet that held that geopolitical stability is maintained by the technological advancement of weapon systems. The society lived "by the motto—peace through superior firepower," referring to itself as "The Arsenal of Freedom" (also the episode title, 1988). Everyone on the planet (Minos) was destroyed by one of its weapon systems. Thus *Star Trek* warns that to engage in imperial strategies—that is, imposing intersubjective agreement—in the modern era is to engage the risk of planetary destruction.[15]

Conclusion

The *Star Trek* franchise taps into the prime philosophical dilemma in modern society: striving for justice (liberal humanism) or settling for stability (pragmatism and neopragmatism). Thus, judging from *Star Trek*, the modern mind (the American mind?) sees that modernity can be used to establish a global regime of justice. The fear, however, is that such visions are utopian (unattainable) and/or implementing such a vision is risky insofar as an effort to revolutionize (profoundly reform) society could result in anarchy (societal/political breakdown). Reflective of these fears, within modes of thought rooted in pragmatism and neopragmatism, is the idea that the best humanity can hope for is stability—that is, sufficient intersubjective agreement—and that it should eschew universal concepts of justice.

Star Trek warns against such reasoning, asserting that pragmatism/neopragmatism are consonant with slavery (original series, "Bread and Circuses"), pacifism (inaction in the face of injustice), political change through assassination, torture, dictatorship, racism, weapons of mass destruction, and so on. Moreover, the "good," stable society is one where citizens are willing to endure great sacrifices/risks for justice. *Star Trek* indicates that regimes that prioritize stability (pragmatism) and intersubjective agreement (neopragmatism) above justice are identifiable through their technologies. Applying this methodology would lead to the conclusion that the United States hews to a politics of empire.

CHAPTER 7

Star Trek: Why Do Soldiers Fight in Modern Warfare?
Preemptive Empire or Federation

Why do people fight in modern warfare? More precisely, why do people agree to serve in militaries (formal and informal) actively engaged in warfare? Why do people risk life and limb in such circumstances—particularly in the modern era, when the technologies of death (fully deployed in war) do inflict high numbers of casualties? The broadcast iterations of the *Star Trek* franchise provide significant insight into the motives of frontline soldiers who engage in war. According to *Star Trek*, there are two prime reasons people engage in large-scale warfare: (1) defense/empire and (2) justice.

Star Trek suggests that pacifism is something of an "unnatural condition" for humanity. This does not mean humanity cannot live in peace and harmony, but that a "victor's peace" is inherently unstable and will lead to more war. Thus only a peace rooted in liberal humanism (justice) will result in truly peaceful human/global relations. According to the academic literature centered on *Star Trek*, justice (liberal humanism) is manifest (exists) as a classless society—free of gender/ethnic biases.[1]

War against Injustice to War for Empire

Outlined in the last chapter, *Star Trek* argues against pacifism (inaction) in the face of injustice (slavery, military occupation, forced captivity, etc.). The *Star Trek* text allows us to comprehend how the impulse against injustice (being subjugated), rather ironically, leads to empire. As noted previously, the epithet *coward* is an insult against those acquiescing to injustice—for example, accepting military occupation—in order to live. Such an epithet is a disincentive against pacifism. The positive incentive for risking life and limb in the face of injustice is glory, or the designation of hero. Thus those that fight and die against military occupation (or those that would enslave) are considered heroes and viewed as dying gloriously. In sharp contrast, to live in injustice and die by natural causes is to be a coward.

Given this reasoning, war in toto could become viewed as an honorable or glorious way to die. In discussing a war between the Federation and the Klingon Empire that was thwarted, a Klingon commander says that the war "would have been glorious" (original series, "Errand of Mercy" 1967). Taking it one step further, the failure to die in battle is to be without honor. During the *Next Generation* episode "Matter of Honor" (1989), a Klingon who dies of old age is described by another Klingon in the following manner: he "will eventually fade of a natural illness and die, weakened and useless. *Honorless.*"

My argument is that the kind of ethos manifest by Klingons can be born of being serially oppressed. In other words, the lauding of fighting against oppression (occupation) is transformed into a general vaunting of war as the ultimate form of bravery (honor). It is important to note that *Star Trek* does not offer this reason to account for the Klingons' tempestuous disposition. Instead, the point is explicitly made that "there is, of course, a *genetic* predisposition toward hostility among all Klingons" ("The Icarus Factor" 1989). Daniel Bernardi, in Star Trek *and History: Race-ing toward a White Future*, focuses on this line and charges that the *Star Trek* series *The Next Generation* (1987–94) conveys racism—or more specifically, an "antiblack" attitude.[2] The Klingons are dark skinned and dark haired. Bernardi writes, "[The] biological notion of blackness is displaced onto the Klingons while a civilized notion of whiteness is ascribed to the Federation."[3]

I think Bernardi is wrong to ascribe racism to *Next Generation*. This is for two reasons. First, as I'll shortly outline, *Star Trek* the franchise, and the *Next Generation* specifically, contains too many positive portrayals of African American actors/characters to ever be justly accused of racism. Second, the assertion of a "genetic predisposition toward hostility among all Klingons" has positive implications for the way the American mind views Arabs, as well as providing insight into the general politics of the nation-state system.

Race Relations in Star Trek

Bernardi specifically holds that *Star Trek* (the original series) and *The Next Generation* are suggestive of an attitude that is hostile toward minorities (people of color). Focusing specifically on *Star Trek* (the original series), Lieutenant Uhura (played by African American actor Nichelle Nichols) was reduced to a bit role—given almost exclusively throwaway lines. Nevertheless, as noted earlier, this character was involved in a scene conveying arguably the clearest stance for ethnic equality and acceptance ever on American television.

With regard to *The Next Generation*, a number of factors militate against the idea that it is antiblack (per se) as indicated by Bernardi. First, the *Enterprise*'s command structure does have prominent, positively portrayed black skinned members: Geordi LaForge (ship's chief engineer) and Worf (ship's chief of security). With these characters (both played by African American actors) consistently demonstrating intellectual prowess/ingenuity and high levels of fortitude, stability, and maturity, it is hard to sustain the charge that *The Next Generation* television series is inherently antiblack.

Second, a character (Guinan) played by African American actor Whoopi Goldberg virtually single-handedly saves the Federation in the episode "Yesterday's *Enterprise*" (1990). Arguably the most jarring episode of *The Next Generation* series, "Yesterday's *Enterprise*" involves an alternate reality/timeline. This alternate reality/timeline is triggered when the *Enterprise-C* emerges from a time wormhole, bringing the ship 22 years into the future and into contact with the *Enterprise-D*—that is, the *Enterprise* of the present. In this new reality, the Federation has been at war with the Klingon Empire for about 22 years. We learn that the Federation is on the verge of losing the war. Except for Guinan, the *Enterprise-D* crew is totally oblivious to the fact that a new timeline was created with the emergence of *Enterprise-C*. It is left to Guinan to argue that the current reality is "all wrong." Guinan is alone in pressing the fact that the "ship from the past . . . it was not supposed to come here. It's got to go back." Captain Jean-Luc Picard is resistant to sending the *Enterprise-C* back through the wormhole because it (and its crew) will face certain destruction once it reaches the other side. In the face of the captain's stern refusal to sending the ship back, Guinan stands her ground: "This war was never meant to be. They *must* return to their own time to correct that." "You've know me a long time," Guinan tells Picard, "This timeline cannot be allowed to continue. I've told you what you must do. You have only your faith in me to help you decide." Picard follows her advice, and the timeline is restored.

With the characters of LaForge, Worf, and Guinan, *The Next Generation* presents a very positive and endearing image of African Americans. It is the politics of the developing world that are ostensibly cast in a negative light in *The Next Generation* series (treated in Chapter 3), and it is this depiction that Bernardi mistakes for a general antiblack attitude. With this understanding of the ethnic politics in *Next Generation*, next I go back to specifically treating the Klingons, who, as I explain in Chapter 3, are metaphors for Arabs.

Klingons as Arabs

Reading the Klingons as Arabs could allow the viewer to have a positive take on the claim that the former have "a genetic predisposition toward hostility." In a literary/artistic/metaphorical sense, for Arabs, this statement could be viewed as a *badge of honor*. This is because Arabs, for centuries, have been a conquered people (the Ottoman Empire and the European mandates after World War I) dominated by corrupt/repressive regimes, and have suffered a diaspora with the creation of Israel and the humiliation of occupation (the West Bank Territories and the Gaza Strip). In the America mind, Arabs have been inherently unwilling to suffer these conditions passively, and responded with violent resistance (including suicide bombings). (In the *Next Generation* episode "Reunion" [1990], a Klingon carries out a suicide attack with a bomb implanted inside his arm.) Perhaps all of us would like to believe that our identity group has "a genetic predisposition toward hostility" against regimes of perpetual repression, injustice, and occupation.

Ascribing a "genetic predisposition toward hostility" to Klingons/Arabs could also have an even broader meaning. Because of the nation-state system—that is, nationalism—humans have a general predisposition toward violence. Put differently, the chauvinistic species identity (nationalism) of the Klingons is something that potentially afflicts the entirety of humanity. This brings us to the ideation of Carl Schmitt.

The "Friend/Enemy" Dichotomy and Star Trek

Carl Schmitt (1888–1985) is in the pantheon of neoconservative thinkers.[4] Schmitt was an architect of the Nazi Germany legal regime and known as the "Crown Jurist" of the Nazis.[5] He held that at the center of politics is the distinction "between friend and enemy."[6] Social and political cohesion is based on this friend/foe dichotomy. Reflective of Schmitt's friend/enemy reasoning, in *The Next Generation* episode "Face of the Enemy" (1993), the point is made that Romulans have an "absolute certainty about . . . who is a friend and who is an enemy." Political scientist Shadia B. Drury renders the following observation: "Schmitt . . . believes that politics is first and foremost about the distinction between WE and THEY. [He] thinks that a political order can be stable only if it is united by an external threat."[7]

The *Star Trek* movie *First Contact* (1996) is predicated on a we/they distinction. The action of the movie takes place in the year 2063, when humanity is immersed in a "Second Dark Age."[8] What rallies humanity from its disarray is its contact with the Vulcans: "*It unites humanity in a way no one ever thought possible when they realize they're not alone in the universe.*" Therefore, the political foundation of humanity in the mid-twenty-first century is the we/they dichotomy, with the Vulcans serving as "they."

While Schmitt emphasizes how the friend/foe bifurcation serves to create unity/political cohesion among identity groups, in fact this ideation is a recipe for perpetual violent conflict. By seeking out (perhaps emphasizing) the difference between "they" and "we" (and worst still, conceptualizing "they" as a potential enemy), Schmitt's ideation can create paranoia—as every "they" is a potential conqueror. Therefore, conquest/destruction could be cast as self-defense—a preemptive strategy to prevent "they" (a potential foe) from conquering, destroying, or attacking "we." The leadership caste of the Dominion (who are liquid creatures) explains its imperial ambitions in terms of preemptive conquest/empire: "The Solids [humanoids] have always been a threat to us. That's the only the justification we need . . . *Because what you control can't hurt you*" (*Deep Space Nine*, "The Search" 1994). In justifying the 2003 invasion of Iraq, the Bush Administration claimed that this country possessed weapons of mass destruction that could be used to attack the United States—*not that there was any plan to do so*. Political scientist Anne Norton notes how such reasoning could be used as a basis for perpetual war: "If a nation could attack because it feared not that it might be attacked tomorrow or the next day, or the next month, but in some vague future, who would be immune?"[9] In fact of matter, the Bush Administration did more that use the concept of "vague future" threat to attack another country, it employed the "they" idea (the potential foe being Iraq under Saddam Hussein) to conquer this country. Therefore, the Bush Administration invoked the idea of preemptive empire. Put differently, "they" were conquered before "they" destroyed/conquered "we," and *"they" must be occupied lest they attack "us" in the future*—or as the Dominion leader put it, "Because what you control can't hurt you."

While Norton takes issue with the Bush administration's rationale leading up to the 2003 Iraq invasion, in fact, the United States in this instance acted upon a logic inherent in the nation-state system—namely, that every nation is different, and every country is a "they" to every other country: "The political enemy is not necessarily morally evil."[10] Instead, Schmitt held that the potential enemy "is merely the other, the stranger, and it is sufficient that according to his nature he is in a special intense way existentially something different and alien, so that in the extreme case conflicts with him are possible."[11] The very claim of nationalism is that every other nation "is in a special intense way existentially something different and alien." Thus "in the extreme case conflicts with him are possible." Therefore, within a nation-state system, military conflict is a constant reality/threat—for example, World War I and II, the Cold War, the India-Pakistan conflict, the Arab-Israeli conflict, and so on—as countries are apt to attack/conquer "the other" (in Schmitt's words) before they themselves are conquered/attacked. In the *Star Trek* movie, *Into Darkness* (2013), elements within Starfleet conduct a false-flag operation to create the public impression that only by preemptively defeating/conquering the Klingons can the Federation be safe/secure.

In a literal sense, with a nation-state system governing the world, humans do have "a genetic propensity toward hostility"—as information about national identity (Hispanic) is regularly compiled/collected along with actual genetically driven characteristics (gender).[12] Notably, according to *Star Trek* (original series), in the 1990s Earth experiences a World War III known as the Eugenics War: "An improved breed of human. That's what the Eugenics War was all about." The war resulted when "young supermen" seized "power simultaneously in over forty nations . . . They were aggressive, arrogant. They began to battle among themselves" ("Space Seed" 1967). Therefore, *Star Trek* makes the claim that the nation-state system is politically/militarily unstable. *The Next Generation* posits an episode with a world divided into two countries that are beset with hostility, loathing, and deep suspicion toward one another ("Attached" 1993). As a result, the creators of *Star Trek* posit a future where Earth replaces the nation-state system with a world government.[13]

The question is, how does such a world government occur? As noted previously, the movie *First Contact* indicates that such a government resulted from the realization that aliens (the Vulcans) were in the region. Prior to *First Contact* and the series *Enterprise*, the *Star Trek* franchise indicated that world government on Earth resulted from the spread of justice (liberal humanism). This brings us to the second reason that people are willing to fight and die in war: justice. In *Star Trek*, justice is embodied in the institution of the Federation, and thus I will speak of federation as representing justice as purported in liberal humanism—a classless society, free of gender/ethnic biases.

Federation

Justice (federation) is the second reason *Star Trek* alludes to that propels people to fight in war. This suggests fighting exclusively for defensive purposes. Within a polity that pursues justice (that is liberal humanism), territorial accrual occurs because of voluntary union, with peoples joining the Federation because it is a paragon of selflessness, social justice, and equality. As noted earlier, "The Federation is made up of over a hundred planets *who have allied themselves* for mutual scientific, cultural and defensive benefits" (*Deep Space Nine*, "Battle Lines" 1993). "The Federation consists of over one hundred and fifty different worlds *who have agreed to share their knowledge and resources in peaceful cooperation*" (*Voyager*, "Innocence" 1996). Kirk, speaking of the founders of the Federation, says, "They were humanitarians and statesmen, and they had a dream. A dream that became a reality and spread throughout the stars, a dream that made Mister Spock and me brothers" ("Whom Gods Destroy" 1969). *Voyager* episode "The Void" provides insight into the normative values and political processes that are at the center of federation. *Voyager* shares its limited food and medical supplies, as well as joins in common defense, to build trust and establish (what Janeway calls) the "Alliance."

The fact that the Federation foregoes cloaking/stealth technology communicates that its starships—to the extent that they have military capabilities—are deployed solely for purposes of defense.[14] With the Federation foregoing offensive weaponry, *Star Trek* indicates that people will only fight for justice when it is defensive. In other words, people will not fight to export justice. Hence while American political leaders will claim to be imposing justice (democracy) through foreign wars (e.g., Iraq),[15] *Star Trek* suggests that it is the security claims—that is, defending against attack or potential attack—that motivates US soldiers to fight.

Next I discuss how fighting for justice (federation), according to *Star Trek*, does not preclude offensive military campaigns. Also, importantly, in the context of a major military threat, a federation is not handicapped/limited by ethics.

Ethics and Justice in Time of War

The last two seasons of *Deep Space Nine* are mostly dedicated to the Dominion War. The Dominion seeks to conquer the Federation because "many years ago we set ourselves the task of imposing order on a chaotic universe" (*Deep Space Nine*, "The Search" 1994). The leaders of the Dominion, the Founders (who oversee a massive military), are cast as ruthless and place no value whatsoever on the lives of humanoids. (The Founders' natural state is one of liquid.) In one noteworthy scene, a Founder decides that a new set of Vorta humanoids should be brought in to research a cure for the affliction she is suffering from. The Founder is informed a "team of Vorta Doctors [is] working night and day to find a cure." The Founder orders, "Have them document their efforts. *Then eliminate them.*" Her Vorta aide asks, "Founder?" She explains, "Activate their clones and order them to continue their predecessors' work. Perhaps a fresh perspective will speed matters along."[16]

In the face of the mortal threat the Federation faces with the Dominion, the Federation can undertake actions that would not be allowed in peacetime. Particularly significant on this score is "Inter Arma Enim Silent Leges" (1999). *Deep Space Nine*'s Doctor Bashir is used as pawn in a game of intrigue that politically destroys a would-be ally, a Romulan Senator Cretak. Bashir confronts Admiral Ross (who oversaw the operation):

> **BASHIR:** And what about your "friend" Senator Cretak? What will happen to her?
> **ROSS:** Dismissed from the [Romulan] Senate—definitely. Imprisoned—most likely.
> **BASHIR:** Executed?
> **ROSS:** I hope not.

When Bashir challenges Ross over the ethical, moral, and legal ramifications of the compromising of Senator Cretak, Ross responds in Latin, "Inter arma enim silent leges" (in time of war, the law falls silent).

According to *Star Trek*, war does allow a federation to pursue the enemy outside of home territory—that is, attacking foes on their territory (an offensive military campaign). In the penultimate episode of *Deep Space Nine* ("The Dogs of War" 1999), the Federation takes the upper hand as the Dominion retreats from enemy space and adopts a defensive posture. The Federation military leadership reason the Dominion's defensive posture is purely intended as an effort to regroup and rebuild its military capabilities for further war.[17] The alliance musters its forces to defeat the Dominion.

After a major space battle, the Dominion is defeated and falls back to its last bastion, the Cardassian home world. Even though it has been defeated, the Dominion retains considerable military resources deployed around Cardassia. The point is made that the Dominion could be "bottled up . . . indefinitely." Nevertheless, the Federation military leadership decides to conquer the last bastion of the Dominion.[18]

If the tactics of empire and federation are no different in the context of war, how does a solider for the federation know they are fighting for protection/defense and not for empire—that is, conquest and control? *Star Trek* presumes a commitment to the truth among the military/political leaders of federation to ensure tactics pursued during war are not used to dupe their populace (and soldiers). This is in sharp contrast to the leaders of empire. In pursuing the invasion of Cardassia, and thereby ending the decades old Klingon-Federation alliance, the Klingon Empire head of government, Chancellor Gowron, declares, "*History is written by the victors*" (*Deep Space Nine*, "The Way of the Warrior" 1995). Contrary to this sentiment that the perception of reality (facts) is malleable and can/should be shaped to serve any (corrupt) agenda, Captain Picard declares, "The first duty of every Starfleet officer is to the *truth*. Whether it's scientific truth, or historical truth, or personal truth. *It is the guiding principle upon which Starfleet is based*" ("The First Duty" 1992). In another instance, Picard, speaking to one of the leading political figures of the Federation ("Sarek" 1992), declares, "Sarek of Vulcan never confused what he wanted with the *truth*."

Star Trek indicates that in the context of federation, the public can trust its leaders. *Deep Space Nine* episode "Paradise Lost" (1996) makes this specific claim. When Captain Sisko comes to understand that his commanding officer is conspiring against the government of Earth, Sisko, along other officers subordinate to the conspirator, reject the chain of command and thwart the conspiracy. Similarly, when the crew of the Federation starship *Pegasus* (*Next Generation*, "Pegasus" 1994) realized that their captain was engaging in illegal research into cloaking technology, they mutinied. Additionally, in the movie *Insurrection* (1998), once Picard et al. from the *Enterprise* learn that the Federation leadership has sanctioned the forced removal of a village, they directly block this removal. Similarly, in the 2013 *Star Trek* movie *Into Darkness*, when the *Enterprise* crew learns that elements within Starfleet conducted a false-flag operation to initiate a war with the Klingons, Kirk et al. successfully expose the subterfuge. Therefore, the embedded institutional commitment to (or ethics of) truth (morality, legality, and fairness) in Starfleet (Federation institutions) serves as an effective prophylactic to conspiracies to bamboozle the public (soldiers). As Picard informed Data, "Starfleet doesn't want officers who will blindly follow orders without analyzing the situation" ("Redemption" 1991).

Star Trek makes the further claim that a prime duty of military officers' (political leaders') within federation is to prevent authoritarian outcomes. The *Deep Space Nine* episode "Past Tense" (1995) features the following exchange: "Are humans really any different than Cardassians ... or Romulans? If push came to shove, if something disastrous happened to the Federation, and we got frightened enough, or desperate enough, how would we react? Would we stay true to our ideals ... or would we just [resort to authoritarian/oppressive means]?"

Captain Sisko responds, "I don't know. But as a Starfleet officer, it's my job to make sure we never have to find out."

Conclusion

Star Trek allows us to see that fighting against injustice (slavery, military occupation, and repression) is not the same as fighting for justice. Rather ironically, in fighting against injustice people can engage in military campaigns to impose injustice on others—that is, preemptive empire. This is because if the only goal of a polity is to prevent its military subjugation, then it can/will subjugate others before it can be subjugated. At least this is the rationale given soldiers, which *Star Trek* indicates they respond to positively (effective fighting). *Star Trek* specifically critiques the current nation-state system, and the nationalism it fosters, for creating perpetual global enmity—as any one nation is "we" and every other is "they." As a result, *Star Trek* expressly argues for world government (see Chapters 2 and 5).

Star Trek offers a definition of justice, labeled liberal humanism. Liberal humanism is a society that is classless and is free of gender/ethnic biases. (I use the term *federation* to indicate a society predicated on liberal humanism.) A key difference between fighting for justice as opposed to fighting against injustice is that those that fight for justice will never fight to impose injustice on others. Therefore, fighting for justice means you are fighting a war of defense, and not one for conquest. *Star Trek* indicates that federation institutions' ethics are calibrated precisely to prevent using the public's fear of injustice from being transformed into wars of conquest—that is, empire.

CHAPTER 8

Star Trek, the Dominant Social Paradigm, and the Lack of an Environmental Ethos

When Eric C. Otto, in *Green Speculations: Science Fiction and Transformative Environmentalism*, identifies concern for the environment in the science fiction genre, he ignores *Star Trek*[1]—the most widely followed science fiction vehicle.[2] This is because the broadcast iterations of the *Star Trek* franchise convey (on environmental issues) the dominant social paradigm.[3] Thus *Star Trek* lacks an environmental ethic, ignores the global warming crisis, and evades profound environmental problems through what can be deemed as fantasy solutions (most especially, utilizing the literary device dilithium crystals). Perhaps most significant, *Star Trek* makes the ostensive point that the Enlightenment is inconsistent with a regime fully intended to protect the environment. The end result is that the viewer is left with the pessimist conclusion that reason and science are incompatible with intact planetary ecosystems.

A Lack of Environmental Ethos

The 1986 *Star Trek* movie *The Voyage Home* does contain a proenvironment message. In the twenty-third century, it is evident that the driving of whales to extinction[4] has put Earth in great danger, as an alien ship is now destroying the planet as it vainly tries to communicate with the now extinct humpback whale. Even though species extinction brought the Earth in the twenty-third century to the brink of destruction, judging from the 1998 movie *Insurrection*, the Federation is seemingly indifferent to environmental matters—since it authorizes the destruction of all life on the planet Ba'ku. Ba'ku is a ringed planet, and its rings contain metaphasic particles that emit a radiation that has antiaging (tissue regeneration) effects. The point is made by a Starfleet admiral: "With metaphasics [radiation treatment], lifespans will be doubled . . . an entire new medical science will evolve . . . We'll be able to use the regenerative properties of this radiation to help billions." In harvesting the metaphasic particles from the planet's rings, all life will apparently be killed: "The concentration in the rings is what makes the whole damned thing work. Don't ask me to explain it. I only know they inject something into the rings that starts a thermolytic reaction. After it's over, *the planet will be unlivable for generations* . . . Every living thing in this [planetary] system will be dead or dying." The planet's surface is presented as beautifully green and mountainous, but no one objects to obliterating this picturesque (seemingly complex) biosphere. The movie's moral dilemma is centered entirely on the forced removal of the six-hundred-person village from the planet. Presumably, if no sentient beings resided on the planet, Picard et al. would not object to the Federation's plans.

We see such indifference to a biosphere's destruction (one devoid of intelligent life) in the 1993 episode "The Chase." A Klingon captain destroys a planet's biosphere (killing all life on it) to prevent others from gaining genetic material from the planet—something that turns out to be futile since he ends up sharing the now rare genetic material with his would-be competitors. The *Enterprise* crew from space witnesses the killing of the biosphere, as it turns from a vibrant green to a dull, lifeless brown. Almost amazingly, no one on the *Enterprise* makes a negative comment on the wanton destruction of all life on a planet. It is left to a Cardassian ship captain to chide the Klingon captain for his complete disregard of nature, "Typical Klingon thinking . . . take what you want and then destroy the rest."

The fact that nature has no legal rights in the Federation is made evident in *The Next Generation* episode "The Measure of a Man" (1989). Data is ordered to submit for disassembly; he chooses to resign his military commission instead of agreeing to be taken apart for examination. Because Data is an android—a thing[5]—he was denied the right to resign. The only hope that Data had to avoid being disassembled was to establish that he is a sentient being. As such, it was found that Data could have the power to resign and escape being forcibly dismembered. Therefore, "The Measure of a Man" indicates that only sentient beings have rights, otherwise they can be wantonly destroyed (à la *Insurrection*).

A lack of concern/empathy for nature is evident in *The Next Generation* episode "Family" (1990). There is a proposal to lift part of the ocean floor on Earth to create a new subcontinent. Again, there is no treatment of the environmental effects (nor moral implications) of so substantially changing the planet's biosphere. Instead, Captain Picard enthuses about the "Atlantis project": "It's really quite exciting, actually, if you understand the potential of exploring a new world on our own planet." Later, Picard acknowledges the monumental aspects (and presumable risks) of such a significant reengineering of the Earth's surface: "How do you plan to accelerate the buildup on the underside of the mantle without increasing the stress on the tectonic plates?" Without raising the issue of the obvious ecological ramifications of the project, Picard looks upon the matter as solely an engineering challenge, offers his knowledge/experience of such endeavors: "On the *Enterprise*, we used harmonic resonators to relieve the tectonic pressures on Drema Four. Obviously, it's not the same problem." Only Picard's brother, who is ostensibly opposed to all change, offers a critical word of the Atlantis project: "I see no good reason why the Earth should have another subcontinent."

Are Modernity and Environmental Protection Incompatible?

Strongly suggesting modernity is incompatible with a regime that values pristine wilderness as an end unto itself is *The Next*

Generation episode "Journey's End" (1994). The action of the episode centers on a group of North American Indians that left Earth two hundred years so they could keep their way of life intact: "The North American Indians were forcibly displaced from their ancestral lands. This group on Dorvan V originally left Earth two hundred years ago because they wanted to preserve their cultural identities." Now they must vacate Dorvan V because of broader geopolitical considerations. Captain Picard is given the distasteful task of forcibly removing the Indian colony. Importantly, the Dorvan V natives don't seemingly have the option of returning to Earth. Instead, if they want "to preserve their cultural identities," they have to reside elsewhere.

The idea that native cultures could not survive intact in the context of modernity (Earth) is rendered in the original series episode "The Paradise Syndrome" (1968). On a faraway planet, the *Enterprise* crew encounters American Indians: "A mixture of Navajo, Mohican, and Delaware . . . All among the more advanced and peaceful tribes." How did North American native tribes come to be on a faraway planet? The tribes were transported by "a superrace known as the Preservers . . . They passed through the galaxy rescuing primitive cultures which were in danger of extinction and seeding them, so to speak, where they could live and grow." Therefore (again), the only way that North American Indian tribes could survive (thrive) was by removing them from Earth.

"Devil's Due"

The incompatibility among science, reason, technology, and a healthy, robust environment is once more asserted in *The Next Generation* 1991 episode "Devil's Due." The action centers on the planet Ventax Two. Significantly, the inhabitants of the planet Ventaxians "a millennium ago . . . turned their backs on technology." Prior to their rejection of technology, "the Ventaxian culture had achieved an extremely advanced scientific level." Today, "new technology has been available to the Ventaxians. They simply are not interested in it." This radical move away from technology resulted in "environmental gains on Ventax Two." As part of the turn from technology, Ventaxians shifted their "economy from an industrial to an agrarian base." They did so because "it was more ecologically sound." Part of this major shift involved "a series of initiatives covering everything from atmospheric contaminants to waste disposal," and this "purified the polluted water and air."

Crucially, the Ventaxians moved away from technology under the guise of religion—hence they seemingly abandoned modernity altogether. According to the fictional Ventaxians' theology, they reformed their society as a result of a "contract" with their version of the devil, known as Ardra. This deity is credited with remedying what is described as the society's socially, politically, and environmentally poor condition: "A thousand years ago, our planet was dying. Overcrowded and dangerous city states warred unceasingly with each other. The air and water were polluted with industrial waste and there was a constant threat of starvation and epidemic." The planet's head of government is asked by the individual impersonating Ardra, "Is there any doubt in your mind, any doubt at all, that if I had not intervened, the terrible conditions here would have continued?" He answers, "No doubt at all."

Global Warming Denial

Very significantly (and disappointingly), the *Star Trek* franchise virtually ignores the global warming phenomenon.[6] This is especially glaring as four discrete *Star Trek* televisions series spanned the late 1980s through to the middle of the first decade of the twenty-first century—that is, 1987 to 2005. During this period, global warming became an accepted scientific fact, as the Intergovernmental Panel on Climate Change issues report after report documenting the link between the warming of Earth and greenhouse gas emissions.[7]

By 1997, the Kyoto Protocol was negotiated by world leaders. Nevertheless, when *Star Trek* characters post-1997 travel back in time to twenty-first-century Earth, no mention is made of the global warming phenomenon. The *Enterprise* episode "Carpenter Street" is set in 2004 Detroit—the historic center of US automobile production. Significantly, the irrationality of the American practice of predicating urban transport (automobile dependency)[8] almost entirely on the profligate use of oil—a finite and limited resource—is commented upon. T'Pol asks Captain Archer, "Were they aware at this time that Earth's supply of fossil fuel was nearing depletion?" Archer starts to answer her question but is distracted by action of the episode, "They had been for thirty years, but it wasn't until 2061 that they finally." Glaringly, what is not mentioned is the irrationality of employing a mode of transportation on a mass scale that is disrupting the planet's biosphere (climate change)—something that was well established/understood when "Carpenter Street" aired in 2004.[9]

One *Star Trek* episode ("Thirty Days" 1998), through the *Voyager* platform, makes a seemingly oblique reference/critique of the global warming phenomenon. The episode (rather unique in the *Star Trek* franchise) expresses sympathy for a natural environment. The *Voyager* crew encounters a planet made entirely of water—an ocean world. One of the inhabitants of the planet tells of his strong emotional connection to this ocean world and for the creatures that live in it: "My family has lived here for ten generations. We protected this ocean, cultivated it, lived in harmony with the animals that inhabit it." One of the *Voyager* crew (Tom Paris) also conveys empathy for this world and strongly objects to the fact that the planet is being destroyed by its inhabitants: "If you don't make some serious changes around here soon, that ocean won't be here much longer." Paris defies Captain Janeway and risks his life to save the ocean world.

There is a certain parallel between the dilemma faced by the inhabitants of the ocean planet and those of us on Earth. Specifically, we are both destroying our respective planets via industrial processes. Moreover, the suggestion is made in "Thirty Days" that these industrial processes will not be terminated even though "the ocean could experience a complete loss of containment in less than five years." This is just like humans who have not stopped emitting dangerous amounts of heat-trapping gases into their atmosphere. The political/economic situation, however, of the ocean planet is completely different insofar as the inhabitants of the world are destabilizing it to produce oxygen (oxygen refineries)—something the residents of the planet obviously cannot do without. The same cannot be said of the residents of Earth. We are destabilizing Earth's biosphere primarily for wealth creation,[10] not life maintenance. Thus the episode "Thirty Days" could confuse (misinform) viewers into believing the global warming phenomenon is the result of processes that are vital for life on the planet.

The Next Generation episode "Force of Nature" (1993) can be viewed as a nod to global warming science and as a swipe to those that call for more scientific certainty before serious sacrifices/actions are taken to address the climate change phenomenon. While the episode mirrors the controversy surrounding climate change politics in the early 1990s, the environmental challenge described in "Force of Nature" bears little to no resemblance to Earth's warming. The action of the episode centers on a corridor of space that ships must use when traversing a particular region. The fact that this corridor is used so much is destabilizing a nearby planet. More specifically, the means used to propel star ships (warp fields),

> SCIENTIST RABAL: cause a dangerous reaction in this region of space.
> SCIENTIST SEROVA: Our planet is already being affected. We have measured large gravitational shifts throughout our system.
> RABAL: If something isn't done, our planet will become uninhabitable.

To bring attention to this issue, the two scientists engage in what can be viewed as ecoterrorism, placing mines that disable ships in the corridor. Serova said, "We were not willing to wait any longer. We knew that if we disabled enough ships, Starfleet would come. Then at least we would be able to present our case." To justify their actions, these scientists point to the lack of resources committed to studying basic science (like that of global warming):

> **Picard:** If you wanted us to review your research, you should have made a request through the Science Council.
> **Rabal:** Their resources are limited. It would have taken over a year before they dispatched a science ship to come and evaluate our work.

Rabal explains that Serova "has sworn to dedicate her life to exposing the dangers of warp drive." This description could be used to describe James Hansen, a leading and longtime champion of climate science.[11] An *Enterprise* crew member, sounding like a defender of fossil fuels, responds, "Warp drive has been around for three centuries. It's a proven technology." After it is concluded that the scientists' arguments could be correct, Captain Picard offers to press for more research on the matter, to which Serova charges, "That's your response? More research? More delays. I suppose I shouldn't have expected anything different."

While the rhetoric conveyed in "Force of Nature" aptly reflects that which occurs around the climate change phenomenon, the environmental conundrum described in the episode bears little resemblance to the global warming dilemma:

> **Data:** There are regions of potential subspace instability within the corridor. They believe that if these regions continue to be exposed to warp field energy, they will rupture. Subspace will extrude into normal space, forming a rift.
> **Picard:** It's like pacing up and down on the same piece of carpet. Eventually you wear it out.
> **Data:** That analogy is essentially correct, sir.

In the end, after having determined that the rebel (oppositional) scientists are correct that warp fields have an adverse effect on space, the policy resolution has no ostensive relation to resolving the global warming phenomenon: "Areas of space found susceptible to warp fields will be restricted to essential travel only, and effective immediately all Federation vessels will be limited to a speed of warp five, except in cases of extreme emergency."

Dilithium Crystals

The world of *Star Trek* evades concerns about emissions resulting from the production of energy through the literary device (fantasy) of dilithium crystals, introduced in the original series. The progressive politics of *Star Trek*, in many ways, follows from these fictitious crystals, which are cast as naturally occurring. According to the *Star Trek* franchise, these minerals contain massive amounts of energy—enough to propel huge star ships at speeds faster than light (warp), and enough to convert matter into energy and vice versa (replicators). These crystals hold enough energy to even take people apart at the molecular level and put them back together in one piece (transporters). It is important to stress that the technology/know-how to accomplish these feats is not necessarily fantasy (outside the realm of possibility). Dilithium crystals are, however, fantasy. These crystals are stable/inert, and when spent, they can readily be disposed of. With dilithium crystals providing such massive amounts of surplus energy with little environmental liabilities, the issue at the core of much of human politics—*who gets what, when, and how?*—is rendered mute. Virtually everyone's material needs/desires can be met with little political (or environmental) friction.

Environment as Instrument

With dilithium crystals serving as the sole source of energy in the world of *Star Trek*, this world is not entirely disconnected from nature. As seemingly consistent with the predominate thinking within the dominant social paradigm,[12] nature within *Star Trek* (e.g., dilithium crystals) is an instrument of modernity. Interestingly, clear instances of labor exploitation/oppression in *Star Trek* occur almost exclusively in connection to mining/mineral processing—positing an enduring relationship between the exploitation of nature and the exploitation of humans.[13]

The most salient instance in *Star Trek* (perhaps in all of American television) of linking resource exploitation and human exploitation/oppression occurs in the original series episode "Cloud Minders" (1969). Captain's Log: "A botanical plague is devastating a planet in the quadrant of the galaxy where the *Enterprise* is operating at present. It threatens to destroy the vegetation on the entire planet, leaving it uninhabitable." The *Enterprise* goes "to the planet Ardana, where the only source of zenite exists. It is the one substance that can halt the plague." Ardana is a seeming stand-in for South Africa. In effective imagery the political, economic, and social realities of the planet are portrayed—with the privileged/governing caste living a life of aesthetic splendor in a "cloud city" (Stratos) floating in the heavens, while the laboring classes (referred to as Troglytes) live on the (barren) planet surface working the mines (extracting zenite). The residents of Stratos are fair skinned, fair haired, and partake in the high arts. The Troglytes are dark haired, dark skinned, and unwashed. The *Enterprise* mission is in jeopardy because of civil/political strife on Ardana. Led by "Disrupters," the Troglytes are blockading the shipment of zenite.

Torture is deployed in an effort to break the Troglytes' political movement. A prisoner screams in agony, discomforting onlookers. Spock, in his famous calm, equanimous voice, observes, "Violence in reality is quite different from theory."

> **RESIDENT OF STRATOS:** But what else can [Troglytes] understand, Mister Spock?
> **SPOCK:** All the little things you and I understand and expect from life, such as equality, kindness, justice.
> **HEAD OF ARDANA GOVERNMENT:** Troglytes are not like Stratos dwellers, Mister Spock. They're a conglomerate of inferior species.

Nature as an Instrument of Geopolitical Control

Space itself is an instrument in *Star Trek*. Whereas Earth has established a world government[14] in *Star Trek*,[15] an interstellar nation-state system, nevertheless, exists. While the Federation is an inclusive political system[16]—allowing new planets (nations) to join on the basis of full equality—the Klingons, Romulans, Cardassians, and so on base their regimes on narrowly construed nationalities (species identities). The result is boundaries between these different political formations (with the Federation and the Romulans having a "neutral zone," or demilitarized zone, as a border). The different states of *Star Trek* compete/fight over territory (space and planets), and the (mineral) resources that inhere in these territories. For instance, in the original series episode "Friday's Child" (1967), the Klingon Empire and the Federation vie for a planet that contains "the rare mineral *topaline*, vital to the life-support systems of planetoid colonies." Thus nature in *Star Trek* is not treated as a collective resource to be managed, cared for, and enjoyed by all, but as a basis of political power—and a perennial source of conflict.

One example of space and natural resources serving as an instrument of power occurs in the *Deep Space Nine* episode "Statistical Probabilities" (1997). The Dominion and the Federation are negotiating a border, and the Dominion is asking for the Kabrel system in exchange for a concession on its part. It is discovered that the Dominion wants this system of planets because it contains yridium bicantizine—a building block of Ketracel-white—a substance vitally needed by Dominion soldiers, who are genetically engineered and bred in mass production. Similarly, in the original series episode "Elaan of Troyius" (1968), the Klingons attack the *Enterprise* in an effort to scuttle peace between two warring planets, as peace between these worlds would weaken the Klingons' claim on a planet rich in dilithium crystals.

Conclusion

Star Trek can be critiqued for lacking a core environmental ethos/ethic. This is most evident in the movie *Insurrection*, where the Federation authorizes the destruction of a planetary ecosystem.

(The project is only stopped because it would forcibly displace a six-hundred-person village.) Additionally, in "The Chase," little is made of the fact that a planet's entire ecosystem was destroyed. In "Measure of a Man," we are told that nature has no legal standing in the Federation. Similarly, no environmental objections are made when the raising of Earth's ocean floor is planned.

The creators of *Star Trek* avoid directly commenting on arguably the greatest challenge ever to civilization: global warming. Those of us that view the *Star Trek* franchise as progressive, penetrating, and farseeing on social and political issues can rightly be disappointed for its deafening silence on climate change. To the extent that *Star Trek* does make reference to the global warming phenomenon, it does so in passing, obliquely, or it misidentifies the problem as caused by vital life giving processes (producing oxygen). Most salient, when *Star Trek* creators had a prime opportunity to invoke global warming (during an episode set in 2004 Detroit), they failed to do so.

The creators of *Star Trek* make the explicit argument that modernity and regimes that center their culture on nature are inherently incompatible. We see this position in episodes where the point is made that native tribes living according to traditional ways cannot coexist with modernity on Earth. In casting this argument, *Star Trek* seemingly holds that technology, reason, and science are overtly hostile to robust environmental protection. This is the reasoning at the core of "Devil's Due."

Looking at *Star Trek* in an optimistic light, one could hold that in lacking an environmental ethos, it is simply conveying the fact that the dominant social paradigm lacks such an ethos. *Star Trek* could be interpreted as arguing that as long as the dominant social paradigm dictates the terms of modernity, an effective environmental protection regime is essentially impossible. More specifically, we will continue to seek quick fixes for our environmental problems (dilithium crystals, nuclear energy, and solar power),[17] and nature will continue to be viewed/treated as an instrument—including as a means of political/hegemonic control.[18] Finally, as conveyed in "Cloud Minders," *Star Trek* does suggest that political regimes that are exploitative of nature will also be exploitative of people—as well as employ racism and torture.

CHAPTER 9

The Politics of State Building
Star Trek: Enterprise

Star Trek: Enterprise the television series is a prequel to the original series. Thus whereas the original series is set in the twenty-third century, *Enterprise* takes place in the twenty-second. *Enterprise*, which was cancelled after four seasons (2001–5), specifically takes up the issue of state-building—that is, the creation of the Federation—with the show concluding with the founding of the interstellar organization. Whereas earlier iterations of the *Star Trek* franchise centered the domestic politics of the Earth in terms consistent with Marxism (e.g., the Bell Uprising), the movie *First Contact* and *Enterprise* seemingly draw their inspiration from the ideation of Carl Schmitt and the German Nazi Party. In the context of Germany's Weimar Republic, Schmitt argued that the basis of politics is the "friend/enemy" dichotomy, and that the core of political stability was a strong executive who had great latitude in declaring states of emergency and decision making in such instances. The Blond Beast existed in Nazi imagery—handsome, chiseled, and honorable—as the best, highest example of the human species. The Nazis cast themselves as freeing the Blond Beast from the constraints imposed on him by the likes of bankers and communists. The *Enterprise* character of Captain Jonathan Archer is the Blond Beast (see Figure 9.1)—being held down by the Vulcans (see Figure 9.2). In the end, the state-building politics underlying *Enterprise* have more in common with the

Figure 9.1 Jonathan Archer, captain of the starship *Enterprise*, twenty-second century

Figure 9.2 Vulcans from *Enterprise*

European experience (the European Union), than the American one. This could account for its early cancellation due to insufficient viewership.

The application of Schmitt's ideas in *Star Trek: Enterprise* indicates how politically dangerous they are—how they are rooted in (and foster) racism, hate, animosity, and genocidal impulses. Moreover, *Star Trek* shows how an excessive fixation on political stability and security can be used by political elites to establish regimes of dictatorship and torture.

The "Friend/Enemy" Dichotomy and *Star Trek*

Carl Schmitt (1888–1985) is in the pantheon of neoconservative thinkers. Schmitt was an architect of the Nazi Germany legal regime and known as the "Crown Jurist" of the Nazis.[1] He was an ostensive mentor to Leo Strauss (1899–1973), who was a German Jew that immigrated to the United States in 1937 because of the Nazis. (Strauss, in particular, is considered to be a lodestone for American neoconservatives.)[2] Schmitt wrote *The Concept of the Political* in 1929, and Strauss a set of sympathetic "Notes" to Schmitt's book.[3] Schmitt provided a letter of recommendation for Strauss that facilitated Strauss's obtaining an academic position at the University of Chicago.[4]

Schmitt held that at the center of politics is the distinction "between friend and enemy."[5] Social and political cohesion is based on this foe/friend dichotomy. Reflective of Schmitt's "friend/enemy" reasoning, in *The Next Generation* episode "Face of the Enemy" (1993), the point is made that Romulans have an "absolute certainty about . . . who is a friend and who is an enemy." The main component of Hitler's and the Nazis' political/propaganda argumentation was directed at an imaginary coalition of Western bankers and Eastern communists conspiring against Germany. According to Nazi mythology (myopia), Jews were at the center of this worldwide anti-Germany coalition. In the face of this global conspiracy directed against Germany, the Hitler regime argued that the German people must be unified (no dissent whatsoever), and strike back (World War II).⁶ In her synthesis of Strauss's writings, Shadia B. Drury renders the following observation: "Like Schmitt, Strauss believes that politics is first and foremost about the distinction between WE and THEY. Strauss thinks that a political order can be stable only if it is united by an external threat."⁷

The *Star Trek* movie *First Contact* (1996) is predicated on a we/they distinction. The action of the movie takes place in the year 2063. The Borg go back in Earth's history to prevent humanity's first contact with the Vulcans. This initial exposure to an alien culture occurs because Zephran Cochrane conducts humanity's first successful warp drive experiment. (Warp speed represents a speed faster than light.) When the Vulcans detect Cochrane's ship achieving warp speed, they decide to introduce themselves to earthlings—first contact. In this iteration (*First Contact*) of *Star Trek*'s historiography of Earth, in 2063 humanity is in what is referred to a "Second Dark Age."⁸ What rallies humanity from its disarray is its contact with the Vulcans:

> **TROI:** *It unites humanity in a way no one ever thought possible when they realize they're not alone in the universe.*

Therefore, the political foundation of humanity in the mid-twenty-first century is the we/they dichotomy—with the Vulcans serving as "they." "The political enemy is not necessarily morally evil." Instead, Schmitt held that the potential enemy "is merely the other, the stranger, and it is sufficient that according to his nature he is in a special intense way existentially something different and alien, so that in the extreme case conflicts with him are possible."⁹

In *Enterprise*, conflict with the Vulcans does occur. "The Andorian Incident" (2001) concludes with the exposure of a Vulcan spy station by Captain Archer, which earns the ire of the Vulcans. The Vulcan ambassador to Earth complains, "The Andorians wouldn't have found the [spy] station if your people hadn't interfered." The *Enterprise* has "been in space for six months and they've already destabilized an entire sector" ("Shadows of P'Jem" 2002). "Fusion" (2002) involves a set of Vulcans who, contrary to Vulcan norms, embrace their emotions. ("I always knew there had to be more to life than just logic and reason.") One of these Vulcans telepathically "rapes" T'Pol (a Vulcan and *Enterprise*'s first officer), and Captain Archer engages in an intense fist fight with the transgressor. The episodes "The Forge" (2004), "Awakening" (2004), and the "Kir'Shara" (2004) make up a story arc whereby Earth's embassy on Vulcan is bombed, killing Admiral Forrest (Archer's mentor), and the *Enterprise* crew gets swept up in internal Vulcan religious and political strife—with an attempt made against Captain Archer's life, and the *Enterprise* and Vulcan military ships coming to a face-off. In the denouement, we learn that elements within the Vulcan government were behind the bombing of the Earth embassy, and that a faction still in the government wants to pull the planet toward a political/military alliance with the Romulans—an intention ominously threatening to Earth.

The we/they or friend/foe dichotomy at the heart of Earth's politics in *Enterprise* and *First Contact* is in sharp contrast to earlier iterations of *Star Trek*, where state-building was accomplished through the progressive expansion of political rights and social justice, like in the American Revolution (original series, "The Omega Glory" 1968), the US Civil War (original series, "The Savage Curtain" 1969), the fight against fascism (original series, "City on the Edge of Forever" 1967), and the Bell Uprising, which takes place in 2024 (*Deep Space Nine*, "Past Tense" 1995). Such an ontology of social/political change through revolutionary moments/events is entirely consistent (if not inspired) by classic Marxism.[10]

It is significant that in *First Contact*, by 2063 San Francisco is destroyed.[11] In "Past Tense" (*Deep Space Nine* 1995), San Francisco is where the antineoliberalism Bell Uprising (the basis of a new global politics) occurs in 2024.

The Neoliberal United Federation of Planets?

This opens the question of how humans come to hold the leadership position in the Federation—a political organization comprising numerous planets and alien species. Starfleet is headquartered on Earth (San Francisco). It is evident in *Enterprise* that earthlings lead in the formation of the Federation—with its founding taking place on Earth ("These Are the Voyages . . ." 2005). In the American mind, US global leadership is ostensibly justified because it is a locus of global justice and freedom—for example, the American Revolutionary War, the US Civil War, the fight against fascism, the New Deal, and the Civil Rights Movement. With the destruction of San Francisco (the negation of the Bell Uprising) and the notion of a Second Dark Age for humanity in the mid-twenty-first century, the idea that a progressive teleology led to the formation of the Federation and human leadership of it is rejected. Far from being impressed by human social practices and political formations, the Vulcans are leery of humanity. T'Pol: "You have yet to embrace either patience or logic. You remain impulsive . . . It remains to be seen whether humanity will revert to its baser instincts" ("Broken Arrow" 2001). Such pronouncements strike against the very foundation of the *Star Trek* franchise—namely, that humans are socially, politically, and technologically progressing toward a utopian ideal (*The Next Generation*, "Transfigurations" 1990).

In *Enterprise*, the argument is made that the Federation is established not as a harbinger of justice and freedom but for pragmatic reasons altogether. This more closely mirrors the formation of the European Union than the history of the creation and strengthening of the American federal government. The effort to create a European-federated structure in the post–World War II period grew predominantly out of two entirely practical considerations: defense (from the Soviet Union) and economic stability—trade, energy security, and so on.[12]

The pressing need for a regional security regime is established in the second *Enterprise* episode, "Fight or Flight" (2001). The

Enterprise comes across an alien ship that has been attacked and whose crew is dead. With no protocol or any officials to notify, the *Enterprise* initially leaves the damaged ship and her dead crew adrift in space.

The need for a regional security protocol is again treated in "Babel One" (2005), "United" (2005), and "The Aenar" (2005). These make up a three-episode arc involving Romulan subterfuge, whereby they launch a remotely controlled ship in an attempt to destabilize Earth's region of space. The Romulan ship can take various forms, and attacks ships under the guise that the offending ship is from one of the other powers in Earth's sector of space.

The economic difficulties created by the lack of a security framework are outlined in two episodes: "Fortunate Son" (2001) and "Marauders" (2002). "Fortunate Son" revolves around the fact that without a protective military presence, cargo ships are regularly subject to raiding (from a species known as Nausicans). Archer to the Nausican raiders: "You're not sneaking up on an old freighter this time. This is an NX Class Starship. Take a good look, because you'll be seeing more of them." In "Marauders," a small alien colony is eking out a living producing and trading a source of energy (deuterium), but a group of Klingon marauders force the colonists to pay them tribute.

Therefore, the prime motive underlying the creation of the Federation is security and trade. This represents the obligations of the neoliberal state—that is, guaranteeing the secure and free movement of goods, services, and capital.

In making the case for a federated interstellar political system, Captain Archer tells an audience of delegates of the would-be United Federation of Planets the following:

> Up until about a hundred years ago, there was one question that burned in every human, that made us study the stars and dream of traveling to them, Are we alone? Our generation is privileged to know the answer to that question. We are all explorers, driven to know what's over the horizon, what's beyond our own shores.

And yet, the more I've experienced, the more I've learned that no matter how far we travel, or how fast we get there, the most profound discoveries are not necessarily beyond that next star. They're within us, woven into the threads that bind us, all of us, to each other. The final frontier begins in this hall. Let's explore it together. ("Terra Prime" 2005)

Thus in advocating for a federation among planets, *Enterprise* does not make any specific justice claims (the elimination of poverty, the promotion of democracy, etc.). Instead, Captain Archer's position is rooted in pragmatism—namely, the logic of coordinating planet members' space travels ("Let's explore [space] together").

We can see the implications of (the minimal) neoliberal political obligations in a federated world system in the original series episode "Cloud Minders" (1969). Captain's Log: "A botanical plague is devastating a planet in the quadrant of the galaxy where the *Enterprise* is operating at present. It threatens to destroy the vegetation on the entire planet, leaving it uninhabitable." The *Enterprise* goes "to the planet Ardana, where the only source of zenite exists. It is the one substance that can halt the plague." In effective imagery, the political, economic, and social realities of the planet are portrayed—with the privileged/governing caste living a life of aesthetic splendor in a "cloud city" (Stratos) floating in the heavens, while the laboring classes (referred to as Troglytes) live on the (barren) planet surface working the mines (extracting zenite). The *Enterprise* mission is in jeopardy because of civil/political strife on Ardana. Led by "Disrupters," the Troglytes are blockading the shipment of zenite. Consistent with a neoliberal conception of international politics, Kirk informs the Ardana leadership that as a member of the Federation, it has an obligation to make the zenite available to other Federation planets. Kirk: "I must concern myself with [the conflict on Ardana] if it should interfere with the delivery of zenite to Merak Two . . . Ardana is a member of the Federation, and it is your council's responsibility that nothing interferes with its obligation to another member of the Federation."

When Kirk directly engages the Troglytes to discuss reforming Ardana's society, Kirk is informed, "Your Federation orders do not entitle you to defy local governments." When Kirk decides to proceed with his plan for reform in the face of the opposition of Ardana's government, Spock warns him, "If you are apprehended deliberately violating the [Ardana] High Advisor's orders, he will be within his rights to have you executed." Evidently, Federation rules do not extend to the treatment of member planet's citizens.

Whereas Kirk in "Cloud Minders" is ostensibly successful in his effort at reforming Ardana, *Enterprise* issues a caution against interventions in the domestic politics of other planets/societies. Charles "Trip" Tucker in "Cogenitor" (2003) tries to liberate a woman whose only role in society is to facilitate the pregnancy of couples. Through Tucker's help, the woman decides she wants more out of life than currently offered to her, and she wants to leave with *Enterprise*. Archer decides against offering the Cogenitor asylum. We learn later that she commits suicide. The captain holds Tucker responsible: "You knew you had no business interfering with those people, but you just couldn't let it alone. You thought you were doing the right thing. I might agree if this was Florida, or Singapore, but it's not, is it. We're in deep space and a person is dead. A person who'd still be alive if we hadn't made First Contact."

Which brings us back to the question of why humans are seemingly at the forefront of the Federation. Consistent with the friend/foe political dynamic identified by Carl Schmitt, humans come to the leadership of the Federation because they appear to be good friends to the other planets/species that make up the Federation. The trustworthiness and fairness of humans is first conveyed in "The Andorian Incident" (2001), the sixth episode of the series. The *Enterprise* makes an unannounced visit to a Vulcan monastery and finds that a group of Andorians are holding the monks at gunpoint. The Andorians suspect that the monastery is a front for a spy operation directed at them. As the Vulcans and the *Enterprise* crew are trying to fend off the Andorians, it turns out that the Andorians were correct—the monastery is a cover for an elaborate spying facility. At this point (with the Vulcans strongly objecting), Captain Archer agrees to end hostilities with the Andorians and allows them to leave the planet unmolested—thereby exposing the Vulcan spy station. Indicating the goodwill Captain Archer gained with the Andorians, the leader of the Andorians says upon leaving, "We're in your debt."

In other episodes, Captain Archer and the *Enterprise* crew take personal risks on behalf of other species to forward the security of the region, showing themselves to be good friends. ("He could've at least mentioned *Enterprise*. Who does he think got the Andorians and Tellarites talking?" ["Demons" 2005].) The United States could be said to have been a good friend to Europe—helping defeat the Kaiser and the Nazis, as well as giving Western/Central Europe huge sums in the post–World War II period in the form of the Marshall Plan. Finally, the United States committed itself to defending Europe from the Soviets during the Cold War through the North Atlantic Treaty Organization. Of course, in carrying out these friendly acts, the United States committed vast resources and incurred massive costs, including the potentially catastrophic risk of nuclear war. Additionally, the United States could take on these tasks because of its immense wealth and national resources. These friendly acts/gestures are arguably the key reasons the United States is the leader of the current world system. Thus the *Enterprise* narrative that the exploits of the *Enterprise* (one ship) would be the prime basis of humanity's leadership of an interstellar federated political system (where political entities surrender [at least part of] their sovereignty) is outside credulity.

The Blond Beast Metaphor

Disturbingly, *Enterprise* invokes the Blond Beast metaphor. In Nazi iconography, the Blond Beast is conspired against (held back) by other races, which prevent the Blond Beast from taking his rightful place as the dominant/superior being. The Nazis held they would unleash the Blond Beast and allow him to exercise his natural dominance.[13] (It is notable that Leonard Nimoy [who is Jewish himself] suggested that Vulcans are a metaphor for Jews.)[14]

During the opening scene of the series, Captain Archer (as a boy) and his father fault the Vulcans for holding back Earth's space program:

> **ARCHER (AS A YOUNG BOY):** Billy Cook said we'd be flying at warp five by now if the Vulcans hadn't kept things from us.
> **ARCHER'S FATHER:** Well they have their reasons. God knows what they are.

In the show's opening episode, "Broken Arrow" (2001), the Vulcans object to the launching of the starship *Enterprise* and initiating a human presence beyond the solar system.

> **ADMIRAL FORREST:** We've been waiting for nearly a century, Ambassador. This seems as good a time as any to get started.
> **VULCAN AMBASSADOR (SOVAL):** Listen to me. You're making a mistake!

The reason for their opposition is condescending and insulting:

> **SOVAL:** Until you've proven you're ready.
> **ARCHER:** Ready to what?
> **SOVAL:** To look beyond your provincial attitudes and volatile nature.

In another instance, the Vulcan ambassador argues for replacing Archer as *Enterprise* captain because "he's too impulsive" ("Shadows of P'Jem" 2002). After an incident where *Enterprise* seemingly destroyed a planet, the Vulcan leadership hold that the *Enterprise* space exploration mission should be put in mothballs: "[Vulcan] Ambassador Soval will use this to convince Starfleet that we need another ten or twenty years before we try this again" ("Shockwave" 2002).

In dealing with the Xindi crisis (discussed later in this chapter), the Vulcans are poor friends. First, space in the Delphic Expanse inflicts severe neurological damage on the Vulcans, with an entire ship's crew being turned into mindless, violent zombies ("Impulse" 2003). In another episode, Captain Archer is incapacitated and T'Pol assumes command. Under her command, the *Enterprise* is gravely damaged, and as a result, it fails in its mission to save Earth. (We see it destroyed, and all remaining humans mercilessly hunted down.) Ultimately, Captain Archer is retroactively cured—whereby he never cedes command to T'Pol—and *Enterprise* is able to carry on with its mission ("Twilight" 2003). In the denouement of the Xindi crisis, when the weapon of mass destruction approaches Earth, the Vulcans are nowhere to be found. Instead, an Andorian ship aids in defending Earth. (Andorian captain Shran: "I anticipated that you'd need some help" ["Zero Hour" 2004].)

Archer, particularly toward the Vulcans, behaves like a Blond Beast. He (irrationally) faults the Vulcans for damaging his father's career. (Archer's father was a spaceship engineer.) Archer: "I watched my father work his ass off while [Vulcan] scientists held back just enough information to keep him from succeeding." Archer tells T'Pol in the opening episode of the show, "You have no idea how much I'm restraining myself from knocking you on your ass" ("Broken Arrow" 2001). He punches out a Vulcan and says, "Boy, did it feel good" ("The Andorian Incident" 2001). Archer manifests open resentment and hostility toward the Vulcans when he says to T'Pol, "Your superiors don't think we can flush a toilet without one of you to assist us . . . I've been listening to you Vulcans tell us what not to do all my entire life . . . Take your Vulcan cynicism and bury it along with your repressed emotions" ("Broken Arrow" 2001).

Strongly reminiscent of the racist elimination of threat ideologies of the Nazi state, the following is opined in the mirror universe of the Empire: "I know Archer. He blames [the Vulcans] for inciting the rebels. If he becomes Emperor, he'll lay waste to

Vulcan." Upon defeating the rebellion, Archer makes a point of destroying a rebellious Vulcan ship (T'Pol: "they're no threat to us"—Archer: "fire when ready") while allowing others to escape. (Member of the bridge: "The last Andorian ship is retreating." Archer: "Let them go. I want the other rebels to know what happened here" ["In a Mirror, Darkly" 2005].)

Consistent with the Blond Beast metaphor, the spirit/mind (katra) of the Vulcans' prophet (Surak) is carried by Archer. The demigod of the Vulcans recognizes his superiority. (A Vulcan says to Archer, "He chose you." ["Awakening" 2004].) Similarly, when T'Pol is forced to choose between the Vulcans and Archer, she selects the Blond Beast. T'Pol is point blank asked: "Does your allegiance lie with the [Vulcan] High Command or with Captain Archer?" T'Pol answered: "I don't wish to return to Vulcan" ("The Expanse" 2003).

Earth Under Attack

The last episode of season two ("The Expanse" 2003) has a terrorist attack committed against Earth on the Florida peninsula. The probe—that upon explosion killed seven million people—was launched from a remote and uncharted area of space known as the Delphic Expanse. The *Enterprise* crew learns that this probe was only a test, and a larger explosive is being planned to destroy the entirety of Earth. This attack is being carried out by the Xindi. Season three is dedicated to *Enterprise*'s effort to stop this threat against humanity.

In the aftermath of the 2001 9/11 attack, the Bush Administration argued for greater political authority to be vested in the White House, including the power to make war. Using the theory of the Unitary Executive, the Bush White House held that the US Constitution empowered the president to act unilaterally—that is, without consultation or authorization from the legislative or judicial branches of government.[15] Carl Schmitt argued that the executive (the President) under the Weimar constitution had broad discretion to declare a state of emergency, even if only a governing majority could not be established in the Reichstag (parliament). When an effort was made to limit the power of the executive during a crisis, Schmitt argued against enumerating the executive's powers during such a crisis—thereby standing for open-ended and unfettered executive authority in such circumstances.[16]

In the *Deep Space Nine* episode "Homefront" (1996), a terrorist bombing occurs on Earth—killing 27 people. In the aftermath of this attack, Starfleet (the military) argues for greater security measures. The President of Earth resists this suggestion: "I understand the need for increased security, but."

> **PRESIDENT:** I believe the Changeling threat is somewhat less serious than Starfleet does.
> **ADMIRAL LEYTON:** Mister President, I assure you the threat is real.
> **PRESIDENT:** For all we know, there was only one Changeling on Earth, and he may not even be here anymore.
> **CAPTAIN SISKO:** But if he is here, we have a problem. There's no telling how much damage one Changeling could do.
> **PRESIDENT:** Forgive me for saying so, Captain, but you sound a little ... paranoid.
> **SISKO:** Do I?

This exchange presages the Bush Administration contention that the al-Qaeda threat required greater political/legal latitude for the military-security apparatus. President Bush took this position even though the 9/11 attack involved only a handful of perpetrators, many of whom died in the attack.

In the end, the Earth President agrees to the enhanced security measures being proposed by the military. Interestingly, the enhanced security measures are seemingly instituted with simply the President's signature—there are no other deliberations presented or discussed.

These increased security measures are cast as necessary defensive measures to protect paradise, or utopia (Earth):

President: I would hate to be remembered as the Federation President who destroyed paradise.
Sisko: We're not looking to destroy paradise, Mister President. We're looking to save it.

Just like Schmitt held that the executive needed emergency powers to protect the Weimar constitution, the Bush Administration argued for enhanced security measures and greater power for the presidency to protect American "freedom and democracy."[17]

In the denouement of "Homefront," Earth experiences a planetary-wide blackout. A state of emergency has been declared. The subsequent *Deep Space Nine* episode, "Paradise Lost" (1996), begins by showing platoons of troops patrolling the street and everyone submitting to security screening (blood tests) to establish that they are not enemies. We learn that the power outage was perpetrated by elements within Starfleet. Thus *Deep Space Nine* issues a caution against the use of national security threats to suspend civil and political rights, as well as democratic decision-making processes:

Sisko: "What you're trying to do is seize control of Earth and place it under military rule."
Admiral Leyton: "If that's what it takes to stop the Dominion."

In 2002, as the neoconservative agenda (invading Iraq) was gaining momentum through both the Bush government and the national media—most prominently the *New York Times*[18]—the *Enterprise* episode "Fallen Hero" aired. The *Enterprise* picks up the Vulcan ambassador from the planet of Mazar—she has been recalled by her government. Soon after *Enterprise* departs, the Mazar government demands that the Vulcan ambassador (V'lar) return, sending ships in pursuit. After initially refusing to tell Captain Archer the cause of the current controversy, V'lar relents and informs the captain why the Mazarites are so eager for her return: "The Mazarites pursuing us are criminals. They are members of an organization that's infiltrated all levels of government, making themselves wealthy and powerful at the expense of many innocent victims. Their methods include eliminating anyone who stands in their way." She adds, "The corruption ran deeper than I thought."

Upon the vanquishing of the Xindi threat, Archer is sent back to the World War II period ("Stormfront" 2004). History has been altered. Time traveling aliens are aiding the Nazis. The Nazis control much of the Northeast United States, including New York City and Washington, DC. Nazis (in full uniform) occupy and operate from the White House: "We are inside the home of a former American President. It seems to me your war effort is going well enough."

In 2001, the Bush Administration declares the War on Terror, and as part of this war, orders the invasion of Afghanistan, where al-Qaeda is headquartered. As the United States is taking prisoners in Afghanistan, the Bush Administration designates many of them to be "enemy combatants," therefore denying them Geneva Convention protections, including the prohibition against torturing prisoners of war.[19] The United States opens the Guantanamo prison camp in 2002 to house these so-called enemy combatants, where aggressive interrogation—that is, torture techniques—against these prisoners were authorized.[20] The movie *Zero Dark Thirty* (2012; made in close collaboration with the US military and the Central Intelligence Agency) indicates that torture is used by the US government in its dealings abroad.[21] Additionally, in 2013, the *New York Times* reported, "A nonpartisan, independent review of interrogation and detention programs in the years after the Sept. 11, 2001, terrorist attacks concludes that 'it is indisputable that the United States engaged in the practice of torture' and that the nation's highest officials bore ultimate responsibility for it."[22]

The *Enterprise* episode "Anomaly" aired in September 2003, and offers a storyline whereby torture is needed to protect Earth from attack. This paralleled Bush Administration arguments at the time that enhanced interrogation techniques were required to protect the United States from further attack.²³ Shortly after entering the Delphic Expanse to stop the planned destruction of Earth, the *Enterprise*'s fuel stock is pirated: "They took every one of our antimatter storage pods." Without these pods, *Enterprise* will run out of fuel in a month "tops." In the raid against *Enterprise*, one of the pirates is captured. Information from this captive (Orgoth) is the only way that *Enterprise* can retrieve its much needed fuel. Archer tries to intimidate Orgoth into cooperating, but Orgoth holds, "I don't think you'd be very comfortable torturing another man. You and your crewmates are far too civilized for that. Too moral." Captain Archer tells him otherwise, "I need what was stolen from me. There's too much at stake to let my morality get in the way." Mockingly, Orgoth asks, "Are you taking me to your torture chamber?" Archer puts Orgoth in an airlock, which Archer uses to suffocate Orgoth. Orgoth relents and tells the captain what he wants to know. *Enterprise* recovers her much needed fuel. The use of suffocation as a torture technique by *Enterprise* is significant in that the most prominent torture technique deployed by the Bush Administration was waterboarding—whereby victims feel as if they are suffocating through simulated drowning.²⁴

In the episode "Cloud Minders," torture and racism are deployed in an effort to break a political movement. A prisoner is pressed to provide the names of the leaders of the Troglyte rebellion:

> **TORTURER:** You still refuse to disclose the names of the other Disrupters.
> **TROGLYTE:** There are no Disrupters!
> **TORTURER:** Very well, if you prefer the rays.

She screams in agony, discomforting onlookers. Spock, in his famous calm, equanimous voice, observes, "Violence in reality is quite different from theory."

> **ONLOOKER:** But what else can [Troglytes] understand, Mister Spock?

Spock: All the little things you and I understand and expect from life, such as equality, kindness, justice.

Torturer: Troglytes are not like Stratos dwellers, Mister Spock. They're a conglomerate of inferior species.

Terra Prime

The *Enterprise* series concludes in 2005, and the penultimate episode, "Terra Prime," centers on the group Terra Prime. Initially, this organization is described as xenophobic: "They want to stop all contact with alien species . . . They believe it's corrupting our way of life." Terra Prime "had a resurgence following the Xindi attack." Later, we learn that Terra Prime is racist: "This is an alien-human hybrid. Living proof of what will happen if we allow ourselves to be submerged in an interstellar coalition. Our genetic heritage . . . That child is a cross-breed freak. How many generations before our genome is so diluted that the word human is nothing more than a footnote in some medical text?" The leader of Terra Prime declares, "I'm returning Earth to its rightful owners." The group seeks to scuttle the formation of the Federation by promising to destroy Starfleet command (in San Francisco) unless all aliens leave Earth. Referring to signs of popular support for Terra Prime and its agenda, the Vulcan Ambassador Soval notes, "The fact that Paxton has the support of so many of your people is . . . troubling." An Andorian ambassador makes the point, "Earthmen talk about uniting worlds, but your own planet is deeply divided. Perhaps you're not quite ready to host this conference [promoting interstellar cooperation]."

Conclusion

Perhaps reflecting the pessimism of the Clinton and Bush Administrations, *Enterprise*, and its precursor *First Contact*, are dominated by pessimism: a Second Dark Age during the twenty-first century, the friend/foe dichotomy as the basis of politics, neoliberalism as the sole motivator of world system politics, the potentiality of Earth's destruction as a narrative foundation, torture as a security necessity, and the prevalence of racism/xenophobia on Earth. Most disconcerting of all is Captain Archer's attitude toward the Vulcans, which is very strongly reminiscent of the Nazi Blond Beast metaphor.

With such pessimistic themes dominating the *First Contact* and *Enterprise* narratives, their creators seem to draw inspiration from the political theory of the likes of Carl Schmitt, the voice of conservatism in the Weimar Republic and, later, the Crown Jurist of the Nazis. This is in sharp contrast to the earlier iterations of *Star Trek*, where Earth's politics is much more in line with the thinking of Karl Marx (the Bell Uprising).

The application of Schmitt's ideas in *Star Trek: Enterprise* indicates how politically dangerous they are—how they are rooted in (and foster) racism, hate, and animosity. Moreover, *Star Trek* shows how an excessive fixation on political stability and security can be used by political elites to establish regimes of dictatorship and torture. Interestingly and importantly, earlier iterations of *Star Trek* issued powerful cautions/critiques against the use of security and stability concerns to establish dictatorship and carry out torture.

CHAPTER 10

Lost in the Developing World
Star Trek: Voyager

Star Trek: Voyager (1995–2001) represents a metaphor of being lost in the so-called Third World. Through this metaphor, *Voyager* focuses on two specific motifs: pragmatism[1] and race relations. The show begins when the star ship *Voyager* is transported seventy thousand light years from Federation space. It is estimated that to get back to Earth it would take *Voyager* 75 years using the propulsion means at its disposal. During the course of its daunting effort to traverse this massive expanse of space, the *Voyager* crew encounters numerous situations fraught with moral/ethnic quandaries. In facing these quandaries/dilemmas, *Voyager* has to decide whether to be expeditious (pragmatic) in trying to get home, or to prioritize their ethical/moral principles (thereby endangering themselves and their chances of getting home). The strength of the show, in my estimation, is that the *Voyager* crew consistently chooses to be ethical even in the face of death (or remaining stranded). Moreover, certain villains in the *Voyager* series are dastardly precisely because they prioritize pragmatism over principle.

As an iteration of the *Star Trek* franchise set almost entirely outside of the Federation—read the advanced parts of the world (Western Europe, the United States, etc.)—*Star Trek: Voyager* can be interpreted as a commentary on the societies and politics of the underdeveloped world. *Voyager* portrays the violence, religiosity, and authoritarianism that putatively characterizes the underdeveloped world. Consistent with neoconservative reasoning—that is, developing world politics as violent and unstable[2]—the Kazon (a species of the Delta Quadrant) are cast as indefatigably and implacably hostile, relentlessly pursuing *Voyager* over the course of the first two seasons of the series.

Antipragmatism

The antipragmatism of *Voyager* starts with its pilot episode ("The Caretaker" 1995) and the setting of the show's premise. *Voyager* and her crew are transported into the Delta Quadrant of the galaxy. (The Federation is in the Alpha Quadrant.) *Voyager* was brought to this part of space by a creature known as the Caretaker. The Caretaker is dying, and he is seeking someone to mate with. The Caretaker finds it particularly imperative to have an offspring because he is manning an array in space that sustains/protects a species known as the Ocampa. An offspring would presumably continue to operate the array. We learn that the Caretaker had brought a number of species from throughout the galaxy in an effort to find a suitable mate.

The Caretaker is in his last moments of life, and failing to have a child, is undertaking an effort to sure up the Ocampa's defenses to prevent the Kazon—a hostile race (more on that to follow)—from overrunning Ocampa society. Upon the Caretaker's death, the Kazon make *Voyager* an offer: they would cease their attack against *Voyager* (allowing it to use the array to return home), and the Kazon could then use the array to invade the Ocampans. Thus from the virtual inception of the show, the *Voyager* crew face a vexing dilemma—make peace with Kazon at the expense of the Ocampa (thereby going home) or destroy the array to protect the Ocampa, hence becoming stranded in a remote part of space. The *Voyager* crew destroys the array.

Outside of the series pilot, three *Voyager* episodes, "False Profits" (1996) "Dreadnought" (1996) and "The Void" (2001), stand out for the ethical, moral, and principled behavior of the crew in an otherwise demoralizing and physically isolated circumstance (75 years from home). In "False Profits," *Voyager* comes across a wormhole that leads directly to the Alpha Quadrant (Federation space). Thus by entering this wormhole, the *Voyager* crew would instantaneously be home. But before they enter this portal, the *Voyager* crew discovers that a planet proximate to it is being exploited by a pair of Ferengi. The Ferengi's presence on the planet relates back to *The Next Generation* series. The starship *Enterprise* was heading a Federation delegation bidding on the rights to a wormhole that linked the Alpha and Delta Quadrant—the wormhole that *Voyager* can now use to get home. In preparation for the bidding, shuttle craft from both the *Enterprise* and a Ferengi ship passed through the wormhole to investigate this phenomenon. The *Enterprise* crew, upon reaching the Delta Quadrant side of the wormhole, conclude that the wormhole is unstable and that the aperture on the Delta Quadrant side will randomly move, thereby threatening to strand anyone on that side of the wormhole. The crew of the *Enterprise* shuttle warn that the wormhole aperture is about to shift to some unknown location, but the Ferengi refuse to listen. So while the *Enterprise* shuttle craft safely returns to the Alpha Quadrant, the Ferengi do not.

In *Star Trek: Voyager*, we learn that since getting stranded in the Delta Quadrant, the two Ferengi, Arridor and Kol, made their way to a nearby planet where they were able to exploit the native population's religious beliefs to attain a dominant political position. The Ferengi are recognized as "The Holy Sages." (Chakotay [*Voyager*'s first officer]: "It seems the people have a myth, an epic poem called the 'Song of the Sages,' which predicts the arrival of two demigods from the sky, the Sages, who would rule over the people as benevolent protectors.") Ferengi, as a species, elevate capitalist ideology to a religion (with their heaven being known as the Divine Treasury, and only those with sufficient profit can enter). As part of their capitalist religion/ideology, Ferengi have what are known as the "Rules of Acquisition," a set of nostrums that Ferengi can putatively rely on in their profit-making endeavors. For example, "Exploitation begins at home," "Expand or die," and, "A wise man can hear profit in the wind." Therefore, when the native population of the Delta Quadrant planet believe the Ferengi to be deities, the Ferengi establish a regime that allows them to economically exploit the planet. "False Profits" is an extension of the *Star Trek* franchise's ongoing criticism of capitalism/neoliberalism. Before the arrival of the Ferengi, the native population (we are told) was "flourishing." Under the Ferengi profit-making regime, Arridor and Kol become very wealthy, and at the same time poverty proliferates among the native population. ("The two Ferengi live in a palatial temple, while the people are lucky to have a roof over their heads.")

The *Voyager* crew feel that they have a moral responsibility to remove the Ferengi from the planet, thereby ending the profit prioritizing government they have created. (Janeway: "The Federation did host the negotiations. And if it weren't for those negotiations, the Ferengi wouldn't be here. So one could say, without being unreasonable I think, that the Federation is partially responsible for what's happened, and therefore, duty bound to correct the situation.") Thus instead of simply going through the wormhole and immediately going home, the *Voyager* crew seek to end the Ferengi's rule in an orderly fashion—in a way consistent with the society's theology. Growing resentful of the Ferengi and their rule, elements of the native population help draw on aspects of their religion to expel the Ferengi. Untrustworthy as ever, in the final instance, the Ferengi use their spaceship to try to return to the planet. Their shenanigans send them through the wormhole, destabilizing it, and leaving *Voyager* stranded.

"Dreadnought" is similar to "False Profits" insofar as events in the distant Alpha Quadrant initiate the action. Dreadnought is a massive missile that is roaming through space in the Delta Quadrant. The missile was programmed and launched in the Alpha Quadrant by *Voyager*'s chief engineer, B'elenna Torres. This is when she was a member of the Maquis—an insurgent movement directed mostly at the Cardassian Alliance, which, according to the Maquis, brutalize their subject peoples. (In the series pilot, a Maquis ship and *Voyager* were pulled to the Delta Quadrant together. Much of *Star Trek: Voyager* involves the process whereby the Maquis are incorporated into the *Voyager* crew—including its command structure [hence Torres becoming *Voyager*'s chief engineer].) The Dreadnought was wantonly launched by Torres into Cardassian space and ended up in the Delta Quadrant. Torres, now a member of the *Voyager* crew, repents for unleashing Dreadnought and undertakes great risks to disarm this weapon of mass destruction. Hence Torres's membership in the *Voyager* crew, and Captain Kathryn Janeway serving as her mentor, develops Torres's moral sensibilities and leads her to the conclusion that blindly launching a weapon of such destructive capacity is ethically/morally wrong—regardless of the circumstance. What is particularly germane for a discussion involving pragmatism is the fact that (in case Torres failed to disarm the missile) *Voyager* is ready to throw itself in the way of Dreadnought to prevent it from devastating a planet it had locked in on.

> **JANEWAY:** I'm prepared to use this ship to detonate the warhead before the missile reaches you.
> **OFFICIAL FROM THREATENED PLANET:** Use your ship? To collide with it?
> **JANEWAY:** Something like that.
> **OFFICIAL:** You would sacrifice yourselves to benefit a people you didn't even know two days ago?
> **JANEWAY:** To save two million lives? That's not a hard decision.

Thus *Voyager* does not take the expedient position that they (nor the Federation) are responsible for Dreadnought. Instead, the *Voyager* crew is ready to sacrifice itself for moral/ethical reasons.

Voyager episode "The Void" makes an explicit claim of the importance of operating on foundational principles—rejecting pragmatism.[3] *Voyager* is trapped in a void in space, where there is no "matter of any kind." Other ships trapped in the void have taken up the practice of attacking/raiding other trapped ships for supplies as a means of surviving. (*Voyager* bridge crew member: "There are more than 150 ships within scanning range but I'm only detecting life signs on 29 of them.")

A captain from one of the other stranded ships advises *Voyager* to abandon her ethical principles in the void: "Wait a few weeks until your resources start to run out. Morality won't keep your life support systems running." Implying that she would die for her principles, Captain Janeway responds, "I'm sorry, General. There are some compromises I won't make."

Nonetheless, in retrieving stolen supplies, members of *Voyager*'s crew suggest that they take supplies from another ship that never belonged to them. Janeway, however, refuses to act unethically—even while acknowledging other ship captains in the void would not limit themselves by ethical considerations.

> **VOYAGER OFFICER:** I'm detecting large quantities of food on his supply deck.
> **VOYAGER OFFICER:** Maybe we should take it while we have the chance.
> **CAPTAIN JANEWAY:** Is it ours?
> **VOYAGER OFFICER:** No, but our own reserves are running out.
> **VOYAGER OFFICER:** Valen (the commander of the ship in question) wouldn't hesitate to take it from us.
> **CAPTAIN JANEWAY:** No, he wouldn't. We've got what's ours. Reverse course.

After Captain Janeway refused to take other than what was taken from *Voyager*, her most senior officers, Tuvok and Chakotay, approach her about this decision.

> **CHAKOTAY:** We want to be clear about what our policy's going to be while we're here in the void.
> **JANEWAY:** You think we should have taken Valen's food.
> **TUVOK:** Logic suggests we may have to be more opportunistic if we intend to survive.

CHAKOTAY: We may not like Valen's tactics but he and his crew are still alive after five years in here.

In response to the conundrum *Voyager* is seemingly facing in the void (to be ethical or to survive), Janeway looks for answers in the foundational document of the Federation, the Federation Charter.

CHAKOTAY: No section on how to exist in a void.
JANEWAY: No, but I've become convinced that we've got to stick to our principles, not abandon them.
CHAKOTAY: Should the crew be ready to die for those principles?
JANEWAY: If the alternative means becoming thieves and killers ourselves, yes.

Thus Janeway reiterates her willingness to die for her (Federation) principles.

However, in a direct rebuke of pragmatic reasoning, Janeway asserts that principled action leads to the optimal outcome. Specifically, she holds that by behaving in a principled manner, *Voyager* can build social capital among the ships trapped in the void. Through collaboration and solidarity, Janeway argues the ships in the void can work together to escape. In shaping this reasoning, Janeway draws inspiration from the example of the Federation: "The Federation is based on mutual cooperation. The idea that the whole is greater than the sum of its parts. *Voyager* can't survive here alone, but if we form a temporary alliance with other ships maybe we can pool our resources and escape." *Voyager* shares its limited food and medical supplies, as well as joins in common defense, to build trust and establish (what Janeway calls) the "Alliance." Through the Alliance, *Voyager*'s food supplies are enhanced ("One of the crews that joined us had technology that tripled our replicator efficiency . . . we can feed five hundred people a day now using half the power it took us a few days ago.") Led by *Voyager*, the Alliance ships escape the void. Those that refused to become members stay behind.

Villainous Pragmatists

Voyager stands out for the fact that a number of its antagonists are villains (or bad guys) precisely because they are pragmatists—that is, elide moral principles. This sets *Voyager* apart from other science fiction/fantasy genres, where villains are dastardly not because they lack moral principles (per se) but because of their ultimate goals (attaining ill-gotten gain [e.g., stealing], inflicting wanton destruction, seeking revenge, capturing political power, etc.).[4] In the case of *Voyager*, the audience can, broadly speaking, sympathize with its pragmatic antagonists' goals (survival, getting home, arriving at a trade deal, and technological advancement), but the villains are bad guys precisely because they show little/no scruples is seeking to attain these goals. Four *Voyager* episodes are noteworthy for their villainous pragmatists: "Phage" (1995), "Future's End" (1996), "Think Tank" (1999), and "*Equinox*" (1999).

"Phage"

As a seeming critique of neopragmatism, the species known as Vidiians is introduced in the episode "Phage" (1995). The Vidiians suffer from a condition called the phage. The phage destroys the organs of the Vidiians. In response, they steal organs from others to survive. ("We are gathering replacement organs and suitable biomatter. It is the only way we have to fight the phage.") Thus the Vidiians have established an intersubjective agreement[5] that does not respect/recognize the rights of others to their bodies/organs. ("Our society has been ravaged. Thousands die each day. There is no other way for us to survive.") Janeway is dismayed that the Vidiians would accept the practice of organ theft: "I can't begin to understand what your people have gone through. They may have found a way to ignore the moral implications of what you are doing, but I have no such luxury." Janeway will not take back the organs that were stolen from one of her crew because it would result in the death of their current recipient.

"Future's End"

"Future's End" takes place in the late twentieth century—the year 1996. The action of this two-part episode centers on Henry Starling (Ed Begley Jr.). By the time *Voyager* comes into contact with Starling, he is a very wealthy technology wizard, like Steve Jobs and Bill Gates. ("Our Mister Starling has built himself quite a corporate empire. Looks like he's got wealth, celebrity, and an ego to match.") Starling is only able to introduce breakthrough technologies to the twentieth century because years earlier (in 1967) he came upon a spaceship from the future. Over time, Starling was able to pilfer technology from the ship.

Voyager's mission in "Future's End" is to discover why a ship from 1996 sought to travel in time, thereby destroying Earth's solar system in the twenty-ninth century. We learn that it will be Starling that will destroy the solar system when he to tries to go to the twenty-ninth century to retrieve more "new" technology for his commercial ventures. He is no longer able to extract usable technology from the ship he found years earlier. ("I've cannibalized the ship itself as much as I can. There's nothing left to base a commercial product on.")

Janeway warns Starling that his attempt to travel into the future will lead to massive catastrophe. Starling, nevertheless, is determined to pursue his goal. Janeway rebukes Starling for his lack of ethics: "You'd destroy an entire city? [Starling threatens to destroy present-day Los Angeles if Janeway tries to stop him.] You don't care about the future, you don't care about the present. Does anything matter to you, Mister Starling?" Starling feels justified in his means and the risk he is creating because his goal is "The betterment of mankind." More specifically, he is driven by technological advancement (at least for his time period):

> **STARLING:** My products benefit the entire world. Without me there would be no laptops, no Internet, no barcode readers. What's good for Chronowerx [Starling's company] is good for everybody. I can't stop now. One trip to the twenty-ninth century

and I can bring back enough technology to start the next ten computer revolutions.

JANEWAY: In my time, Mister Starling, no human being would dream of endangering the future to gain advantage in the present.

In response, Starling takes an openly pragmatic stance—that is, centered on the short-term: "Captain, the future you're talking about, that's nine hundred years from now. I can't be concerned about that right now. I have a company to run and a whole world full of people waiting for me to make their lives a little bit better." *Voyager* destroys Starling and his ship.

"Think Tank"

In "Think Tank," *Voyager* finds itself being pursued by a species known as the Hazari. It is unable to elude them, and *Voyager* is in serious danger of being destroyed. As they face this peril, an organization that Janeway dubs the "Think Tank" ("a small group of minds") appears, offering *Voyager* the knowledge necessary to escape the Hazari. But in exchange for this knowledge, the Think Tank wants Seven of Nine to join their group. We learn that the Think Tank regularly offers knowledge/help in exchange for some prize (normally knowledge).

MEMBER OF THE THINK TANK: We have helped hundreds of clients. We turned the tide in the war between the Bara Plenum and the Motali Empire. Reignited the red giants of the Zai Cluster. Just recently, we found a cure for the Vidiian phage... Just last month we helped retrieve a Lyridian child's runaway pet. A subspace mesomorph, I might add. We had to invent a whole new scanning technology just to find it.

JANEWAY: And what did you ask for as compensation?

THINK TANK: One of their transgalactic star charts. The best map of the known galaxy ever created. When we helped the citizens of Rivos Five resist the Borg, all we asked for was the recipe for their famous zoth-nut soup.

Janeway probes the Think Tank's moral/ethical boundaries by asking, "Tell me, is there any job you won't do?" The spokesperson for the group (Kurros, played by Jason Alexander [of *Seinfeld* fame]) explains, "We will not participate in the decimation of an entire species, nor will we design weapons of mass destruction."

Nevertheless, the Think Tank has few scruples in seeking to attain prizes—in this case Seven of Nine. (While human, she is a former member of the Borg collective. Borg modifications have made Seven highly intelligent and capable of telepathic communication.) It was the Think Tank that set the Hazari on *Voyager* (by placing a bounty on it). In the end, *Voyager* is able to outmaneuver the Think Tank. But before it is forced to flee, Kurros tells Seven of Nine that she will be dissatisfied living on *Voyager*, and would have been happier with them—living a life of contemplation and knowledge seeking. ("You know you will never be satisfied here among these people.") Seven of Nine, in response, chides the Think Tank for its lack of principles: "Acquiring knowledge is a worthy objective, but its pursuit has obviously not elevated you."

"Equinox"

Arguably the most powerful critique of pragmatism/neopragmatism—that is, prioritizing stability and intersubjective agreement over actual justice—in the *Star Trek* franchise (and perhaps in all US television history) is the two-part *Voyager* episode "*Equinox*" (1999). The *Equinox* is a Federation ship that, like *Voyager*, was pulled into the Delta Quadrant by the Caretaker. The captain of the *Equinox* (Captain Rudy Ransom) explains that its isolation and the damage (and loss of life) the ship suffered has eroded the crew's (and his) moral framework: "When I first realized that we'd be traveling across the Delta Quadrant for the rest of our lives, I told my crew that we had a duty as Starfleet officers to expand our knowledge and uphold our principles. After a couple of years, we started to forget that we were explorers, and there were times when we nearly forgot that we were human beings."

It turns out that the *Equinox* killed an intelligent "nucleagenic" life-form and harvested it as a power source. (These nucleagenic creatures look like glowing bats; Ransom: "We constructed a containment field that would prevent the life-form from vanishing so quickly, but something went wrong.") These life-forms contain "high levels of antimatter."

> **RANSOM:** We examined the remains and discovered it could be converted to enhance our propulsion systems. It was already dead. What would you have done? We traveled over ten thousand light years in less than two weeks. We'd found our salvation. How could we ignore it?
>
> **JANEWAY:** By adhering to the oath you took as Starfleet officers to seek out life, not destroy it.

Ransom defends his actions by pointing to the desperate circumstances that the *Equinox* found herself: "It's easy to cling to principles when you're standing on a vessel with its bulkheads intact, manned by a crew that's not starving."

Janeway rejects this reasoning: "It's never easy, but if we turn our backs on our principles, we stop being human. I'm putting an end to your experiments and you are hereby relieved of your command. You and your crew will be confined to quarters."

Ransom and his crew escape from *Voyager* and resume their journey home. Before they depart, they steal *Voyager*'s force field generator—thereby seemingly dooming *Voyager* to destruction by the nucleagenic life forms that are now seeking revenge for the death caused by the *Equinox* crew.

In part two of "*Equinox*," Captain Ransom and his crew continue to do whatever it takes to reach home. They continue to capture and kill the nucleagenic creatures:

> **EQUINOX OFFICER:** We're going to need more fuel. We've only got enough left to jump another five hundred light years.
>
> **RANSOM:** Fuel. Is that the euphemism we're using now? You mean we need to kill more life forms.
>
> **OFFICER:** Several more.

Seven of Nine was on *Equinox* as it fled. Ransom tries to entice her to join his crew by arguing, "Janeway clung to her morality at the expense of her crew." Seven of Nine refuses and will not give the *Equinox* vital information. The decision is made to forcibly extract the information, even though doing so will cause Seven of Nine permanent and massive brain damage. (Equinox doctor: "I'm going to extract her cortical array. It contains an index of her memory engrams, but once I've removed it, her higher brain functions, language, cognitive skills will be severely damaged.")

Janeway is determined to capture Ransom and his crew: "You're right, I am angry. I'm damned angry. He's a Starfleet captain, and he's decided to abandon everything this uniform stands for. He's out there right now . . . torturing and murdering innocent life-forms just to get home a little quicker. I'm not going to stand for it. I'm going to hunt him down no matter how long it takes, no matter what the cost. If you want to call that a vendetta, go right ahead."

Voyager captures one of *Equinox*'s crew, and in order to get him to cooperate, Janeway comes close to letting the nucleagenic creatures kill him. (He relents in time to save himself.)

Captain Janeway communicates with the nucleagenic creatures and enlists their help in stopping *Equinox*. Janeway explains to the creatures: "We have rules for behavior. The *Equinox* has broken those rules by killing your species. It's our duty to stop them." The creatures demand, "Give us the *Equinox*. Give us the *Equinox!*" ("They insist on destroying the ones who are responsible.") In the face of Commander Tuvok's objection ("We will punish them according to our own rules. They will be imprisoned. They will lose their freedom"), Janeway agrees to deliver *Equinox* to the creatures. In the denouement of "*Equinox*," Ransom and his ship are destroyed.

As *Voyager*'s crew are ostensibly acting as paragons of virtue and morality—willing to die (and even kill) for their ethics—the politics of the developing world is (metaphorically) conveyed. While *Voyager* is traveling through the Delta Quadrant, hostility,[6] authoritarian politics, religiosity,[7] scientific obscurantism,[8] and military adventurism[9] is depicted. The most significant, in my estimation, of the *Voyager* episodes that convey one of these motifs is "Resistance"—discussed in the next section. Perhaps the most disconcerting feature of the metaphorical politics portrayed in *Voyager* involves race relations. Specifically, the argument is made that racial hate in the developing world is so deeply embedded that politics in this region are hopelessly unstable. This neoconservative argument is centered on the Kazon and is sharply made in the episode "Alliances" (1996).

Politics of the Developing World

"Resistance"

"Resistance" (1995) is noteworthy because it depicts a planet with an authoritarian regime, where a heavy-handed police/military presence is evident in poor neighborhoods. Moreover, the regime inflicts torture—as Tuvok is tortured for information. The stark and powerful depiction of authoritarian regimes is something that *The Next Generation* generally avoided. Thus in one episode, an uprising on a Klingon-controlled world is at the center of the action, but the subject peoples are never shown, and their conditions and treatment by the Klingons is never depicted.[10] In another *Next Generation* episode ("The High Ground" 1990), an insurgency on a planet is at the center of the action. But while the rebels "are demanding autonomy and self-determination for their homeland," no effort is made to explore their demands or the reasons underlying them. To show an oppressive Klingon regime or to depict one on "The High Ground" (1990) is to implicate the Federation (the United States) in these repressive systems. The Federation is a long-standing military/political ally of the Klingons. In "The High Ground," the point is made that the Federation maintains active relations with the governing (putatively repressive) regime. ("Although nonaligned, the planet has enjoyed a long trading relationship with the Federation.")

The most significant treatment of a brutal regime in *Next Generation* involves the Cardassians. The Cardassians lure and capture Captain Picard. In an effort to gain his cooperation, Picard is tortured by the Cardassians.[11] With regards to potentially critiquing Federation (US) foreign policy, more germane is the Cardassian multidecade occupation of the planet Bajor. The Federation and Cardassians were recently at war and maintain an uneasy peace. The criticism that is leveled at the Federation is that it stands idly by as the Cardassians occupied and brutalized Bajor. Hence the argument/critique is not that the Federation fosters/sponsors oppressive/repressive regimes (as the United States does) but that it does not intervene to stop such regimes maintained by hostile governments. A Bajorian leader renders the following criticism: "The Federation is pledged not to interfere in the internal affairs of others. How convenient that must be for you, to turn a deaf ear to those who suffer behind a line on a map."[12] *Deep Space Nine* is centered on the Federation protecting Bajor from potential Cardassian aggression postoccupation.

Thus the *Voyager* episode "Resistance" is significant insofar as it powerfully portrays repressive government policies. In the case of *The Next Generation* and the Cardassian occupation of Bajor, what the audience sees is not the occupation regime but a refugee camp composed of Bajorans fleeing the occupation.[13] "Resistance" is also noteworthy in that the action takes place in the Delta Quadrant. Hence the oppressive regime depicted holds no moral/ethical implications for the Federation.

The Kazon

During the first two seasons of *Voyager*, the prime nemesis is the Kazon. The racial overtones surrounding the Kazon are hard to ignore. The Kazon are brown/red skinned and have dreadlocks (see Figure 10.1). They are divided into sects (tribes). Additionally, the Kazon have a rigid patriarchy—the fact that Janeway is a woman hampers efforts to make peace ("I won't have a woman dictate terms to me" ["Alliances"]). The audience is introduced

Figure 10.1 Kazon leaders

to the Kazon (as noted previously) during the series pilot ("Caretaker"), as they are determined to overrun the Ocampa. The Ocampa are fair skinned and live only to be nine years of age. Hence the Kazon want to pillage (and seemingly do worse to) a society whose members have the chronological age of young children.

In part because Captain Janeway destroyed the Caretaker Array (as noted earlier), the Kazon persist in trying to capture *Voyager*. Most of *Voyager*'s dealings with the Kazon involve the sect known as Nistrim—who plot, scheme, and attack over several episodes in an effort to commandeer *Voyager* and its advanced technology.[14] In the denouement of *Voyager*'s involvement with the Kazon, the Nistrim finally take control of *Voyager*—stranding the crew on a barren/hostile planet, where crew members do perish ("Basics" 1996). One key factor in allowing Janeway and company to regain control of *Voyager* involves a murderous sociopath who was part of the Maquis that was brought into the *Voyager* crew. After it was discovered that this person murdered another crew member, he (Ensign Lon Suder) was permanently interned in his quarters ("Meld" 1996). Now that the Kazon-Nistrim are in control of the ship, the white-skinned Suder is unleashed and massacres virtually all the brown/red-skinned Kazon on *Voyager*. A case of "white hate" being given dramatic vent?

A more obvious, and more important, political message involving the Kazon is made in the episode "Alliances." This episode can be viewed as a comment on South African politics. Interestingly, this is arguably the second *Star Trek* episode that treats South Africa. The original series episode, "Cloud Minders," is ostensibly a commentary on the South African apartheid system. It is noteworthy that "Cloud Minders" (1969) concludes on an optimistic note—indicating that racial harmony can be achieved in South Africa (and presumably between blacks/whites throughout the developing world.) "Alliances" ends on a much darker and highly pessimistic stance, indicating that racial hate/divisions simply run too deep in the developing world to arrive at harmonious social relations.

Voyager meets the Trabe in "Alliances." The Trabe leader explains that, like *Voyager*, they are being attacked by the Kazon. As a result of this ceaseless hostility, the Trabe cannot even settle on a planet and instead are forced to live in wondering convoys of ships. We learn that the source of the Kazon's hostility toward the Trabe (who are fair skinned [see Figure 10.2]) stems from the fact that, in the past, the Trabe maintained a caste system wherein the Kazon were brutally treated. The Trabe leader (Mabus) acknowledges the harsh treatment meted out to the Kazon under their rule. This ultimately led to the Kazon violently overthrowing the Trabe social order: "The Trabe treated [the Kazon] like animals—fenced them in, encouraged them to fight amongst themselves so they wouldn't turn on us, and sat by while they turned into a violent, angry army. When they finally realized we were their true enemy, we didn't stand a chance." We are further told that the Kazon uprising occurred over a generation ago, but they are still determined to "punish" the Trabe:

Figure 10.2 Trabe leader

> **VOYAGER OFFICER:** It happened over thirty years ago and the Kazon are still trying to punish you?
>
> **MABUS:** Remarkable, isn't it? Most of the Trabe who persecuted the Kazon are either dead or old men by now. Most of us were children when the uprising occurred, and our children are innocent, but the Kazon's desire for revenge is as strong as ever.

Ultimately, Janeway and Mabus agree to an alliance for purposes of achieving a negotiated settlement with the Kazon. *Voyager* and the Trabe call for a conference with the leaders of all the Kazon sects in order to establish a lasting peace. Kazon hate toward the Trabe, however, is seemingly too deeply embedded to allow for an effective treaty. One of the Kazon leaders declares, "The Trabe have always wanted peace for themselves, but we paid the price. They lived in luxury and we lived in squalor and misery." Another Kazon leader describes the Trabe as "the greatest villains this quadrant has ever known."

It is the Trabe, however, who brought a murderous intent to the conference, as they execute a plot to kill all the Kazon leaders at the meeting—which Janeway and *Voyager* foils. Trabe hate is just as deeply embedded: "You don't know the Kazon. There's no dealing with them. Violence is all they understand."

Conclusion

Star Trek: Voyager is metaphorically lost in the developing world. This allows its creators to explore motifs and themes different than those dealt with in other iterations of the *Star Trek* franchise. The strength of *Voyager*—in my view—as a piece of art/literature is the deep commitment to ethics and morality that Janeway and her crew display throughout the series. Of course, this is particularly admirable because losing one's morality/ethics is presumably easy when one is in a very difficult circumstance, like *Voyager* found herself. Thus *Voyager* offers an argument for moral/principled behavior and a rejection of pragmatism even in demoralizing and dangerous circumstances. Episodes like "The Void" very powerfully deliver this argument. Similarly, when confronted with daunting circumstances, people may construct intersubjective agreements that result in the victimization (death/murder) of others. *Voyager* is particularly critical of an approach to politics that evades ethics and solely relies on intersubjective agreement to attain stability/success. This critique is especially pointed in the episodes "Phage," "Future's End," and "*Equinox*."

While *Voyager* is optimistic on the ability (indeed the need) for Americans/Westerns to behave morally/ethically, it is pessimistic with regard to politics in the developing world. Reading the Delta Quadrant as a metaphor for the developing world, *Voyager* stands out for the fictional species the Kazon (dark skinned with dread locks). The Kazon wantonly assail the fair-skinned Ocampa, and persistently seek to take/steal *Voyager*—advanced (Western) technology. Moreover, the episode "Alliances" conveys black/white relations in the developing world as inherently contentious and inevitably destabilizing. This is consistent with neoconservative biases/reasoning.

CONCLUSION

Star Trek
From Cold War to Post–Cold War

As noted in the Introduction, the *Star Trek* franchise represents something of a natural experiment—where one iteration of the franchise is produced during the height of the Cold War, in the midst of the Civil Rights era and the student protest movements (Chapter 1), and later iterations are produced during the politically conservative Reagan Era and the denouement of the Cold War (Chapter 3). In comparing *Star Trek* during the Cold War and after the Cold War, we can note an outright rejection of any triumphalism of the West's victory over the Soviet Union.

Instead, the optimism of the original series gives way to pessimism in *The Next Generation*. This shift into pessimism is the result of the fact that *Star Trek* is not pro-American but promodernism. *Star Trek* correctly envisioned that the end of the Soviet Union would not settle the debate over the future political course of the planet ("the end of history"). Quite the contrary, *Star Trek* presciently foresaw that the demise of the Soviet project would see a resurgence of traditionalism (patriarchy, ethnic identity as the basis of political legitimacy, and political religion), which would invoke greater (not less) global political instability and conflict (Chapter 4).

In this way, *Star Trek* views Reaganism (and its victory over the Soviet Union) as part of the demoralization of the modern world-system. Philosophically, it represents a move away from justice (liberal humanism) and principled action, and toward the prioritization of stability—that is, pragmatism and intersubjective agreement (Chapters 2 and 10). Put differently, globalism (modernism)—in the absence of the social justice politics of the New Deal or Soviet socialism—prompts cynicism and a turn to traditionalism by communities, in part to protect themselves from what amounts to socially and politically corrosive neoliberalism (Chapter 2). *Star Trek* in the 1990s critiqued Nazism as a form of traditionalism and warned about the dangers of this extreme traditionalism.

Significantly, while *Star Trek* of the 1960s focused on criticisms of US foreign policy and meditations on incorporating premodern societies into the modern world system, later *Star Trek* focuses on the threat of dictatorship, torture, and military adventurism. Presumably, in a world system seemingly permanently cleaved into multiple civilizations, the perennial security threat that exclusionist nation-states (civilizations) creates/fosters an environment where militarism and authoritarianism can thrive (Chapters 6, 7, and 9). This is a prime caution of *Star Trek* of the 1980s and beyond.

Star Trek and the Cold War

Significantly, in the pilot of *Next Generation*, Captain Picard calls the Cold War "nonsense" ("Encounter at Farpoint" 1987). Later in the first season, Picard again calls the Cold War "nonsense" ("Lonely among Us" 1987). From the perspective of modernism, the Cold War was nonsense. Both the Soviet Union and the United States were modernist projects. Even from the perspective of the current period, it may be hard to understand what the Cold War was about—whether the modern economy was going to be controlled by the state or private individuals. Especially considering that the height of the Cold War coincided with the state-managerial outlook of the New Deal,[1] the fact that the United States and the Soviet Union came close to destroying the world is somewhat baffling. The incredulity surrounding the Cold War is conveyed in the original series episode "Errand of Mercy" (1967). When Captain Kirk insists that the Federation and the Klingons have the right to go to war, the Organian spokesman points out the absurdity of his position: "To wage war, Captain [Kirk]? To kill millions of innocent people? To destroy life on a planetary scale? Is that what you're defending [i.e., arguing for]?"

While *Star Trek* the original series indicates that peace is entirely possible between the United States and the Soviet Union (Chapter 1), it casts a prominent component of traditionalism (premodernism), theocracy (political religion), as dangerous and stunting human intellectual development. Hence political religion (theocracy) is something to be avoided. "All Our Yesterdays" (1969) is an episode where Captain Kirk is transported back to the Puritan period, and comes close to being burned alive for being a "witch." When the *Enterprise* (in *The Next Generation*) is involved in rekindling religious beliefs among a group of primitive people, the point is made "that religion could degenerate into inquisitions, holy wars, chaos" ("Who Watches the Watchers" 1989).

Perhaps the strongest critique of theocracy in the history of American television is posited in "The Apple" (1967). Significantly, the people of Vaal are quite dimwitted, as they are completely dependent on Vaal and unable to take care of themselves. Kirk makes the following observation of the natives: "These people aren't living, they're existing. They don't create, they don't produce, they don't even think. They exist to service a machine [i.e., a god]."

Star Trek, Traditionalism, and the Post–Cold War

With neoliberalism serving as the global hegemonic paradigm in the aftermath of the Cold War, *Star Trek*'s creators foresee the resurgence of traditionalism throughout the world (Chapter 3). The *Star Trek* series *Deep Space Nine* (1993–99) is especially centered on the danger and dysfunction of religion in politics. Much of this series deals with the Bajorans. The Bajorans are governed by a theocracy, with religious figures composing the government.

The Bajoran Kai is both the highest religious and political official. The legislative body is the Vedek Assembly. A Vedek is akin to a priest or monk. Captain Sisko in *Deep Space Nine* is recognized by the Bajorans as the Emissary to the Prophets. The Prophets are the Bajorans' gods, and thus Sisko is deemed their direct representative. The Emissary, through his pronouncements, can profoundly shape Bajor's government and society. In one episode, Sisko, through revelation from the Prophets, decides that Bajor should not join the Federation, and this alone reverses the government's decision to do so.[2] Another episode has Sisko replaced as the Emissary, and the new emissary reinstates the Bajoran caste system.[3] Perhaps the most disturbing manifestation of religion in all *Star Trek* occurs in "Covenant" (1998), whereby a Bajoran cult forms around the evil version of the Prophets (referred to as the Pah wraiths). The leader of this cult (Dukat) rapes one of the members, impregnates her as a result, and attempts to kill her to cover this up. He finally orders his followers to commit mass suicide, and they obey. (They are stopped.) As part of the denouement of *Deep Space Nine*, the Bajorian Kai (Wynn) becomes a follower of the evil Pah wraiths.

A great deal of *Deep Space Nine* revolves around the Dominion and the Federation/Klingon/Romulan war against it. The Dominion (from the Gamma Quadrant) is a violently ruthless empire populated by genetically engineered and mass-produced technicians (Vorta) and soldiers (Jemh'dar) who are totally subservient to the Founders (Changelings capable of adopting any shape). During season five, the Dominion invades the Alpha Quadrant intent on conquering the Federation (along with the entire quadrant) and eradicating the Earth's population.[4]

Significantly, the Dominion's social order is founded on the idea that the Founders are gods. Hence both the Vorta and the Jemh'dar view them as deities. In their religious fervor, the Jemh'dar commit kamikaze-style suicide during battle,[5] and the Vorta commit suicide upon the command of the Founders. (The Vorta are breed with suicide pills implanted behind their ear, which they can engage on command.)[6]

Post–Cold War Politics of the Developing World

Star Trek suggests that in the absence of a general framework advocating social justice, interventions into the developing world are bound to fail. Whereas Kirk in "Cloud Minders" (1969) is ostensibly successful in his effort at reforming "Ardana," *Star Trek*'s creators in the series *Enterprise* issue a caution against interventions in the domestic politics of other planets/societies in "Cogenitor" (2003). *Star Trek: Voyager* indicates the extreme degree to which relations between the developed and underdeveloped world could deteriorate, where the starship *Voyager* is stranded in the Delta Quadrant—that is, the so-called Third World. *Voyager* introduces the Kazon, with which peace is ostensibly not possible (Chapter 10).

With hate and animosity ostensibly deeply embedded in the world system, it is almost inevitable that democratic norms will come under threat as societies increasingly prioritize security concerns over democratic precepts (Chapters 5, 6, 7, and 9). Moreover, even as the global warming crisis is evidently coming to a head, the modern world-system is predominately focused on the politics of hegemony and seemingly deaf to impending ecological disaster (Chapter 8).

Democracy in Retreat

With global relations hopelessly marked by animosity and mutual suspicions, authoritarianism and militarism become more and more the norm. As *Star Trek* notes, the fact that national security (and not progressive politics) has become the key concern of the global system means that even the so-called advanced democracies are susceptible to antidemocratic (authoritarian) outcomes and preemptive empire building (Chapters 5, 6, 7, and 9). *Deep Space Nine* specifically posits that a "state within the state" is a common practice throughout the world system. For the Federation, the state within the state is Section 31.

Section 31

Deep Space Nine introduces Section 31—a secret intelligence agency that is outside the law. It is described in the following terms: "We don't submit reports or ask for approval for specific operations, if that's what you mean. We're an autonomous department." In another instance, Section 31 is cast as "judge, jury and executioner." Section 31 justifies its existence and means in terms consonant with national security: "We deal with threats to the Federation that jeopardize its very survival . . . If you knew how many lives we've saved, I think you'd agree that the ends do justify the means."[7]

Section 31 operatives have no scruples. Prior to the advent of open hostilities between the Dominion and the Federation, it infects the Changeling Odo (Chief of Security for *Deep Space Nine*) with a deadly disease in the hopes that he will infect the other Changelings (the Founders).[8] (While Odo is a Changeling like the Founders, he rejects the Dominion and allies himself with the Federation.) Section 31 kidnaps a Starfleet officer (Julian Bashir, Chief Medical officer of *Deep Space Nine*), tortures him (through sleep deprivation), and psychologically disorients him into believing he is a Dominion spy. When Bashir states in disbelief, "Is it possible that the Federation would condone this kind of activity?" A *Deep Space Nine* crew member cynically responds, "I find it hard to believe that they wouldn't. Every other great power has a unit like Section 31"[9]—an all-powerful, lawless secret security organization. The 2013 *Star Trek* movie, *Into Darkness*, has Section 31 conduct a false-flag operation to initiate war with the Klingons.

We learn that the Cardassians also operate a secret, autonomous intelligence service—the Obsidian Order. In theory, the Obsidian Order "answer[s] to the political authority . . . just as the military does. In practice, [they] both run [their] own affairs" (*Deep Space Nine*, "Defiant" 1994). Later, it is discovered that the Cardassian Obsidian Order and the Romulan Tal Shiar (another intelligence agency) secretly constructed a fleet of military ships and unilaterally undertake an attack on the Dominion home world. ("If you attack the Dominion . . . You'll be taking Romulus and Cassandra into war" [*Deep Space Nine*, "Improbable Cause" 1995].)

Arguably, the most extreme and dangerous/destructive example of traditionalism and militarism/authoritarianism in human history is that of the German Nazi regime. *Star Trek* warns that Nazism and fascism pose profound threats for humanity and civilization.

Nazism as Traditionalism and Global Threat

Star Trek: Voyager casts Nazism as a traditionalist project. In "The Killing Game" (1998), a German Nazi officer emphasizes the putative greatness of Germany's past to justify its push for worldwide conquest:

> He's never embraced the Fuhrer or his vision. One does not cooperate with decadent forms of life, one hunts them down and eliminates them. The Kommandant speaks of civilization. The ancient Romans were civilized. The Jews are civilized. But in all its moral decay, Rome fell to the spears of our ancestors as the Jews are falling now. Look at our destiny! The field of red, the purity of German blood. The blazing white circle of the sun that sanctified that blood. No one can deny us, no power on Earth or beyond. Not the Christian Savior, not the God of the Jews. We are driven by the very force that gives life to the universe itself!

The kind of hypernationalism (traditionalism) advocated by the likes of the Nazis is extremely dangerous in the modern era. Therefore, the parable of the Xindi and the fact that they destroyed their own planet must be taken seriously.

Conclusion

The *Star Trek* franchise is significant insofar as it spans the Cold War and the post–Cold War period. As a result, the franchise lends credible insight into the politics and policies of the world system throughout much of the modern era. In the original series, produced in the late 1960s, an optimism about modernity is evident—as *Star Trek*'s creators argue that Soviet/US relations could/should readily improve. The original series is not entirely sanguine, however, as it provides critical meditations on US foreign policy and the wisdom of imposing modernism on the premodern regions of the world.

My argument is that the *Star Trek* franchise can only be legitimately read as promodernism, not pro-American. Thus *Next Generation* laments that the Cold War occurred at all, referring to it as "nonsense" on two separate occasions. *Star Trek*, beginning in the 1980s, can be critiqued for turning away from criticisms of US foreign policy and for proffering negative portrayals of peoples of the developing world (Chapters 3 and 10). Nevertheless, my view is that the franchise takes arguably an even deeper critical stance on the politics of the world system in the ongoing Reagan Era.[10] More specifically, the collapse of the New Deal and Soviet socialism (as well as the institution of the neoliberalism on the global scale) has caused a crisis of confidence in modernism and a concomitant resurgence of traditionalism. In a context where meaningful worldwide political unity is less likely than ever, national security is taking political priority. Under this circumstance democracy is under threat, and extreme forms of nationalism (Nazism) appear as ever more likely to become manifest. In the worst case scenario, the planet itself could fall victim to the geopolitical machinations that seemingly predominate the current world-system (the fate of the planet Xindi). The *Star Trek* franchise is analytically useful/insightful, as it allows viewers to reason through these momentous issues. Through the Nazis, the Klingons, the Bajorans, the Dominion, the Kazon, the Cardassians, the Romulans, Section 31, and the Xindi, the *Star Trek* franchise shows us how politics worldwide is becoming more and more regressive and devastatingly dangerous.

Notes

Introduction

1. Theodor W. Adorno, *The Culture Industry: Selected Essays on Mass Culture*, ed. J. M. Bernstein (New York: Routledge Classics, 2001); Howard Eiland and Michael W. Jennings, *Walter Benjamin: A Critical Life* (Cambridge, MA: Belnap, 2014).
2. Daniel Leonard Bernardi, Star Trek *and History: Race-ing toward a White Future* (New Brunswick, NJ: Rutgers University Press, 1998).
3. *Star Trek* (original series), "The Ultimate Computer," 1968.
4. Bernardi, Star Trek *and History*, 130.
5. Ibid., 134.
6. Ibid., 127.
7. Ibid., 136.
8. Ibid., 116.
9. For example, see Robin Roberts, *Sexual Generations: "Star Trek: The Next Generation" and Gender* (Chicago: University of Illinois Press, 1999).
10. David Greven, *Gender and Sexuality in* Star Trek*: Allegories of Desire in the Television Series and Films* (Jefferson, NC: MacFarland, 2009).
11. The animated television series *Justice League (Unlimited)* is sharply critical of US foreign policy in the contemporary period. George A. Gonzalez, "*Justice League* (*Unlimited*) and the Politics of Globalization," *Journal of Foundation: The International Review of Science Fiction* 45, no. 123 (forthcoming 2016).
12. Jacques Rancière, *Aesthetics and Its Discontents*, trans. Steve Corcoran (Malden, MA: Polity, 2009).

Chapter 1

1. Rick Worland, "Captain Kirk: Cold Warrior," *Journal of Popular Film and Television* 16, no. 3 (1988): 110.

2. Mark P. Lagon, "'We Owe It to Them to Interfere:' *Star Trek* and U.S. Statecraft in the 1960s and the 1990s," in *Political Science Fiction*, ed. Donald M. Hassler and Clyde Wilcox (Columbia: University of South Carolina Press, 1997), 235.
3. Keith M. Booker, "The Politics of *Star Trek*," in *The Essential Science Fiction Reader*, ed. J. P. Telotte (Lexington: University Press of Kentucky, 2008), 197.
4. Nicholas Evan Sarantakes, "Cold War Pop Culture and the Image of U.S. Foreign Policy: The Perspective of the Original *Star Trek* Series," *Journal of Cold War Studies* 7, no. 4 (2005), 74–103.
5. Modernism is a set of normative values that privileges reason and secularism, as opposed to obscurantism and political religion (i.e., theocracy). Peter Childs, *Modernism* (New York: Routledge, 2007).
6. Jacques Rancière, *Aesthetics and Its Discontents*, trans. Steve Corcoran (Malden, MA: Polity, 2009).
7. Daniel Bernardi, Star Trek *and History: Race-ing toward a White Future* (Newark, NJ: Rutgers University Press, 1998).
8. The invocation of Abraham Lincoln is arguably reflective of a globalist outlook insofar as his persona is admired worldwide as a great liberator. Richard Carwardine and Jay Sexton, eds., *The Global Lincoln* (New York: Oxford University Press, 2011).
9. Roland Vegso, *The Naked Communist: Cold War Modernism and the Politics of Popular Culture* (New York: Fordham University Press, 2013).

    Star Trek's creators appear to challenge the putative normative argument that ostensibly served as the basis of the Cold War in "Errand of Mercy" (1967) when a Klingon commander says to Captain Kirk: "You of the Federation, you are much like us."

    KIRK: We're nothing like you. We're a democratic body.

    KLINGON: Come now. I'm not referring to minor ideological differences. I mean that we are similar as a species . . . Two tigers, predators, hunters, killers, and it is precisely that which makes us great.

10. *The Next Generation*, "Encounter at Farpoint," 1987.
11. Kirk tells the Yangs that the United States Constitution "was not written for chiefs or kings or warriors or the rich and powerful, but for all the people!"

12. While Nicholas Evan Sarantakes thoughtfully acknowledges that *Star Trek* cannot be reduced to pro-American propaganda, he nevertheless holds that "in episodes involving foreign policy, the Klingons represent the Soviet Union." Sarantakes, "Cold War Pop Culture," 78.
13. Christian Domenig, "Klingons: Going Medieval on You," in *Star Trek and History*, ed. Nancy R. Reagin (Hoboken, NJ: John Wiley & Sons, 2013).
14. Jacqueline S. Ismael, *Kuwait: Dependency and Class in a Rentier State* (Gainesville: University of Florida Press, 1993); Giovanni Arrighi with Beverly Silver, *Chaos and Governance in the Modern World System* (Minneapolis: University of Minnesota Press, 1999); Immanuel Wallerstein, *World-Systems Analysis: An Introduction* (Durham: Duke University Press, 2004); Harold Kerbo, *World Poverty: The Roots of Global Inequality and the Modern World System* (New York: McGraw-Hill, 2005).
15. John Dickie, *Cosa Nostra: A History of the Sicilian Mafia* (New York: Palgrave Macmillan, 2005); Selwyn Raab, *Five Families: The Rise, Decline, and Resurgence of America's Most Powerful Mafia Empires* (New York: St. Martin's Griffin, 2006); Letizia Paoli, *Mafia Brotherhoods: Organized Crime, Italian Style* (New York: Oxford University Press, 2008).
16. Booker, "Politics of *Star Trek*," 205–6.
17. Ibid.
18. Ibid., 202–3.
19. Lagon, "'We Owe It to Them to Interfere,'" 246.
20. Michael E. Latham, *Modernization as Ideology: American Social Science and "Nation Building" in the Kennedy Era* (Chapel Hill: University of North Carolina Press, 2000); and *The Right Kind of Revolution: Modernization, Development, and U.S. Foreign Policy from the Cold War to the Present* (Cornell University Press, 2010); Nils Gilman, *Mandarins of the Future: Modernization Theory in Cold War America* (Baltimore, MD: John Hopkins University Press, 2007).
21. Arthur M. Schlesinger Jr., *Robert Kennedy and His Times* (Boston: Houghton Mifflin, 1978); Robert J. McMahon, *The Cold War: A Very Short Introduction* (New York: Oxford University Press, 2003); Jason K. Duncan, *John F. Kennedy: The Spirit of Cold War Liberalism* (New York: Routledge, 2013).

22. Expressing the selfless politics of twenty-third-century earth (speaking to Edith Keeler in 1930s in New York City), Captain Kirk explains, "Let me help. A hundred years or so from now, I believe, a famous novelist will write a classic using that theme. He'll recommend those three words even over I love you" ("City on the Edge of Forever" 1967).

Chapter 2

1. Jennifer E. Porter, "To Boldly Go: *Star Trek* Convention Attendance as Pilgrimage," in Star Trek *and Sacred Ground: Explorations of* Star Trek, *Religion, and American Culture*, ed. Jennifer E. Porter and Darcess L. McLaren (Albany: State University of New York Press, 1999); Karen Anijar, *Teaching Toward the 24th Century:* Star Trek *as Social Curriculum* (New York: Routledge, 2000); Lincoln Geraghty, *Living with* Star Trek: *American Culture and the* Star Trek *Universe* (New York: I. B. Tauris, 2007).
2. Karin Blair, *Meaning in* Star Trek (New York: Warner, 1977); and "The Garden in the Machine: The Why of *Star Trek*," *Journal of Popular Culture* 13, no. 2 (1979): 310–19; Ina Rae Hark, "*Star Trek* and Television's Moral Universe," *Extrapolation* 20, no. 1 (1979): 20–37; Jane Elizabeth Ellington and Joseph W. Critelli, "Analysis of a Modern Myth: The *Star Trek* Series," *Extrapolation* 24, no. 3 (1983): 241–50; Taylor Harrison et al., eds., *Enterprise Zones: Critical Positions on* Star Trek (Boulder, CO: Westview, 1996); Richard Hanley, *The Metaphysics of* Star Trek, *or, Is Data Human?* (New York: Basic Books, 1997); Jon Wagner and Jan Lundeen, *Deep Space and Sacred Time:* Star Trek *in the American Mythos* (Westport, CT: Praeger, 1998); Robin Roberts, *Sexual Generations: "*Star Trek: The Next Generation*" and Gender* (Chicago: University of Illinois Press, 1999); Nicholas Evan Sarantakes, "Cold War Pop Culture and the Image of U.S. Foreign Policy: The Perspective of the Original *Star Trek* Series," *Journal of Cold War Studies* 7, no 4 (2005): 74–103; David Greven, *Gender and Sexuality in* Star Trek: *Allegories of Desire in the Television Series and Films* (Jefferson, NC: MacFarland, 2009).
3. John Corry, "Something about *Star Trek* Talks to Every Man," *New York Times*, June 10, 1984, H25.
4. Carlin Romano, *America the Philosophical* (New York: Simon & Schuster, 2012).

5. William Tyrrell, "*Star Trek* as Myth and Television as Mythmaker," *Journal of Popular Culture* 10, no. 4 (1977): 711–19; Lincoln Geraghty, ed., *The Influence of Star Trek on Television, Film and Culture* (Jefferson, NC: MacFarland, 2007).
6. Gregory Claeys, ed., *The Cambridge Companion to Utopian Literature* (New York: Cambridge University Press, 2010).
7. Donald M. Hassler and Clyde Wilcox, eds., *New Boundaries in Political Science Fiction* (Columbia: University of South Carolina Press, 2008).
8. Freedman, Carl, "Science Fiction and Utopia: A Historico-Philosophical Overview," in *Learning from Other Worlds*, ed. Patrick Parrinder (Durham: Duke University Press, 2001), 74, emphasis in original; also see Tom Moylan, ed., *Demand the Impossible: Science Fiction and the Utopian Imagination* (New York: Methuen, 1986).
9. Peter Singer, *Marx: A Very Short Introduction* (New York: Oxford University Press, 2001).
10. Gérard Klein, "From the Images of Science to Science Fiction," in *Learning from Other Worlds*, ed. Patrick Parrinder (Durham: Duke University Press, 2001).
11. Alan Shapiro, Star Trek: *Technologies of Disappearance* (Berlin: Avinus, 2004).
12. *Star Trek,* the original series, "Space Seed," 1967.
13. "The Borg gain knowledge through assimilation. What they can't assimilate, they can't understand" ("Scorpion" 1997; *Star Trek: Voyager*).
14. During *The Next Generation* episode "Attached" (1993), it is noted that Earth's world government was formed in 2150.
15. Ibid.
16. V. I. Lenin, *Imperialism: The Highest Stage of Capitalism* (New York: Pluto, 1996 [1917]).
17. Christopher Read, *Lenin: A Revolutionary Life* (New York: Routledge, 2005).
18. Ulrich Beck and Ciaran Cronin, *Cosmopolitan Vision* (Cambridge: Polity, 2006).
19. Daryl Johnson and Mark Potok, *Right-Wing Resurgence: How a Domestic Terrorist Threat Is Being Ignored* (Lanham, MD: Rowman & Littlefield, 2012); Joseph E. Uscinski and Joseph M. Parent, *American Conspiracy Theories* (New York: Oxford University Press, 2014).

20. Mark Mozower, *Governing the World: The History of an Idea* (New York: Penguin Press, 2012), 26–30.
21. Frank Biermann, *Earth System Governance: World Politics in the Anthropocene* (Cambridge, MA: MIT Press, 2014).
22. Mark Maslin, *Global Warming: A Very Short Introduction* (New York: Oxford University Press, 2009); James Lawrence Powell, *The Inquisition of Climate Science* (New York: Columbia University Press, 2011).
23. Justin Gillis, "Ending Its Summer Melt, Arctic Sea Ice Sets a New Low That Leads to Warnings," *New York Times*, September 20, 2012, A8; Jason Mark, "Climate Fiction Fantasy," *New York Times*, December 10, 2014, A35.
24. John M. Broder, "Climate Talks Yield Commitment to Ambitious, but Unclear, Actions," *New York Times*, December 9, 2012, A13.
25. Justin Gillis and John M. Broder, "With Carbon Dioxide Emissions at Record High, Worries on How to Slow Warming," *New York Times*, December 3, 2012, A6.
26. Kurkpatrick Dorsey, *Whales and Nations: Environmental Diplomacy on the High Seas* (Seattle: University of Washington Press, 2013).
27. John Firor and Judith Jacobsen, *The Crowded Greenhouse: Population, Climate Change, and Creating a Sustainable World* (New Haven, CT: Yale University Press, 2002).
28. Walter K. Dodds, *Humanity's Footprint: Momentum, Impact, and Our Global Environment* (New York: Columbia University Press, 2008); Thomas Robertson, *The Malthusian Moment: Global Population Growth and the Birth of American Environmentalism* (New Brunswick, NJ: Rutgers University Press, 2012); Kerryn Higgs, *Collision Course: Endless Growth on a Finite Planet* (Cambridge, MA: MIT Press, 2014).
29. Matthew Connelly, *Fatal Misconception: The Struggle to Control World Population* (Cambridge, MA: Harvard University Press, 2008).
30. Michael Egan, *Barry Commoner and the Science of Survival: The Remaking of American Environmentalism* (Cambridge, MA: MIT Press, 2009); Paul Sabin, *The Bet: Paul Ehrlich, Julian, and Our Gamble over Earth's Future* (New Haven, CT: Yale University Press, 2013).
31. Eric D. Smith, *Globalization, Utopia, and Postcolonial Science Fiction* (New York: Palgrave Macmillan, 2012).

32. Arthur M. Schlesinger, *The Disuniting of America: Reflections on a Multicultural Society* (New York: W. W. Norton, 1988); Derek Rubin and Jaap Verheul, eds., *American Multiculturalism after 9/11: Transatlantic Perspectives* (Amsterdam: Amsterdam University Press, 2010); Denis Lacorne, *Religion in America: A Political History* (New York: Columbia University Press, 2001); Alexis de Tocqueville, *Democracy in America*, trans. Harvey C. Mansfield and Delba Winthrop (Chicago: University of Chicago Press, 2011 [1835]).
33. Gene Roddenberry et al., *Star Trek: Nemesis*, dir. Stuart Baird, 2002.
34. *The Next Generation*, "Transfigurations," 1992.
35. Harlow Giles Unger, *Lafayette* (Hoboken, NJ: Wiley, 2003); Craig Nelson, *Thomas Paine: Enlightenment, Revolution, and the Birth of Modern Nations* (New York: Penguin, 2007); Joseph F. Kett, *Merit: The History of a Founding Ideal from the American Revolution to the Twenty-First Century* (Ithaca, NY: Cornell University Press, 2013).
36. James M. McPherson, *Battle Cry of Freedom: The Civil War Era* (New York: Oxford University Press, 2003).
37. Gérard Duménil and Dominique Lévy, *Capital Resurgent: Roots of the Neoliberal Revolution*, trans. Derek Jeffers (Cambridge, MA: Harvard University Press, 2004); Daniel Stedman Jones, *Masters of the Universe: Hayek, Friedman, and the Birth of Neoliberal Politics* (Princeton, NJ: Princeton University Press, 2012).
38. Guin A. McKee, *The Problem of Jobs: Liberalism, Race, and Deindustrialization in Philadelphia* (Chicago: University of Chicago Press, 2009); Timothy Williams, "For Shrinking Cities, Destruction Is a Path to Renewal," *New York Times*, November 12, 2013, A15; Paul Krugman, "Twin Peaks Planet," *New York Times*, January 2, 2015, A21.
39. Thomas J. Sugrue, *The Origins of the Urban Crisis: Race and Inequality in Postwar Detroit* (Princeton, NJ: Princeton University Press, 2005); Joe Drape, "Bankruptcy for Ailing Detroit, but Prosperity for Its Teams," *New York Times*, October 14, 2013, A1.
40. Carol Poh Miller and Robert Wheeler, *Cleveland: A Concise History* (Bloomington: Indiana University Press, 2009).
41. Susan M. Wachter and Kimberly A. Zeuli, eds., *Revitalizing American Cities* (Philadelphia: University of Pennsylvania Press, 2013); Monica Davey, "A Picture of Detroit Ruin, Street by Forlorn Street," *New York Times*, February 18, 2014, A1; Jon Hurdle, "Philadelphia Forges Plan To Rebuild From Decay," *New York Times*, January 1, 2014, B1.

42. "The Affordable Housing Crisis," *New York Times*, December 5, 2012, A30; "How to Fight Homelessness," *New York Times*, December 17, 2012, A28; "Washington: More Tent Cities Sought for Homeless in Seattle," *New York Times*, January 16, 2015, A20.
43. Kristin S. Seefedt and John D. Graham, *America's Poor and the Great Recession* (Bloomington: Indiana University Press, 2013).
44. Erik Brynjolfsson and Andrew McAfee, *Race against the Machine: How the Digital Revolution Is Accelerating Innovation, Driving Productivity, and Irreversibly Transforming Employment and the Economy* (San Francisco: Digital Frontier, 2012); Cecilia Kang, "New Robots in the Workplace: Job Creators or Job Terminators?," *Washington Post*, March 6, 2013, http://www.washingtonpost.com/business/technology/new-robots-in-the-workplace-job-creators-or-job-terminators/2013/03/06/a80b8f34-746c-11e2-8f84-3e4b513b1a13_story.html; Claire Cain Miller, "Smarter Robots Move Deeper into Workplace," *New York Times*, December 16, 2014, A1; Farhad Manjoo, "Uber's Business Model Could Change Your Work," *New York Times*, January 29, 2015, B1; Zeynep Tufekci, "The Machines Are Coming," *New York Times*, April 19, 2015, SR4.
45. Paul Krugman, "Robots and Robber Barons," *New York Times*, December 10, 2012, A27.
46. Sam Polk, a former hedge fund trader, posited a critical assessment of the ethos that dominates the American finance community in a 2014 op-ed piece: "Wall Street is a toxic culture that encourages the grandiosity of people who are desperately trying to feel powerful." Sam Polk, "For the Love of Money," *New York Times*, January 19, 2014, SR1.
47. Karl Marx, *The Critique of the Gotha Programme* (London: Electric Book, 2001 [1875]), 20.
48. *Deep Space Nine*, "Little Green Men," 1995.
49. Karl Marx, *On the Jewish Question*, 1844, http://www.marxists.org/archive/marx/works/1844/jewish-question/.
50. Marx, *Critique of the Gotha Programme*, 20.
51. Robert Danisch, *Pragmatism, Democracy, and the Necessity of Rhetoric* (Columbia: University of South Carolina Press, 2007); Larry A. Hickman, *Pragmatism as Post-Modernism: Lessons from John Dewey* (New York: Fordham University Press, 2007); Alan Malachowski, *The New Pragmatism* (Montreal: McGill-Queen's University Press, 2010); Michael Bacon, *Pragmatism* (Cambridge, MA: Polity, 2012).

52. Louis Menand, *The Metaphysical Club* (New York: Farrar, Straus, and Giroux, 2001), xii.
53. Richard Tuck, *Hobbes: A Very Short Introduction* (New York: Oxford University Press, 2002); Noel Malcolm, ed., *Thomas Hobbes: Leviathan* (New York: Oxford University Press, 2012 [1668]).
54. Richard Rorty, *Philosophy and the Mirror of Nature* (Princeton: Princeton University Press, 1981); Michael Bacon, *Richard Rorty: Pragmatism and Political Liberalism* (Lanham: Lexington Books, 2007); Neil Gross, *Richard Rorty: The Making of an American Philosopher* (Chicago: University of Chicago Press, 2008).
55. *Deep Space Nine*, "Crossover," 1994.
56. John F. Burns, "U.N. Panel to Assess Drone Use," *New York Times*, January 25, 2013, A4; Lloyd C. Gardner, *Killing Machine: The American Presidency in the Age of Drone Warfare* (New York: New Press, 2013); Thom Shanker, "Simple, Low-Cost Drones a Boost for U.S. Military," *New York Times*, January 25, 2013, A12; Declan Walsh and Ihsanullah Tipu Mehsud, "Civilian Deaths in Drone Strikes Cited in Report," *New York Times*, October 22, 2013, A1.
57. Stephen Eric Bronner, *Rosa Luxemburg: A Revolutionary for Our Times* (University Park: Pennsylvania State University Press, 1993).
58. James M. McPherson, *Abraham Lincoln and the Second American Revolution* (New York: Oxford University Press, 1992); James Oakes, *Freedom National: The Destruction of Slavery in the United States* (New York: W. W. Norton, 2012).
59. Sidney Hook, *Towards the Understanding of Karl Marx* (New York: John Day, 1933), 294–95.
60. James P. Cannon, *The History of American Trotskyism: Report of a Participant* (New York: Pioneer Publishers, 1944); Constance Ashton Myers, *The Prophet's Army: Trotskyists in America, 1928–1941* (Westport, CT: Greenwood Press, 1977); A. Belden Fields, *Trotskyism and Maoism: Theory and Practice in France and the United States* (New York: Praeger, 1988), chapter 4; Bryan D. Palmer, *James P. Cannon and the Origins of the American Revolutionary Left, 1890–1928* (Urbana: University of Illinois Press, 2010).
61. In the midst of a labor strike (*Deep Space Nine*, "Bar Association" 1996), a character reads directly from the *Communist Manifesto*: "Workers of the world, unite. You have nothing to lose but your chains."
62. Mark P. Lagon, "'We Owe It to Them to Interfere:' *Star Trek* and U.S. Statecraft in the 1960s and the 1990s," in *Political Science*

Fiction, ed. Donald M. Hassler and Clyde Wilcox (Columbia: University of South Carolina Press, 1997); Keith M. Booker, "The Politics of *Star Trek*," in *The Essential Science Fiction Reader*, ed. J. P. Telotte (Lexington: University Press of Kentucky, 2008).
63. Please see Chapter 1.
64. See *The Next Generation*, "Transfigurations," 1990.
65. Daniel Leonard Bernardi, Star Trek *and History: Race-ing toward a White Future* (New Brunswick, NJ: Rutgers University Press, 1998), chapter 4.
66. I take issue with this claim in the Introduction of this volume.
67. Gillian Brock, ed., *Cosmopolitanism versus Non-Cosmopolitanism: Critiques, Defenses, Reconceptualizations* (New York: Oxford University Press, 2013).
68. *The Next Generation*, "Code of Honor," 1987.

Chapter 3

1. Samuel P. Huntington, *The Clash of Civilizations and the Remaking of World Order* (New York: Simon & Schuster, 1996); Martin Hall and Patrick Thaddeus Jackson, eds., *Civilization Identity* (New York: Palgrave Macmillan, 2007).
2. See Chapter 1, note 22.
3. Daniel Leonard Bernardi, Star Trek *and History: Race-ing toward a White Future* (New Brunswick, NJ: Rutgers University Press, 1998), chapter 4.
4. Bernardi, Star Trek *and History*, 107.
5. Ibid., 111.
6. Ibid.
7. Ibid., 133.
8. Christian Domenig, "Klingons: Going Medieval on You," in Star Trek *and History*, ed. Nancy R. Reagin (Hoboken, NJ: John Wiley & Sons, 2013), 295.
9. Domenig, "Klingons."
10. *The Next Generation*, "Sins of the Father," 1990; *The Next Generation*, "Redemption" 1991.
11. Rick Berman and Michael Piller, "Unification Part I," *Star Trek: The Next Generation*, dir. Cliff Bole, http://www.st-minutiae.com/academy/literature329/207.txt.

Chapter 4

1. Samuel P. Huntington, *The Clash of Civilizations and the Remaking of World Order* (New York: Simon & Schuster, 1996), 56; David Brooks, "Saving the System," *New York Times*, April 29, 2014, A23; Stephen Benedict Dyson, *Otherworldly Politics: The International Relations of Star Trek, Game of Thrones, and Battlestar Galactica* (Baltimore, MD: Johns Hopkins University Press, 2015), chap. 5.
2. Huntington, *The Clash of Civilizations*, 21.
3. Issac Deutscher, *The Prophet Armed: Trotsky 1879–1921*, vol. 1 (New York: Oxford University Press, 1963); Leon Trotsky, *History of the Russian Revolution* (New York: Pathfinder, 1980 [1933]).
4. Huntington, *Clash of Civilizations*, 184.
5. This is also true of Vulcan-human and Romulan-human pairings.
6. For a full list of Klingon rituals, see "Klingon Rituals and Traditions," *Klingon Imperial Diplomatic Corps*, http://www.klingon.org/database/rituals.html#anchor714236.
7. Daniel Leonard Bernardi, Star Trek *and History: Race-ing toward a White Future* (New Brunswick, NJ: Rutgers University Press, 1998), chapter 4.
8. Ibid., 133.
9. Robert C. Scharff and Val Dusek, eds., *Philosophy of Technology: The Technological Condition*, 2nd ed. (New York: Wiley-Blackwell, 2014).
10. Huntington, *Clash of Civilizations*, 21, emphasis added.
11. Huntington, *The Clash of Civilizations*.
12. The following is in the 1995 movie script:

    SCRIMM (2063 RESIDENT OF EARTH): Where are you from most recently?
    PICARD: California. San Francisco.
    SCRIMM: Beautiful city. Used to be, anyway. I didn't think anyone still lived there.

    Star Trek Minutiae, September 29, 1995, http://www.st-minutiae.com/academy/literature329/fc.txt.
13. Huntington, *Clash of Civilizations*, 20, emphasis added.

Chapter 5

1. Karin Blair, *Meaning in* Star Trek (New York: Warner, 1977); and "The Garden in the Machine: The Why of *Star Trek,*" *Journal of Popular Culture* 13, no. 2 (Fall 1979): 310–19; Ina Rae Hark, "*Star Trek* and Television's Moral Universe," *Extrapolation* 20, no. 1 (Spring 1979): 20–37; Taylor Harrison et al., eds., *Enterprise Zones: Critical Positions on* Star Trek (Boulder, CO: Westview, 1996); Thomas Richards, *The Meaning of* Star Trek (New York: Doubleday, 1997); Daniel Bernardi, Star Trek *and History: Racing toward a White Future* (Newark, NJ: Rutgers University Press, 1998); Jon Wagner and Jan Lundeen, *Deep Space and Sacred Time:* Star Trek *in the American Mythos* (Westport, CT: Praeger, 1998); Robin Roberts, *Sexual Generations: "Star Trek: The Next Generation" and Gender* (Chicago: University of Illinois Press, 1999); Alan N. Sharpio, Star Trek*: Technologies of Disappearance* (Berlin: Avinus, 2004); David Greven, *Gender and Sexuality in* Star Trek*: Allegories of Desire in the Television Series and Films* (Jefferson, NC: MacFarland, 2009).
2. Thomas L. Jeffers, *Norman Podhoretz: A Biography* (New York: Cambridge University Press, 2010); C. Bradley Thompson with Yaron Brook, *Neoconservatism: An Obituary for an Idea* (Boulder, CO: Paradigm, 2010); Justin Vaïsse, *Neoconservatism: The Biography of a Movement* (Cambridge, MA: Harvard University Press, 2010); Jean-François Drolet, *American Neoconservatism: The Politics and Culture of a Reactionary Idealism* (New York: Columbia University Press, 2011).
3. Terry H. Anderson, *Bush's Wars* (New York: Oxford University Press, 2011).
4. David Rohde, "The World: Managing Freedom in Iraq; America Brings Democracy: Censor Now, Vote Later," *New York Times*, June 22, 2003, http://www.nytimes.com/2003/06/22/weekinreview/world-managing-freedom-iraq-america-brings-democracy-censor-now-vote-later.html.
5. Joseph M. Parent, *Uniting States: Voluntary Union in World Politics* (New York: Oxford University Press, 2011), chapter 8; Sebastian Rosato, *Europe United: Power Politics and the Making of the European Community* (Ithaca, NY: Cornell University Press, 2011); Michelle Egan, *Single Markets: Economic*

Integration in Europe and the United States (New York: Oxford University Press, 2012); George A. Gonzalez, *Energy and the Politics of the North Atlantic* (Albany: State University of New York Press, 2013).
6. "The specific political distinction to which political actions and motives can be reduced is that between friend and enemy." Carl Schmitt, *The Concept of the Political*, expanded ed. (Chicago: University of Chicago Press, 2007 [1929]), 26.
7. Shadia B. Drury, *Leo Strauss and the American Right* (New York: St. Martin's Press, 1997), 23.
8. The script notes the following in the movie: "A Third World War. Nuclear explosions, environmental disasters, tens of millions dead. The United States ceases to exist. All political authority vanishes. Humanity teetering on the edge of the Second Dark Age," Star Trek Minutiae, September 29, 1995, http://www.st-minutiae.com/academy/literature329/fc.txt.
9. Schmitt, *Concept of the Political*, 27.
10. See Chapter 4, note 12.
11. Michael H. Hunt, *The American Ascendancy: How the United States Gained and Wielded Global Dominance* (Chapel Hill: University of North Carolina Press, 2007), chapter 8.
12. Gérard Duménil and Dominique Lévy, *Capital Resurgent: Roots of the Neoliberal Revolution*, trans. Derek Jeffers (Cambridge: Harvard University Press, 2004); Daniel Stedman Jones, *Masters of the Universe: Hayek, Friedman, and the Birth of Neoliberal Politics* (Princeton, NJ: Princeton University Press, 2012); Adrian Parr, *The Wrath of Capital: Neoliberalism and Climate Change Politics* (New York: Columbia University Press, 2013).
13. Norman Podhoretz, *Present Danger* (New York: Simon & Schuster, 1980); James Graham Wilson, *The Triumph of Improvisation: Gorbachev's Adaptability, Reagan's Engagement, and the End of the Cold War* (Ithaca, NY: Cornell University Press, 2014).
14. Michael Wines, "Reagan Birthday Is a Gift to His Party," *New York Times*, February 4, 1994, http://www.nytimes.com/1994/02/04/us/reagan-birthday-is-a-gift-to-his-party.html.
15. Francis X. Clines, "Reagan Denounces Ideology of Soviet as 'Focus of Evil,'" *New York Times*, March 9, 1983, http://www.nytimes.com/1983/03/09/us/reagan-denounces-ideology-of-soviet-as-focus-of-evil.html.

16. William Safire, "Islamofascism," *New York Times*, October 1, 2006, sec. 6, p. 20; Norman Podhoretz, *World War IV: The Long Struggle against Islamofascism* (New York: Doubleday, 2007).
17. Samuel P. Huntington, *The Clash of Civilizations and the Remaking of World Order* (New York: Simon & Schuster, 1996 [2011]).
18. John McCain, "Obama Made America Look Weak," *New York Times*, March 15, 2014, A21.
19. Paul Krugman, "Fearing Fear Itself," *New York Times*, October 29, 2007, A19.
20. Jane Caplan, *Nazi Germany* (New York: Oxford University Press, 2008); Jeffrey Herf, *The Jewish Enemy: Nazi Propaganda during World War II and the Holocaust* (Cambridge, MA: Harvard University Press, 2008).
21. Leonard Nimoy, *I Am Spock* (New York: Hyperion, 1995); Bernardi, Star Trek *and History*, 140–41; David Van Biena, "Spock's Jewish Roots," in *Leonard Nimoy (1931–2015): Remembering the Man behind Spock* (New York: Entertainment Weekly, 2015), 24–25.

Chapter 6

1. Karin Blair, *Meaning in* Star Trek (New York: Warner, 1977); and "The Garden in the Machine: The Why of *Star Trek*," *Journal of Popular Culture* 13, no. 2 (Fall 1979): 310–19; Ina Rae Hark, "*Star Trek* and Television's Moral Universe," *Extrapolation* 20, no. 1 (Spring 1979): 20–37; Taylor Harrison et al., eds. *Enterprise Zones: Critical Positions on* Star Trek (Boulder, CO: Westview, 1996); Thomas Richards, *The Meaning of* Star Trek (New York: Doubleday, 1997); Daniel Bernardi, Star Trek *and History: Race-ing toward a White Future* (Newark, NJ: Rutgers University Press, 1998); Jon Wagner and Jan Lundeen, *Deep Space and Sacred Time:* Star Trek *in the American Mythos* (Westport, CT: Praeger, 1998); Robin Roberts, *Sexual Generations: "Star Trek: The Next Generation" and Gender* (Chicago: University of Illinois Press, 1999); Alan N. Sharpio, Star Trek: *Technologies of Disappearance* (Berlin: Avinus, 2004); David Greven, *Gender and Sexuality in* Star Trek: *Allegories of Desire in the Television Series and Films* (Jefferson, NC: MacFarland, 2009).
2. "The Cage" was subsequently broadcast via the two-part episode *Star Trek* (original series), "The Menagerie," 1966.

3. Richard Rorty, *Philosophy and the Mirror of Nature* (Princeton: Princeton University Press, 1981); Michael Bacon, *Richard Rorty: Pragmatism and Political Liberalism* (Lanham: Lexington Books, 2007); Neil Gross, *Richard Rorty: The Making of an American Philosopher* (Chicago: University of Chicago Press, 2008).
4. As quoted in Mark Mazzetti, "'03 U.S. Memo Approved Harsh Interrogations," *New York Times*, April 2, 2008, http://www.nytimes.com/2008/04/02/washington/02terror.html.
5. Scott Shane, "Waterboarding Used 266 Times on 2 Suspects," *New York Times*, April 20, 2009, A1; Jonathan Hafetz, "Don't Execute Those We Tortured," *New York Times*, September 25, 2014, A31; Mark Mazzetti, "Panel Faults C.I.A. Over Brutality Toward Terrorism Suspects," *New York Times*, December 10, 2014, A1.
6. Daniel Headrick, *The Tools of Empire: Technology and European Imperialism in the Nineteenth Century* (New York: Oxford University Press, 1981).
7. Benjamin F. Jones and Benjamin A. Olken, "Do Assassins Really Change History?" *New York Times*, April 12, 2015, SR12.
8. In the *Star Trek: Voyager* episode "Author, Author" (2001), Klingon politics are referred to as "palace intrigue."
9. Robert Dallek, *Lyndon B. Johnson: Portrait of a President* (New York: Oxford University Press, 2005); James N. Giglio, *The Presidency of John F. Kennedy* (Lawrence: University of Kansas Press, 2006).
10. Jack David, *B-2 Stealth Bombers* (New York: Torque Books, 2007); Christopher Drew, "Costliest Jet, Years in Making, Sees the Enemy: Budget Cuts," *New York Times*, Nov. 29, 2012, A1.
11. Adam B. Schiff, US House of Representatives member (who serves on the House Permanent Select Committee on Intelligence), noted in 2014, "The United States is the only country with a significant armed drone capability." Adam B. Schiff, "Let the Military Run Drone Warfare," *New York Times*, March 13, 2014, A27. Also see Joe Cochrane, "At Asia Air Show, Plenty of Competition for Sales of Drones," *New York Times*, February 17, 2014, B2.
12. John F. Burns, "U.N. Panel to Assess Drone Use," *New York Times*, January 25, 2013, A4; Lloyd C. Gardner, *Killing Machine: The American Presidency in the Age of Drone Warfare* (New York: New Press, 2013); Thom Shanker, "Simple, Low-Cost Drones a Boost for U.S. Military," *New York Times*, January 25, 2013, A12; Declan

Walsh and Ihsanullan Tipu Mehsud, "Civilian Deaths in Drone Strikes Cited in Report," *New York Times*, October 22, 2013, A1; Christopher Drew and Dave Philipps, "Burnout Forces U.S. to Curtail Drone Flights," *New York Times*, June 17, 2015, A1.
13. Joseph Cirincione, *Bomb Scare: The History and Future of Nuclear Weapons* (New York: Columbia University Press, 2007); Jeremy Bernstein, *Nuclear Weapons: What you Need to Know* (New York: Cambridge University Press, 2008); Thomas M. Nichols, *No Use: Nuclear Weapons and U.S. National Security* (Philadelphia: University of Pennsylvania Press, 2014); William J. Broad and David E. Sanger, "U.S. Ramping Up Major Renewal in Nuclear Arms," *New York Times*, September 22, 2014, A1.
14. Nicolas Evan Sarantakes, "Cold War Pop Culture and the Image of U.S. Foreign Policy: The Perspective of the Original *Star Trek* Series," *Journal of Cold War Studies* 7, no 4 (2005): 74–103.
15. I argue that the global warming phenomenon is a direct result of US hegemonic strategies. George A. Gonzalez, *Urban Sprawl, Global Warming, and the Empire of Capital* (Albany: State University of New York Press, 2009); *Energy and Empire: The Politics of Nuclear and Solar Power in the United States* (Albany: State University of New York Press, 2012); and *Energy and the Politics of the North Atlantic* (Albany: State University of New York Press, 2013).

Chapter 7

1. Karin Blair, *Meaning in* Star Trek (New York: Warner, 1977); and "The Garden in the Machine: The Why of *Star Trek*," *Journal of Popular Culture* 13, no. 2 (Fall 1979): 310–19; Ina Rae Hark, "*Star Trek* and Television's Moral Universe," *Extrapolation* 20, no. 1 (Spring 1979): 20–37; Taylor Harrison et al., eds. *Enterprise Zones: Critical Positions on* Star Trek (Boulder, CO: Westview, 1996); Thomas Richards, *The Meaning of* Star Trek (New York: Doubleday, 1997); Daniel Bernardi, Star Trek *and History: Race-ing toward a White Future* (Newark, NJ: Rutgers University Press, 1998); Jon Wagner and Jan Lundeen, *Deep Space and Sacred Time:* Star Trek *in the American Mythos* (Westport, CT: Praeger, 1998); Robin Roberts, *Sexual Generations: "Star Trek: The Next Generation" and Gender* (Chicago: University of Illinois Press, 1999); Alan N. Sharpio, Star Trek: *Technologies of Disappearance* (Berlin:

Avinus, 2004); David Greven, *Gender and Sexuality in* Star Trek*: Allegories of Desire in the Television Series and Films* (Jefferson, NC: MacFarland, 2009).
2. Bernardi, Star Trek *and History*, chapter 4.
3. Ibid., 133.
4. Anne Norton, *Leo Strauss and the Politics of American Empire* (New Haven, CT: Yale University Press, 2004).
5. Joseph W. Bendersky, *Carl Schmitt: Theorist for the Reich* (Princeton, NJ: Princeton University Press, 1983).
6. "The specific political distinction to which political actions and motives can be reduced is that between friend and enemy." Carl Schmitt, *The Concept of the Political*, expanded ed. (Chicago: University of Chicago Press, 2007 [1929]), 26.
7. Shadia B. Drury, *Leo Strauss and the American Right* (New York: St. Martin's Press, 1997), 23.
8. See Chapter 5, note 8.
9. Norton, *Leo Strauss*, 143.
10. Schmitt, *Concept of the Political*, 27.
11. Ibid.
12. Carl Zimmer, "Racial Boundaries Grow Fuzzy as Ancestry Map Emerges From Study," *New York Times*, December 26, 2014, A20.
13. During *The Next Generation* episode "Attached" (1993), it is noted that Earth's world government was formed in 2150.
14. This matter is elaborated in Chapter 6.
15. David Rohde, "The World: Managing Freedom in Iraq; America Brings Democracy: Censor Now, Vote Later," *New York Times*, June 22, 2003; see Chapter 5, note 4 for web address.
16. *Deep Space Nine*, "Penumbra," 1999.
17. When it is suggested that "the wiser course would be to simply contain them within their perimeter," Sisko retorts, "That's what they're hoping we'll do—so they'll have time to rebuild their forces" (*Deep Space Nine*, "The Dogs of War" 1999).
18. *Deep Space Nine*, "What You Leave Behind," 1999; in the last instance, Odo is able to convince the Dominion leader to surrender, and the final conquest does not take place.

Chapter 8

1. Eric C. Otto, *Green Speculations: Science Fiction and Transformative Environmentalism* (Columbus: Ohio State University Press,

2012). Also see Richard Pérez-Peña, "College Classes Use Arts to Brace for Climate Change," *New York Times*, April 1, 2014, A12.
2. John Corry, "Something about *Star Trek* Talks to Every Man," *New York Times*, June 10, 1984, H25.
3. Lester W. Milbrath, *Envisioning a Sustainable Society: Learning Our Way Out* (Albany: State University of New York Press, 1989).
4. Kurkpatrick Dorsey, *Whales and Nations: Environmental Diplomacy on the High Seas* (Seattle: University of Washington Press, 2013).
5. Jane Bennett, *Vibrant Matter: A Political Ecology of Things* (Durham, NC: Duke University Press, 2010).
6. On an alien planet, the point is made: "We've spend years, decades, trying to avoid anything that would lead to a greenhouse effect and now here we are about to create one on purpose." In an effort to keep the planet warm, the *Enterprise* crew works to increase the amount of carbon dioxide in the planetary atmosphere (*The Next Generation*, "A Matter of Time" 1991).
7. Catherine Gautier, *Oil, Water, and Climate: An Introduction* (New York: Cambridge University Press, 2008); Catherine Gautier and Jean-Louis Fellous, eds., *Facing Climate Change Together* (New York: Cambridge University Press, 2008); Spencer R. Weart, *The Discovery of Global Warming*, 2nd ed. (Cambridge, MA: Harvard University Press, 2008); John Houghton, *Global Warming: The Complete Briefing*, 4th ed. (New York: Cambridge University Press, 2009); Mark Maslin, *Global Warming: A Very Short Introduction* (New York: Oxford University Press, 2009); James Lawrence Powell, *The Inquisition of Climate Science* (New York: Columbia University Press, 2011).
8. Matthew Paterson, *Automobile Politics* (New York: Cambridge University Press, 2007).
9. George A. Gonzalez, *Urban Sprawl, Global Warming, and the Empire of Capital* (Albany: State University of New York Press, 2009).
10. Adrian Parr, *The Wrath of Capital: Neoliberalism and Climate Change Politics* (New York: Columbia University Press, 2013).
11. Justin Gillis, "Climate Maverick to Retire From NASA," *New York Times*, April 2, 2013, D1.
12. Milbrath, *Envisioning a Sustainable Society*.
13. For instance, movie *Star Trek: The Undiscovered Country*, dir. Nicholas Meyer, 1991; Gene Roddenberry et al., *Star Trek: Nemesis*, dir. Stuart Baird, 2002; *Enterprise*, "Judgement," 2003.

14. Mark Mozower, *Governing the World: The History of an Idea* (New York: Penguin Press, 2012).
15. During *The Next Generation* episode "Attached" (1993), it is noted that Earth's world government was formed in 2150.
16. Joseph F. Kett, *Merit: The History of a Founding Ideal from the American Revolution to the Twenty-First Century* (Ithaca, NY: Cornell University Press, 2013).
17. George A. Gonzalez, *Energy and Empire: The Politics of Nuclear and Solar Power in the United States* (Albany: State University of New York Press, 2012).
18. George A. Gonzalez, *Energy and the Politics of the North Atlantic* (Albany: State University of New York Press, 2013).

Chapter 9

1. Joseph W. Bendersky, *Carl Schmitt: Theorist for the Reich* (Princeton, NJ: Princeton University Press, 1983).
2. Anne Norton, *Leo Strauss and the Politics of American Empire* (New Haven, CT: Yale University Press, 2004); Francis Fukuyama, "After Neoconservatism," *New York Times Magazine*, February 19, 2006, 62.
3. Leo Strauss, "Notes on Carl Schmitt, *The Concept of the Political*," in *The Concept of the Political*, expanded ed., by Carl Schmitt (Chicago: University of Chicago Press, 2007 [1932]).
4. Daniel Tanguay, *Leo Strauss: An Intellectual Biography* (New Haven: Yale University Press, 2007); Steven B. Smith, "Leo Strauss: The Outlines of a Life," in *Cambridge Companion to Leo Strauss*, ed. Steven B. Smith (New York: Cambridge University Press, 2009), 18.
5. "The specific political distinction to which political actions and motives can be reduced is that between friend and enemy." Carl Schmitt, *The Concept of the Political*, expanded ed. (Chicago: University of Chicago Press, 2007 [1929]), 26.
6. Jane Caplan, *Nazi Germany* (New York: Oxford University Press, 2008); Jeffrey Herf, *The Jewish Enemy: Nazi Propaganda during World War II and the Holocaust* (Cambridge, MA: Harvard University Press, 2008).
7. Shadia B. Drury, *Leo Strauss and the American Right* (New York: St. Martin's Press, 1997), 23.
8. See Chapter 5, note 8.

9. Schmitt, *Concept of the Political*, 27.
10. Peter Singer, *Marx: A Very Short Introduction* (New York: Oxford University Press, 2001).
11. See Chapter 4, note 12.
12. Joseph M. Parent, *Uniting States: Voluntary Union in World Politics* (New York: Oxford University Press, 2011), chapter 8; Sebastian Rosato, *Europe United: Power Politics and the Making of the European Community* (Ithaca, NY: Cornell University Press, 2011); Michelle Egan, *Single Markets: Economic Integration in Europe and the United States* (New York: Oxford University Press, 2012); George A. Gonzalez, *Energy and the Politics of the North Atlantic* (Albany: State University of New York Press, 2013).
13. Susan Bachrach and Steven Luckert, *State of Deception: The Power of Nazi Propaganda* (Washington, DC: United States Holocaust Memorial Museum, 2009), 44.
14. Leonard Nimoy, *I Am Spock* (New York: Hyperion, 1995); Daniel Leonard Bernardi, *Star Trek and History: Race-ing toward a White Future* (New Brunswick, NJ: Rutgers University Press, 1998), 140–41; David Van Biena, "Spock's Jewish Roots," in *Leonard Nimoy (1931–2015): Remembering the Man Behind Spock* (New York: Entertainment Weekly, 2015), 24–25.
15. Jonathan Mahler, "After the Imperial Presidency," *New York Times Magazine*, November 9, 2008, MM42; Ryan J. Barilleaux and Christopher S. Kelley, eds., *The Unitary Executive and the Modern Presidency* (College Station: Texas A&M University Press, 2010).
16. Bendersky, *Carl Schmitt*, chapter 4.
17. "After the Attacks: Bush's Remarks to Cabinet and Advisers," *New York Times*, September 13, 2001, http://www.nytimes.com/2001/09/13/us/after-the-attacks-bush-s-remarks-to-cabinet-and-advisers.html; also see Jim Rutenberg and Sheryl Gay Stolberg, "In Prime-Time Address, Bush Says Safety of U.S. Hinges on Iraq," *New York Times*, September 12, 2006, http://www.nytimes.com/2006/09/12/us/12bush.html.
18. Don Van Natta, Jr., Adam Liptak, and Clifford J. Levy, "The Miller Case: A Notebook, A Cause, a Jail Cell and a Deal," *New York Times*, October 16, 2005, sec. 1, p. 1.

19. "Rewriting the Geneva Conventions," *New York Times*, August 14, 2006, A20.
20. Richard W. Stevenson, "White House Says Prisoner Policy Set Humane Tone," *New York Times*, June 23, 2004, A1.
21. Scott Shane, "Portrayal of C.I.A. Torture in Bin Laden Film Reopens a Debate," *New York Times*, Dec. 13, 2012, A1; "About Those Black Sites," *New York Times*, February 18, 2013, A16.
22. Scott Shane, "U.S. Practiced Torture After 9/11, Nonpartisan Review Concludes," *New York Times*, April 16, 2013, A1; also see Mark Mazzetti, "Panel Faults C.I.A. over Brutality toward Terrorism Suspects," *New York Times*, December 10, 2014, A1; "Dark Again after the Torture Report," *New York Times*, December 12, 2014, A34.
23. "Effort to Prohibit Waterboarding Fails in House," *Associated Press*, March 12, 2008, http://www.nytimes.com/2008/03/12/washington/12torture.html?pagewanted=all.
24. Scott Shane, "Waterboarding Used 266 Times on 2 Suspects," *New York Times*, April 20, 2009, A1.

Chapter 10

1. Robert Danisch, *Pragmatism, Democracy, and the Necessity of Rhetoric* (Columbia: University of South Carolina Press, 2007); Larry A. Hickman, *Pragmatism as Post-Modernism: Lessons from John Dewey* (New York: Fordham University Press, 2007); Alan Malachowski, *The New Pragmatism* (Montreal: McGill-Queen's University Press, 2010); Michael Bacon, *Pragmatism* (Cambridge: Polity, 2012).
2. Leo Strauss is considered to be a lodestone for American neoconservatives. Anne Norton, *Leo Strauss and the Politics of American Empire* (New Haven, CT: Yale University Press, 2004); Francis Fukuyama, "After Neoconservatism," *New York Times Magazine*, February 19, 2006, 62; Strauss held, "The only restraint in which the West can put some confidence is the tyrant's fear of the West's immense military power." As quoted in James Atlas, "The Nation: Leo-Cons; A Classicist's Legacy: New Empire Builders," *New York Times*, May 4, 2004, sec. 4, p. 1.
3. Michael Walzer, *Thinking Politically: Essays in Political Theory*, ed. David Miller (New Haven: Yale University Press, 2007), chapter 1.

4. Daniel H. Nexon and Iver B. Neuman, *Harry Potter and International Relations* (Lanham, MD: Rowman & Littlefield, 2006); Daniel W. Drezner, *Theories of International Politics and Zombies* (Princeton: Princeton University Press, 2011); Jason Dittmer, *Captain America and the Nationalist Superhero* (Philadelphia: Temple University Press, 2012)
5. Richard Rorty, writing in the early 1980s, argues that societies are based on "intersubjective agreement." Thus what is required for societal stability is enough consensus on a set of ideas—any set of ideas. Hence what matters is consensus, and not the ideas themselves. Richard Rorty, *Philosophy and the Mirror of Nature* (Princeton: Princeton University Press, 1981); Michael Bacon, *Richard Rorty: Pragmatism and Political Liberalism* (Lanham: Lexington Books, 2007); Neil Gross, *Richard Rorty: The Making of an American Philosopher* (Chicago: University of Chicago Press, 2008).
6. *Voyager*, "Year of Hell," 1997.
7. "Sacred Ground," 1996.
8. "Distant Origin," 1997.
9. "Scorpion," 1997.
10. *Star Trek: The Next Generation*, "The Mind's Eye," 1991.
11. *Star Trek: The Next Generation*, "Chain of Command," 1992.
12. *Star Trek: The Next Generation*, "Ensign Ro," 1991.
13. Ibid.
14. *Voyager*, "State of Flux," 1995; *Voyager*, "Maneuvers," 1995; *Voyager*, "Investigations," 1996; *Voyager*, "Basics," 1996.

Conclusion

1. Eric Rauchway, *The Great Depression and the New Deal: A Very Short Introduction* (New York: Oxford University Press, 2008).
2. *Deep Space Nine*, "Rapture," 1996.
3. *Deep Space Nine*, "Accession," 1996.
4. The Vorta (Weyoun) in charge of the Dominion war effort opines that after its victory the Dominion should "eradicate" the Earth's "population" to prevent any "organized resistance" (*Deep Space Nine*, "Sacrifice of Angels," 1997).
5. See *Deep Space Nine*, "The Jem'Hadar," 1994; and *Deep Space Nine*, "Behind the Lines," 1997.

6. *Deep Space Nine*, "Treachery, Faith, and the Great River," 1998.
7. *Deep Space Nine*, "Inquisition," 1998.
8. *Deep Space Nine*, "Extreme Measures," 1999.
9. *Deep Space Nine*, "Inquisition," 1998.
10. Jeffrey L. Chidester and Paul Kengor, eds., *Reagan's Legacy in a World Transformed* (Cambridge, MA: Harvard University Press, 2015); Doug Rossinow, *The Reagan Era: A History of the 1980s* (New York: Columbia University Press, 2015).

Index

"Aenar, The" (2005) (*Star Trek: Enterprise*), 93, 151
Afghanistan, 34
"Allegiance" (1990) (*Star Trek: The Next Generation*), 104
"Alliances" (1996) (*Star Trek: Voyager*), 181–82
"All Our Yesterdays" (1969) (*Star Trek*, original series), 187
"Andorian Incident, The" (2001) (*Star Trek: Enterprise*), 97, 148–49, 153–54
Angel of the Revolution (Wells), 35
"Anomaly" (2003) (*Star Trek: Enterprise*), 160–61
"Apple, The" (1967) (*Star Trek*, original series), 23, 27, 51
"Arena" (1967) (*Star Trek*, original series), 21
"Arsenal of Freedom, The" (1988) (*Star Trek: The Next Generation*), 114
"Awakening" (2004) (*Star Trek: Enterprise*), 83, 97, 149

"Babel One" (2005) (*Star Trek: Enterprise*), 93, 151
"Balance of Terror" (1966) (*Star Trek*, original series), 18–19
"Basics" (1996) (*Star Trek: Voyager*), 180–81
"Birthright" (1993) (*Star Trek: The Next Generation*), 81
"Bread and Circuses" (1968) (*Star Trek*, original series), 45
"Broken Arrow" (2001) (*Star Trek: Enterprise*), 155

Bush (George W.) Presidential Administration (US), 92, 108, 122, 157

"Cage, The" (unaired) (*Star Trek*, original series), 104–5
"Caretaker, The" (1994) (*Star Trek: Voyager*), 166
"Carpenter Street" (2004) (*Star Trek: Enterprise*), 136
"Chain of Command" (1992) (*Star Trek: The Next Generation*), 68, 79
"Chase, The" (1993) (*Star Trek: The Next Generation*), 5, 132
"City on the Edge of Forever" (1967) (*Star Trek*, original series), 25, 38–39
"Cloud Minders" (1969) (*Star Trek*, original series), 94, 108–9, 140, 152, 161–62
"Code of Honor" (1987) (*Star Trek: The Next Generation*), 61
"Cogenitor" (2003) (*Star Trek: Enterprise*), 152
Cold War, 17
"Conscience of the King, The" (1967) (*Star Trek*, original series), 36
"Covenant" (1998) (*Star Trek: Deep Space Nine*), 188
"Crossover" (1994) (*Star Trek: Deep Space Nine*), 111

"Day of the Dove" (1968) (*Star Trek*, original series), 18, 65–66
"Devil's Due" (1991) (*Star Trek: The Next Generation*), 134–35
Dewey, John, 44

dilithium crystals, 139
"Dreadnought" (1996) (*Star Trek: Voyager*), 168–69

"Elaan of Troyius" (1968) (*Star Trek*, original series), 141
"Encounter at Farpoint" (1987) (*Star Trek: The Next Generation*), 57
"Enemy, The" (1989) (*Star Trek: The Next Generation*), 69
"Equinox" (1999) (*Star Trek: Voyager*), 175–78
"Errand of Mercy" (1967) (*Star Trek*, original series), 17, 58–59
European Union, 35
"Expanse, The" (2003) (*Star Trek: Enterprise*), 157

"Face of the Enemy" (1993) (*Star Trek: The Next Generation*), 109–10
"Fallen Hero" (2002) (*Star Trek: Enterprise*), 159–60
"False Profits" (1996) (*Star Trek: Voyager*), 167–68
"Family" (1990) (*Star Trek: The Next Generation*), 133
"Far Beyond the Stars" (1998) (*Star Trek: Deep Space Nine*), 89
"Fight or Flight" (2001) (*Star Trek: Enterprise*), 93, 150–51
"Force of Nature" (1993) (*Star Trek: The Next Generation*), 137–38
"Forge, The" (2004) (*Star Trek: Enterprise*), 83, 97, 149
"Fortunate Son" (2001) (*Star Trek: Enterprise*), 93, 151
"Friday's Child" (1967) (*Star Trek*, original series), 26, 141
"Fusion" (2002) (*Star Trek: Enterprise*), 149
"Future's End" (1996) (*Star Trek: Voyager*), 173–74

Gaza Strip (Israel/Palestine), 121
Georgia, Republic of, 35
global warming, 135–39

"High Ground, The" (1990) (*Star Trek: The Next Generation*), 57

"Homefront" (1996) (*Star Trek: Deep Space Nine*), 106, 158–59
Hook, Sidney, 50
Huntington, Samuel P., 73, 78, 80
Hussein, Iraq President Saddam, 122

"In a Mirror, Darkly" (2005) (*Star Trek: Enterprise*), 46–47, 108
"Inter Arma Enim Silent Leges" (1999) (*Star Trek: Deep Space Nine*), 112, 126
"In the Cards" (1997) (*Star Trek: Deep Space Nine*), 43
Iraq (US Invasion of), 34, 35, 92, 122, 123
Israel, 121

James, William, 44
Johnson, US President Lyndon B., 112
"Journey's End" (1994) (*Star Trek: The Next Generation*), 58, 134

Kennedy, US President John F., 112
"Killing Game, The" (1998) (*Star Trek: Voyager*), 191
"Kir'Shara" (2004) (*Star Trek: Enterprise*), 83, 97, 149
Kuwait, 34

Lenin, V. I., 34
Libya, 35
"Little Green Men" (1995) (*Star Trek: Deep Space Nine*), 43

"Marauders" (2002) (*Star Trek: Enterprise*), 93, 151
"Mark of Gideon, The" (1969) (*Star Trek*, original series), 36
Marx, Karl, 32, 43–44, 75, 88
McCain, US Senator John, 99
"Measure of a Man, The" (1989) (*Star Trek: The Next Generation*), 133
"Mind's Eye, The" (1991) (*Star Trek: The Next Generation*), 64
"Mirror, Mirror" (1967) (*Star Trek*, original series), 27–28, 46, 108

Nazism, 191; the Blond Beast metaphor of, 154–57
"Neutral Zone, The" (1988) (*Star Trek: The Next Generation*), 42–43
"Next Phase, The" (1992) (*Star Trek: The Next Generation*), 69
Nimoy, Leonard, 99, 155

"Omega Glory, The" (1968) (*Star Trek*, original series), 18, 49

"Paradise Lost" (1996) (*Star Trek: Deep Space Nine*), 106–7, 127, 159
"Paradise Syndrome, The" (1968) (*Star Trek*, original series), 25–26, 134
"Past Tense" (1995) (*Star Trek: Deep Space Nine*), 39–42, 48, 105
"Patterns of Force" (1968) (*Star Trek*, original series), 21–22, 24
"*Pegasus*, The" (1994) (*Star Trek: The Next Generation*), 113
Persian Gulf War (1990–91), 34
"Phage" (1995) *(Star Trek: Voyager)*, 172
"Piece of the Action, A" (1968) (*Star Trek*, original series), 22
Prime Directive, 26–27
"Private Little War" (1968) (*Star Trek*, original series), 20–21
Protocols of the Elders of Zion, 35

Reagan, US President Ronald, 99
"Resistance" (*Star Trek: Voyager*), 178–79
"Return of the Archons" (1967), 51
"Reunion" (1990) (*Star Trek: The Next Generation*), 65
"Rightful Heir" (1993) (*Star Trek: The Next Generation*), 63–64, 78
Roddenberry, Gene, 9
Rorty, Richard, 45–46, 107
Russia, 35. *See also* Soviet Union

"Savage Curtain, The" (1969) (*Star Trek*, original series), 16, 49–50
Schmitt, Carl, 95–96, 121, 147, 157–58
Section 31, 189–90
"Sins of the Father" (1990) (*Star Trek: The Next Generation*), 64–65

Soviet Union, 34. *See also* Russia
Star Trek (2009), 56
Star Trek: First Contact (1996), 83, 96, 121–22, 148
Star Trek: Insurrection (1998), 127, 132
Star Trek: Into Darkness (2013), 123, 127
Star Trek: Nemesis (2002), 69–70
Star Trek: The Voyage Home (1986), 36, 131–32
Star Trek: Wrath of Kahn (1982), 105
"Statistical Probabilities" (1997) (*Star Trek: Deep Space Nine*), 141
"Stormfront" (2004) (*Star Trek: Enterprise*), 160
Strauss, Leo, 147

"Terra Prime" (2005) (*Star Trek: Enterprise*), 84, 98, 162
"Thirty Days" (1998) (*Star Trek: Voyager*), 136
"This Side of Paradise" (1967) (*Star Trek*, original series), 24, 25, 51
"Time's Arrow" (1992) (*Star Trek: The Next Generation*), 29–30, 113
Trotsky, Leon, 75, 88

Ukraine, 35
"Unification" (1991) (*Star Trek: The Next Generation*), 68
Unitary Executive (theory of), 157
"United" (2005) (*Star Trek: Enterprise*), 93, 151
United Nations, 35
United States, 12, 35, 113–14, 115

"Void, The" (2001) (*Star Trek: Voyager*), 76–77, 169–71

West Bank Territories (Israel/Palestine), 121
"Who Watches the Watchers" (1989) (*Star Trek: The Next Generation*), 187
"Wounded, The" (1990) (*Star Trek: The Next Generation*), 67

"Yesterday's Enterprise" (1990) (*Star Trek: The Next Generation*), 119

Zero Dark Thirty (2012), 160

Printed in the USA
CPSIA information can be obtained
at www.ICGtesting.com
LVHW011957160324
774517LV00004B/451